THIS
WAS ALMOST SAME

Reya responded just as fiercely, holding him tightly. She was so aroused that, if he'd desired, they could have made love right there, in front of the campfire, for all the world to see. She didn't care; all she wanted was him. The tension that had existed between them almost from the moment they'd met exploded now, and they clutched at each other.

Uttering a groan, Colin pulled back. "You don't know what you're getting into," he said hoarsely.

She smiled shakily. "Neither do you."

"This is crazy...."

"I know. I don't care."

He groaned again and buried his face in her hair. "I don't, either," he whispered, then reached down and literally swept her off her feet. Holding her in his arms, he started toward the house....

ABOUT THE AUTHOR

Genetic engineering is making headlines around
the world today, but that's only part of the reason
Risa Kirk decided to explore the issue in *Tempting
Fate*. Before she picked up a pen to write full-
time, Risa was a medical technologist for ten
years, and her fascination with science has never
deserted her. This dynamic, gripping love story is
Risa's second Superromance, and her third is in
the works.

Books by Risa Kirk

HARLEQUIN SUPERROMANCE
200–BEYOND COMPARE

These books may be available at your local bookseller.

Don't miss any of our special offers. Write to us at the
following address for information on our newest releases.

Harlequin Reader Service
901 Fuhrmann Blvd., P.O. Box 1397, Buffalo, NY 14240
Canadian address: P.O. Box 603,
Fort Erie, Ont. L2A 5X3

Risa Kirk

TEMPTING FATE

Harlequin Books

TORONTO • NEW YORK • LONDON
AMSTERDAM • PARIS • SYDNEY • HAMBURG
STOCKHOLM • ATHENS • TOKYO • MILAN

Published December 1986

First printing October 1986

ISBN 0-373-70238-8

PROLOGUE

"YOU'VE GOT TO DO SOMETHING, Colin," Richard Carlyle said. "Now. Before it's too late."

Colin Hughes's jaw tightened, and with a sigh, Richard sat back in his chair and watched as Colin got up from his. The latest edition of The *Rocky Mountain Tribune*, one of Denver's major newspapers, was on the desk between them, and the headline caught Richard's eye again: "Geneticon—Progress, or a Nightmare Glimpse into the Future?"

Grimacing, Richard glanced quickly away. He'd done all he could; it was up to Colin now.

Colin had gone to the broad expanse of plate-glass window behind the desk. Staring out at the sprawling brick buildings that housed the laboratories, his handsome face took on a brooding expression as he recalled the way Geneticon had looked five years ago when he'd first come to Denver. There had been only one building then, a squat, unimposing structure where some of the finest young minds in the country were working in cramped conditions, carrying on advanced experiments in molecular biology despite outdated equipment. All the big financial grants were being siphoned off then toward larger, more prestigious institutions; funding here had been severely restricted. He had changed all that. Today, Geneticon's scientists worked with the finest equipment money could buy, and that single building had mushroomed into a scientific complex where experiments were carried on without interruption.

At least, that's the way it had been, Colin amended darkly, until those articles started appearing in the paper. The first had been published last week; the second, today. If it hadn't been so infuriating, he would have laughed at the absurdity. It was obvious that the reporter knew little or nothing about genetic research; every statement had reeked of innuendo and conjecture, if not outright lies. How anyone could believe that Geneticon was trying to clone human beings, or was involved in creating a master race, was beyond him, but it seemed someone did, and his mouth tightened again. Without turning around, he muttered, "When you say I have to do something, are you speaking as my friend, or as Geneticon's attorney?"

"Which would you prefer?" Richard asked.

Colin didn't answer for a moment; his glance had shifted to the main entrance, where the electronically controlled wrought-iron gates and high brick walls guarded the complex. He couldn't see it from here, but as he pictured the bronze plaque set unobtrusively into one of the walls by those gates, he unconsciously clenched his fist. He'd been so filled with hope when he'd designed the logo for Geneticon five years ago— the caduceus wrapped with the two interlocking strands of the DNA molecule seemed to represent the future—but now...

His gaze shifted to the mountains in the distance. He hadn't known much about genetic research when he'd first come here, he remembered. He'd come to see the place at a friend's request. But as Stefan Benadi had shown him through the crowded laboratories, he knew he had found a new purpose. He hadn't realized until that day that he'd been existing in a frozen, nightmare state, so stricken by grief that he couldn't feel anything else. But something deep within him had been impressed by the intensity of Stefan's young scientists; he'd recalled almost wistfully that he'd once felt the same way. He'd been just as dedicated, just as fiercely determined to succeed, when he'd started his own computer company eight years before. He hadn't let anything stop him from making Hughes Tech-Craft a reality, even though he'd been only twenty-five at the time. The computer chip he'd designed had replaced older, slower versions, and the company had been a huge success—so much so that he'd been touted as a young genius. But as he'd looked around at Stefan's group that day, he had realized that true genius was right here. As Stefan had known, it had been impossible for him not to be fired by their enthusiasm, impossible to walk away, pretending other concerns.

Colin's mouth twisted. He hadn't had any other concerns at the time, had he? He'd only had more money than he'd ever need after selling the company. More rolled in all the time because of the patents he'd kept, but all the money in the world couldn't bring back what he had lost, and Stefan Benadi had known that. His old friend had died last year, but Colin would always be grateful to him. Stefan had given him Geneticon, and Geneticon had given him back his life.

Abruptly he turned back to the room. "I'm not going to be browbeaten into admitting reporters into my laboratories," he said. "Let them think what they like."

Richard tried not to look alarmed. "But that's what they're doing right now, Colin. If you would only issue a simple statement—"

Colin's dark eyes raked the newspaper on the desk with contempt. "I've no intention of issuing any statement at all," he said. "These rumors about some kind of Frankensteinian experiments going on at Geneticon are so absurd I refuse to dignify them with a reply."

"But that's just the point," Richard pressed. "There *are* rumors, and unless you do something right now to dispel them..." He saw Colin's eyes narrow and tried another approach. "Look, I know after what happened in California, you've got good reason to distrust the press. I can't blame you. But this situation is entirely different. If you won't think of yourself, at least think of the people who work for you. How can they possibly concentrate with all this other business going on?"

Colin hesitated at that, and Richard felt hopeful for the first time since entering the office. Perhaps he'd found the key. Colin was fiercely protective of his scientists; he guarded their privacy almost as ferociously as he guarded his own. If he thought they might be disturbed by these articles, he might listen to reason.

"All right," Colin said irritably. "What do you suggest?"

Richard didn't hesitate. He knew Colin would never voluntarily speak to the press, not after that traumatic experience in California five years ago, but something had to be done to rescue Geneticon from the adverse publicity, and he was sure he'd found a solution. "I think you should hire a public relations firm."

Colin looked at him as though he were out of his mind. "That's the most ridiculous idea I've ever heard. It's bad enough that someone is publishing lies about our experiments here, now you want us to advertise?"

"I'm not talking about advertising," Richard said. "What you need, what Geneticon needs, is a way of informing the public about genetic research." He gestured at the newspaper on the desk to emphasize his point. "You have to counteract this kind of negative publicity, Colin—"

"Which I fully intend to do once I find out who is responsible for spreading all these rumors! In case you've forgotten, we *try* to keep our experiments under wraps just to prevent this kind of thing from happening!"

"I know, and when we find out who started all this, we can take appropriate steps. But until then, we have to deal with the effect of these articles, and a skilled agency will be able to do that."

"And I suppose you have one in mind."

"As a matter of fact, I do," Richard said, undaunted by Colin's sarcasm. "One of my clients is Auguste Weidmar, of Weidmar Foods, you know, and without telling him why, I asked him for an opinion. As it happens, he's just decided to sign with the Clendenin Agency, and he maintains it's the best in the city."

Colin threw himself into the chair behind the desk. "I'll think about it."

Richard leaned forward and turned the paper so that the headline faced Colin. "When?"

Colin made an angry gesture. "I'll have my secretary look into it. Is that good enough?"

Richard shook his head. Pulling a card from his pocket, he held it out so that Colin was forced to take it. "The number is right here," he said, "and Auguste said the person you want to talk to is Reya Merrill."

Colin glared at him. "I suppose you want me to call her right now," he growled.

"No time like the present," Richard agreed pleasantly, and tried not to smile when Colin uttered a sound of exasperation and reached for the phone.

CHAPTER ONE

THE CHAMPAGNE CORK POPPED with a bang, shooting straight up to the ceiling where it left a crescent-shaped mark. Eyes sparkling, Reya Merrill snatched it out of the air one-handed as it came down again. Holding it aloft, she laughed in delight.

She was a slender young woman, just thirty, with a determined chin, a straight nose, and a mouth that lent even more animation to her expressive face. Sable hair brushed her shoulders, and the eyes that were deep blue in repose were brilliant sapphire now with excitement. Leaning forward with a quick movement that was so characteristic of her, she held her glass under the frothing spout as her equally excited assistant, Sally Dean, grandly splashed the wine up to the rim.

"A toast!" she said after Sally filled her own glass. "To—"

"To Auguste Weidmar!" Sally cried, waving the overflowing bottle in victory. "Bless his shriveled little old heart!"

"Sally!"

But Reya was too jubilant to be scandalized for long, and an instant later she was laughing as she and Sally clinked glasses and drank. She smiled as her assistant began dancing around the room; she felt like doing a jig herself.

This was a day for celebration. After months of working to land the Weidmar Foods account, she'd finally succeeded. The patriarchal head of Denver's oldest and finest food packaging company—"Weidmar Foods, bringing old-fashioned goodness right to your table"—had called a while ago to tell her solemnly and with a great deal of important throat-clearing that he had graciously decided to sign with the Clendenin Agency. Reya had barely prevented herself from giving a whoop of joy before she hung up the phone, and Sally had taken one look at her face and dashed to the lounge for the bottle of champagne she'd hidden in the refrigerator in anticipation. It wasn't every day that Reya landed a plum account like Weidmar, and as Sally generously added more champagne to her glass, Reya thought that if she could get one more like that, just one, her promotion would be ensured.

"Is this a private party, or can anyone join?"

Both women whirled around at the sound of that voice, Sally flushing guiltily when she saw the head of the agency, Joseph Clendenin, standing in the doorway. Reya smiled when she noticed her assistant discreetly trying to hide the champagne bottle behind her back. Grabbing an extra glass from the edge of her desk, Reya held it out with a laugh that was more effervescent than the champagne.

She'd never been intimidated by Joseph Clendenin, as so many of his employees had. She had known from that first interview with him two years ago that he was a fair man behind that stern facade. He expected results from his people, and he got them. Which was why the Clendenin Agency, even with its relatively small staff of ten, had such a fine reputation. It was the top public relations firm in Denver, and after that debacle she'd suffered in New York, she'd been surprised that anyone had responded to her letters of inquiry, much less the head of an agency like Clendenin. So she'd taken the first plane to Denver for an interview, determined not to let him know how badly she wanted the job.

But she hadn't wanted it so badly that she was prepared to compromise her principles, as Dayton and Associates had expected her to do in New York. She had boldy told Clendenin at the outset that she'd work hard for him if he hired her, but she wasn't going to be part of any fraudulent campaigns. If he expected that, he could find someone else.

Thankfully he'd been amused at this brash approach from a then twenty-eight-year-old marketing supervisor who'd just been fired from her last positon. He knew what had happened, he'd said. All he asked was that she give her best and the rest would take care of itself. It had.

Clendenin smiled as he accepted the glass she held out. "Don't mind if I do. Congratulations, Reya. That was a fine piece of work you did, bringing Weidmar into the fold."

"I'll say!" Sally blurted excitedly. "Who would have ever thought that old—" She stopped abruptly, turning beet red. "Oh, dear...."

Fortunately the phone rang just then in the outer office, and Reya grinned as her assistant dashed thankfully out to answer it. "I guess we're both excited, Mr. Clendenin. Sally didn't mean—"

Clendenin's eyes sparkled behind his thick glasses. He was a big man, broad shouldered and white haired, and he seemed to fill the entire office. "I know what she meant," he said, "and she's right. Auguste Weidmar might be the head of one of Denver's most respected firms, but he's still an old curmudgeon. I imagine you're going to have quite a time with him."

Reya smiled. "Oh, I have a few ideas."

His eyes glinted again. "I suspected you did."

"In fact—"

Sally appeared just then in the doorway, a strange expression on her face. "I'm sorry to interrupt, but there's a call for you, Reya."

"Not now, Sally."

Swallowing, the assistant looked from Reya to Clendenin and back again. "I really think you should take this call, Reya. It's Colin Hughes, and he wants to talk to you about representing Geneticon."

Reya was startled. Everyone in the city who read the paper knew about the recent articles on Geneticon. She remembered glancing at a headline about it today before she rushed out of the apartment. She hadn't taken the time to do more than skim the article because she was late, and now she looked uncertainly at her boss. "Maybe you should take the call...."

Clendenin raised a white eyebrow. "He asked for you."

"Yes, but obviously—"

Draining his glass, he handed it back to her. "Might as well start getting your feet wet," he said with a smile.

Surprised, Reya stared after him as he left the office. Her eyes met Sally's, and she knew they were both thinking the same thing. As head of the agency, Joseph Clendenin fielded all initial calls from prospective clients. It was he who decided whether to accept an account or not, and what to do with it if he did. Everyone who worked for him was free to make suggestions or come up with ideas of their own after that. He not only encouraged such response, he expected it. But he was still the one who made all the important decisions, and the thought that he had handed this to her just now could only mean one thing. Hardly daring to believe it, Reya felt excitement bubbling up inside her again.

"Might as well start getting your feet wet."

Did that really mean that he was ready to trust her with an account decision, that he was testing her to see how well she would handle it? Her promotion to account executive seemed just a phone call away, and as Reya glanced away from the grinning Sally to the instrument on her desk, she took a deep breath to steady herself.

Geneticon would be a big account, an important account, for until those recent articles in the paper, the research center had occupied a respected position among Denver's elite companies. There was a mystique attached to a private institute engaged in such esoteric pursuits as finding a cure for cancer or producing new vaccines to fight disease, and Denverites had spoken about it in hushed tones of awe, almost of reverence. Reya had heard it proudly proclaimed that one day Geneticon would rival even that bastion of genetic research, Cold Spring Harbor on Long Island, whose scientists came from all over the world to work under the famous Nobel laureate James Watson, co-discoverer of the structure of the DNA molecule.

So as Reya approached the phone, her heart began to beat a little faster. Her hand shaking slightly, she lifted the receiver, willing her voice under control.

"Reya Merrill."

The deep voice would have been pleasant if the owner hadn't been so abrupt. "This is Colin Hughes," he said curtly, as though he didn't care whether she knew who he was or not. "I'd like to make an appointment to discuss the possibility of your representing Geneticon."

"Certainly, Mr. Hughes," Reya answered, and tried not to notice that her hand was trembling as she began to flip through her appointment book. She saw with dismay that she was booked solid through the rest of the week and made a few rapid calculations. She could change the breakfast production meeting with Simmons Hardware to lunch, which would leave her free to reschedule the publicity meeting with Sayers Market for later in the week. Then if she moved the budget meeting with Hayes' Emporium to—

"I'll be in my office tomorrow morning at nine," Colin Hughes said brusquely, interrupting her frantic juggling.

"Tomorrow at nine?" she repeated weakly, staring down at her calendar. A bold red circle highlighted a conference with Auguste Weidmar at that time and Reya wondered how she could possibly put that off after his call today.

"Is there some problem with that?" the curt voice asked. "Because if there is—"

"No, no," Reya assured hastily. She would just have to reschedule Weidmar. "There's no problem at all. Tomorrow at nine is fine."

"Good," he said, sounding as though it wasn't at all. "Do you know how to get to Geneticon?"

"Yes, of course," she said smoothly, trying to hide her irritation at his tone. "It's just off Highway 36, toward Boulder, isn't it?"

"Yes. I'll leave word at the gate."

"The gate? Oh, I see. Well, fine. I'll see you to-morrow morning, then, Mr.—" But before she could finish, Colin Hughes said an abrupt goodbye and hung up.

Sally had been hovering in the doorway during most of the conversation, unashamedly eavesdropping. As Reya replaced the receiver with a frown, Sally exploded. "I can't believe it! Oh, Reya, if you get the Geneticon account..."

Reya couldn't help but feel piqued at the way Geneticon's owner had spoken to her. Normally she wouldn't have minded rearranging her schedule to accommodate a client; she did that willingly all the time. But Colin Hughes's manner was irritating. It was almost as though he resented having to contact her in the first place, and she wondered if he felt like that, why he had bothered to call at all. Annoyed, she looked at her assistant. "Don't hold your breath."

"What do you mean?" Sally asked. "He wanted an appointment, didn't he?"

"It was more like a summons to the royal presence," Reya replied, still irked. "Who is this man, anyway? Do we have any bio information on him?"

"Not much. I checked with research while you were on the phone. But we do have a picture of him...."

Sally handed it to her, a grainy newspaper print accompanied by an article dated five years earlier, when Colin Hughes had bought Geneticon. Staring down at the handsome, aloof face with the shaded eyes and arrogant nose, Reya was surprised. She had expected from his voice that he would be an older man, but if this picture had been taken at the time and wasn't a publicity print, it was obvious that he was only in his late thirties now. Scanning the article that gave little information beyond the bare details of his acquiring the research center, she muttered, "We must have more than this."

Sally had been reading the article over her shoulder. "Not really. I've heard he keeps a pretty low profile. But I'll have research see what else they can find." She hesitated, and then said with a sigh, "He's sure good-looking, isn't he?"

Reya had been thinking the same thing. Her glance had been drawn again and again to that face as she read the brief article, and she wished the picture had been clearer. But because she was still annoyed, she handed the paper back to Sally with a shrug. "If you like cold, overbearing men, I guess he is."

Sally peered more closely at the paper. "I don't know, Reya. There's something about his eyes..." She looked up again and grinned. "He isn't like Darren, is he?"

At the mention of her fiancé's name, Reya whirled around and looked at the clock. When she saw that it was after six-thirty, she groaned. She was supposed to be meeting Darren right now at Larimer Square for dinner; with all the excitement, she'd completely forgotten about their date. So punctual himself, Darren Enderly abhorred tardiness in others, and he'd be annoyed that she was late.

He was annoyed, all right; or as irritated as he ever allowed himself to be. She saw his petulant expression when she drove into the parking lot adjacent to the restaurant a few minutes later. By the time she locked the classic little powder blue '57 Thunderbird she was so proud of and walked to where he was standing outside the square, he was tapping his foot and staring pointedly at his watch.

"Hi," she said, determinedly ignoring his gesture. "Sorry I'm late."

"Where have you been? I've been standing here almost a half hour!"

Wondering why he simply hadn't waited for her in the restaurant, Reya decided not to ask. She hated it when he adopted that peevish tone, but because she was too eager to share her success today, she didn't want to spoil the evening with an argument. Smiling, she took his arm. "Let's go inside. I've got some wonderful news, and I'm dying to tell you."

He looked at her suspiciously, an attractive man with every blond hair in place, his round face closely shaven again, she knew, before he'd left his law office. Even at the end of a workday, his trousers remained perfectly pressed, his button-down shirt absolutely unwrinkled. His tie was tied just so, and she could have done her makeup by the shine of his shoes. He always looked as though he'd stepped from the pages of a fashion magazine, and normally she found these traits somewhat endearing. Tonight, for some reason, they irritated her.

Darren was still annoyed himself. Grudgingly, he asked, "What happened?"

She smiled again. "I'll tell you inside."

They had reservations at a restaurant in Larimer Square, one of the revitalized sections of the city. The buildings in this area were a century old and had been beautifully restored. The restaurant itself was part of a quaint little building that retained the original wainscoting and parquet floors. Dark green flowered wallpaper decorated the walls, and the intimate tables and booths boasted white linen with pink accents and fresh flowers. Reya and Darren had been here before and she'd been enchanted with the place, but tonight she was too preoccupied with her news to pay much attention to the decor. As they were seated in one of the booths, she looked across the table at Darren and wondered suddenly whether she should tell him about the Weidmar account after all.

She knew he wasn't going to be happy about it. He'd been pressuring her since they became engaged about the time she spent at her job. He couldn't seem to understand why her work meant so much to her, and she'd tried in vain to explain that her career was just as important to her as his was to him. Even so, they had just barely avoided a serious quarrel the last time they had discussed the agency. Wishing that she hadn't said anything about her exciting day, she was trying to decide how to broach the subject when Darren brought it up himself.

"So what's your news?" he asked.

He'd been studying the wine list with the intensity of a cryptologist examining the Dead Sea Scrolls, but now, obviously having made his choice, he set it aside to give her the same thoughtful, calm consideration he gave everything else. She thought fleetingly that this attention to detail was what probably made him a good attorney, and she knew that was what had drawn her to him in the first place. She had needed a stablizing influence in her life when she'd first come to Denver; being fired from her job had been a blow, and she'd lost confidence in herself. She was so determined to do well at Clendenin, so eager and anxious and unnerved about the move and the new job that being with Darren was like coming in from a storm.

She had been delighted to discover when they met through a friend that he enjoyed the symphony, one of her passions. And when she learned that he was also an avid hunter of antiques, she thought she had found the perfect mate. Now she wasn't so sure. This blind spot he had about her career was more than the irritant it had been in the beginning; it had become a widening gulf between them, and the main reason she had put off setting a wedding date.

"I got the Weidmar Foods account today," she said, and couldn't prevent the quiver of excitement in her voice. She looked at him, knowing he wouldn't be as thrilled about her coup as she was, but hoping he would at least be pleased for her.

"I see," he said, and picked up the wine list again. "Would you prefer the Montrachet, or the Château Lafite?"

She stared at him in disbelief. "Didn't you hear what I said?"

"Yes," he said calmly. "Now, I'd like a good red tonight, but if you're really in the mood for white, we'll order the Montrachet."

"Darren!"

Frowning, he looked at her over the top of the wine list. "I really don't think this is something we should discuss over dinner, do you?"

She was so annoyed at his reaction that she couldn't prevent a sarcastic reply. "When do you think we should discuss it? After we're married, and it's too late?"

He looked aggrieved at that. "I told you before how I felt about your devoting so much time to your work. I assumed you would take that into consideration."

"I have," she said, trying vainly to remain as calm as he. "It's just that I don't think you understand how important this is to me."

"More important than I am?"

"Of course not!"

"Well, then?"

"Well, what?" she sputtered. "Darren, you sound as though you expect me to quit my job and just stay at home after we're married!"

"Why not? Other women do."

"And others continue satisfying careers—"

"Not the wives of the partners."

He said that as if the last two words should be capitalized and engraved in gold, and she compressed her lips to prevent another sarcastic retort. He was referring to the wives of the men in the law firm he worked for: Auman, Gustafson and Waite. She had met *the wives* and hoped she'd never have to endure another evening like that again. They'd been like three peas in a pod, all perfectly groomed and coiffed, with finishing school accents and the conversational range of newts.

"Darren," she said, "you enjoy being a lawyer, don't you?"

"What does that have to do with it?"

"Just answer the question."

"Of course I do, but what—"

"Would you resign from your job just because you got married?"

He looked uncomfortable. "Of course not. But—"

"Then why do you think I should give up mine?"

He looked away. "It's not the same thing."

"Why isn't it?" she pressed. "You enjoy your work, and I enjoy mine. We've both trained hard for what we do, and we're both good at it. Tell me what the difference is.''

He turned back to her, his fair skin suddenly flushed. "It's just not . . . seemly, that's all!"

"Seemly! What does that mean?"

He leaned forward to emphasize his point. "Listen, Reya, you might not realize it, but I work for a very important, influential law firm. I expect to be invited to become a partner very soon. How do you think it would look if my wife was the only one who worked?"

She was losing her temper; she could feel it. "Why should you care how it *looks*? Isn't the important thing how *I* feel about it?"

"And what about *my* feelings?" he asked. "Haven't you thought about that?"

They seemed to have reached an impasse. Reya fought her temper as Darren took several sips from his water glass. As always, he was the first to compose himself.

"I told you this wasn't the time or place to discuss this," he said stiffly.

She was still trying to deal with her seething temper. "You're right about that," she said tightly. "Especially since we seem to have a difference of opinion about your work and mine!"

He flushed again, but to her annoyance was determined to remain calm. He *always* remained calm, she thought balefully; maybe that was part of the problem. If just once they could have a knock-down-and-drag-out fight about something, maybe she wouldn't feel as though she were beating her fists against a brick wall.

"I see that you're upset," he said. "Maybe you need time to think about this."

"*I* need time! Don't you think we both do?"

"No," he said simply. "You know that I love you, Reya. I've asked you to be my wife."

"So—"

But just then the wine steward came up to the table, and as if nothing had happened, Darren began an animated discussion about the wine selection with him. Fuming, Reya suddenly remembered the newspaper article Sally had shown her and the picture of Colin Hughes. *He* looked like a man who wouldn't care what anyone thought, she mused, and then was annoyed enough at the thought to turn her attention to Darren again. As a gesture of apology, he'd ordered the Montrachet for her after all, and she tried to feel warmed by that. They touched glasses in a silent toast, but as she drank, she saw that other face in her mind again and she frowned. Why was it that the wine, expensive as it was, suddenly tasted flat?

CHAPTER TWO

REYA STOPPED THE THUNDERBIRD before the high wrought-iron gates at Geneticon the next morning, wondering how she was going to get in. A solid brick wall surrounded the place, and the April morning was so quiet she could hear a bird chattering to itself somewhere to her right. The gates in front of her remained stubbornly shut, and she tapped her fingers impatiently against the steering wheel as she peered down the driveway ahead. Was she supposed to shout, honk the horn, get out and do a little dance on the hood of the car so someone would notice her and let her in? She glanced at her watch and frowned. It was five minutes to nine, and if someone didn't come soon, she'd be late. With a sigh, she got out of the car and looked around. Hoping there was a button to push or a siren to sound, she was just starting forward when a voice came out of nowhere, making her jump.

"State your business, please."

Feeling a little foolish talking to someone she couldn't see, she said, "This is Reya Merrill. I have an appointment with Mr. Hughes," and added pointedly, "at nine."

"Thank you, Ms Merrill," the voice said politely. "Mr. Hughes's office is in the first building to your right at the end of the driveway."

"Thank you," she said, and felt even more foolish. The voice sounded mechanical and flat and she still couldn't see where it was coming from.

"Our pleasure," came the response. Then, "Welcome to Geneticon."

Rolling her eyes, she walked the few steps back to the car, imagining a camera somewhere swinging around to follow her, recording every movement on tape. She was sure of it when the gates began to swing silently open just as she started the engine again, and she wondered if the camera was still following her as she drove through.

The driveway was a few hundred feet long, curving around to the right, shaded by a canopy of trees. Closely trimmed grass covered the grounds and Reya couldn't help wondering in amusement if the gardener had to have a security clearance to work here. Her good humor restored, she was still smiling as the collection of brick buildings appeared in front of her through the trees. A few moments later she was being ushered into Colin Hughes's office by a secretary who looked at her suspiciously before she announced, "Miss Merrill to see you, Mr. Hughes."

He was standing by a huge window behind his desk, staring out at a magnificent view of the Rocky Mountains that ringed Denver. He turned at her entrance, but for a second or two as he continued to stand there, the light behind him shaded his face and Reya instantly felt at a disadvantage. Secure behind the momentary anonymity, he was obviously scrutinizing her while she couldn't see him, and unconsciously she straightened. Glad that she had dressed carefully for this occasion in a pale lemon suit with an apricot silk blouse and matching heels, she decided to take the initiative. She came forward, holding out her hand.

"Good morning, Mr. Hughes. It's a pleasure meeting you."

He had no choice but to come forward himself to take her hand, and as the light fell on his face, Reya drew in a breath. That newspaper picture hadn't done him justice. With that high forehead and hawkish nose and dark eyes, he looked as though he'd walked out of a Brontë novel, an illusion heightened by the black hair waving back from a widow's peak, just grazing his ears and touching his collar in back. He was wearing a dark suit, a crisp white shirt with a blue-striped tie that had to be French silk, and the body under the perfect tailoring was tall and lean. Even though she was wearing heels, she had to look up at him, and as he took her hand in his, she tried not to stare. He was one of the most handsome men she'd ever seen, and his voice was as deep as she remembered it, and just as abrupt.

"Thank you for coming," he said in a tone that suggested he'd rather she hadn't come at all. He gestured her to a chair in front of the desk. "Shall we get down to business?"

Reya had brought a portfolio with her, an oversize leather case containing promos and press releases from work she had done for other companies. Vowing not to be disturbed by his abruptness, she began to open it. "I thought you might like to see what Clendenin has done for—"

"I'm not interested in what you've done for someone else," he interrupted, seating himself behind his desk. "I want to know what you can do for me."

Reya appeared calm as she placed the portfolio beside her chair, but inwardly she was growing more tense by the second. Reminding herself how important this account was to her, she summoned a smile. "That depends on what you want, Mr. Hughes. Clendenin is a full service agency, of course. We can help with everything from preparing annual budget reports to promoting new products. We will assist in producing company newsletters, and—"

"My accounting department is perfectly capable of handling Geneticon's financial statements, Miss Merrill, and as for the rest, we don't advertise and we don't need or want a company magazine. What we want is to be left alone!"

She sat back, startled by the vehemence of his last statement, though she didn't know why she should be. He was obviously angry about the publicity Geneticon had been receiving, and after having reread the articles herself, she couldn't blame him. "I assume you're referring to those recent articles in the paper," she said, and went on quickly when she saw his expression. "What you want, then, is an antipublicity campaign. Well, that can be arranged, too."

For the first time since she'd entered the room, he seemed taken aback. "It can?"

"Of course," she replied, and hoped she sounded more confident than she felt. For something like this to succeed, she needed the full cooperation of the client, and from what she'd seen of Colin Hughes so far, she wondered if she'd get it. Brushing away that thought, she continued, determined to make a convincing presentation. "One of the functions of a public relations firm is to counteract a negative image, and there are several ways of doing that. One is—"

Before she could say more, the office door opened and a man hurried in, apologizing to Colin for being late and turning to Reya with a smile.

"I'm Richard Carlyle, Geneticon's legal department," he said, wrapping her hand in his. "And you're Reya Merrill, of course. Colin and I are both grateful that you could take the time to talk with us today. We've been looking forward to meeting you."

Reya doubted from what Colin Hughes had said so far that he'd been looking forward to this meeting at all, but she smiled, thinking how different Richard Carlyle was from the members of Darren's stolid law firm. There was an openness about him, a glint of humor in his gray eyes that was appealing, and she was suddenly glad he'd arrived. The tense atmosphere seemed to lift at his entrance and she felt more confident. She sensed that he would be an ally, and from her conversation so far with Colin Hughes, it seemed she might need one.

"Thank you, Mr. Carlyle," she said with a smile as he took the chair beside her. "It's nice to meet you, too."

"Call me Richard, please. And don't let me interrupt."

Reya nodded in acknowledgment, and then aware of Colin's impatient expression, went on quickly. "Mr. Hughes and I were just discussing an antipublicity campaign for Geneticon."

Richard looked confused. "An antipublicity campaign?"

Reya nodded. "A device to counteract the effects of the recent newspaper articles."

Colin erupted at that. "It's beyond me," he said angrily, "how anyone with any intelligence at all could believe that we're trying to create a master race, or attempting to produce wings on dogs and webbed feet on cats! It's obvious that reporter doesn't have the faintest idea of what genetic research is all about.''

Reya, who had gone back to her office after ending that uncomfortable dinner with Darren last night to read everything she could find on Geneticon, looked at Colin calmly. "If you hire Clendenin, we'll take care of that. It will be our job to inform the public, to tell them about Geneticon so that they won't have to wonder—''

Colin sat back forcefully in his chair. "Let them wonder what they like. If the public is stupid enough to believe that kind of drivel, it doesn't deserve to be informed!''

"Now, Colin," Richard said with a quick glance at the startled Reya. "This is the reason we called Miss Merrill in the first place. Why don't we listen to what she has to say?''

Colin stood abruptly, his tanned face flushed with anger. "No. I think this meeting was a mistake. I'm sorry, Miss Merrill, but I don't see any purpose in continuing this discussion.''

Reya hid her dismay. She knew it would be fruitless to argue with him right now; he'd only become more antagonistic, more certain that he didn't need her. But she wasn't going to give up so easily; this account meant too much to her. She couldn't go back to the office and admit to Joseph Clendenin that she'd failed to get the first account he had entrusted her with, not without a fight, anyway. But there were other weapons she could use, and she drew on her arsenal now. Reaching for her portfolio again, she grasped the handle and stood.

"I'm sorry you feel that way, Mr. Hughes," she said. "My agency could have helped you a great deal. Countering the effect of those newspaper articles would have been difficult, but not impossible, and of course we're trained in that sort of thing. But if you prefer to handle this yourself . . ." She let that sink in a second or two as she turned to Richard Carlyle, who had risen with her, obviously distressed. Holding out her hand again, she said to him, "It was nice meeting you, Mr. Carlyle."

"Miss Merrill . . ."

She saw the pleading look in his eyes and wished she could reassure him before she turned to Geneticon's owner again. Satisfied to see the doubt in his dark glance, she smiled at him, too. "I would suggest, however," she said, "that if you intend to negate the effect of the publicity you've received so far, you should do something soon, before the situation gets worse. We're all aware that rumors have the unfortunate ability to solidify into fact unless challenged, and you wouldn't want that to happen."

With that, she turned to go.

"Wait!"

Almost at the door, Reya nearly sagged with relief. She'd seen the struggle on Colin's face as she turned away, but she'd really thought she'd lost him until she'd heard that peremptory command.

"Yes?" she said politely, and looked over her shoulder in time to catch the swift look the two men exchanged. Richard was glaring at Colin, obviously willing him to say something to keep her, and Colin was returning his look with an exasperated one of his own. She waited.

"I..." Colin began, and cleared his throat, looking more aggravated than before. He obviously wasn't accustomed to apologizing, and he had to try again. "I'm sorry," he said finally. "This business with the papers has been irritating, but I shouldn't have snapped at you like that. Please accept my apologies."

His eyes met hers just then, and without warning, Reya felt the effect of the dark glance all the way to her toes. The air seemed to become still, taut with some expectation that made her feel breathless without knowing why. It was as though a powerful current was drawing her to him against her will, and for a horrified instant as she stared at him, she couldn't even remember why she was here.

Then Richard stepped into her line of vision, and the spell, or whatever it had been, was broken. "I'm afraid we've all been affected by the recent publicity, Miss Merrill," he said. "You'll have to forgive us if things seem a little... tense."

Still dazed, Reya managed to nod. "I understand," she said, and wondered if she did. She wanted to turn around and leave before she became more involved, and it took a deliberate effort to thrust the impulse away. Reminding herself again how much this account could mean to her, she walked back to the desk. Richard held the chair for her and she sat down again. Pretending that nothing had happened, she took a pen and notepad from her purse and hoped neither man would notice that her hand was shaking.

"I believe you were going to tell us about an anti-publicity campaign," Richard said.

Reya took a deep breath, trying to arrange her scattered thoughts. "Yes," she began, and commanded herself to put everything else from her mind. "But in order for me to do that most effectively, I have to be conversant with the type of work Geneticon is doing, the experiments you're involved in here, that type of thing." She forced herself to look at Colin again. "Is it possible for you to give me some background material, Mr. Hughes?"

Colin studied her for a moment, his expression unreadable. "How much do you know about genetic research, Miss Merrill?" he asked finally.

Reya thought of how she'd spent half the night studying as much as she could about the subject. "I'm not a scientist, if that's what you're asking."

"Then I don't see how the details of the experiments in progress here could possibly be of any help, or interest, to you," he said flatly.

Richard was glaring again; she could see him out of the corner of her eye. But her confidence was returning; this was her job, after all. "Everything you do here at Geneticon is of interest to me, Mr. Hughes," she said calmly, and meant it. Before she committed herself, and the agency, to defending Geneticon, she had to be absolutely certain the rumors surrounding the center were untrue. If Colin agreed to give her full access to whatever information she required, she'd know he had nothing to hide. She went on before she lost courage. "And whatever files or documents you can provide will certainly be of help in proving that the accusations in the paper are . . . unfounded, don't you agree?"

For a few seconds, she was sure she had gone too far. She saw a muscle clench along Colin's jaw as he struggled to control himself, but before he could order her out of his office, she continued. "I think it would be a good idea for me to take a tour of the laboratories, as well.''

"That's an excellent idea!" Richard exclaimed before Colin could reply. Blithely ignoring the glare Colin directed at him, he looked at Reya. "If you have time now, I'm sure Colin wouldn't mind showing you around. He really is an excellent guide. Sometimes I think he knows more about those experiments than his scientists do. It's fascinating listening to him. He's almost a walking encyclopedia on genetic research."

In one of those lightning changes of mood that would so disorient her in the future, Colin leaned back in his chair and shook his head in mock disbelief. "These Machiavellian tactics don't suit you, Richard," he said dryly, and glanced at Reya. She was completely taken aback to see a glint of humor in his eyes before he looked at Richard again. "And I'm afraid it's too late to try to sell me to Miss Merrill. I'll show her around if you'll stop trying to make me sound like a reincarnation of Louis Pasteur."

Richard grinned. "You shouldn't have stopped me. The next thing I was going to say was that you'd worked with Watson and Crick on the discovery of DNA."

Reya looked from one man to the other in complete astonishment. The mood had changed so swiftly that she felt as though she'd missed something and didn't know what it was. Colin saw her confusion and smiled at her, disconcerting her even more. "Are you ready for the grand tour, Miss Merrill? Now that I've been manipulated into it, we might as well get started."

Richard left them in the hallway outside the office with a wave and an excuse that he had work to do, and as she watched him walk away, Reya was tempted to call him back. She still felt off balance, and confused thoughts about Colin were whirling in her mind. She never would have believed he was capable of poking fun at himself. After the introduction she'd had, she would have found it difficult to think he ever smiled. He was obviously a man of many facets, and suddenly she was uncomfortable at the thought of being alone with him.

Then she told herself she was being ridiculous. Why shouldn't she be alone with him? They weren't on a date. This was a business meeting, and he was a prospective client. She had a job to do, a job she was good at, and just because Colin Hughes had surprised her just now was no reason to let herself get so rattled.

But she was very aware of him all the same as he gestured and they began walking in the opposite direction Richard had gone, and as he held the outer door and she passed by him, she noticed again how tall he was. He seemed to tower over her as they paused on the top step of the administration building, and for some absurd reason, she remembered that Darren was barely five foot ten, and that she could look him in the eye if she was wearing heels.

Wondering why that thought had occurred to her, she shook her head and said, "Where are we going first?"

Now that he had agreed to show her around, Colin had obviously decided to be an amiable guide. Staring down at her, he asked, "Where would you like?"

His unwavering gaze made her even more uncomfortable and she looked quickly round at the scattered brick buildings linked by concrete walkways, choosing the nearest. "How about that one?"

He nodded. "Good choice. That's the cell biology unit."

Like many laymen, Reya had pictured a scientific laboratory as a dark, mysterious place where white-coated scientists labored unceasingly over microscopes, occasionally stirring smoking concoctions that bubbled above Bunsen burners. The cell biology lab was so different from that image that she stopped on the threshold and stared around in surprise.

There were microscopes, of course, scattered about the long counters, even one with a camera attached in a complicated arrangement that allowed two people to gaze into it while the lens acted as a third pair of eyes. And there were refrigerators, and labeled jars and bottles lining the shelves, and round machines she knew were centrifuges, and aluminum boxes that had to be incubators. She recognized all these things, but the biggest surprise was the young man who looked up as they entered. Wearing jeans and a T-shirt, he had sandals on his feet and a mop of hair that hadn't seen a barber in months. Behind him, light spilled in from open windows that framed another view of the Rockies, and he grinned as he saw Colin. Reaching out, he switched off the tape cassette that had been blaring some kind of rock music, and said, "If I'd known we had a visitor, I would have dressed."

"In a lab coat?" Colin said dryly. "I didn't think you owned one. Reya, this is Rick Demeo, the head of our cell biology department."

Reya was embarrassed. She'd thought from his appearance that he was a lab assistant, or even a janitor, and she was chagrined at her hasty judgment. Pulling herself together, she said hello, and thought as they shook hands that he couldn't have been more than twenty-five. He seemed very young to have such responsibility, and she wondered if he'd been some kind of prodigy.

"Miss Merrill is with the Clendenin Agency," Colin said, and added when Rick looked blank, "a public relations firm."

Instantly a guarded expression came into the young man's eyes. He looked at Colin suspiciously. "What do we need public relations for?"

"I wondered that myself until this morning," Colin said as Reya stared at him in surprise. "But after talking to Miss Merrill, I think she can help with the current, er, situation."

Rick looked at her again. "If you can get those reporters off our backs, you'll be doing us all a favor, Miss Merrill."

Reya smiled. "I'm certainly going to try. And since we might be working together, why don't you both call me Reya?"

Rick nodded. "Suits me—we're all on a first name basis here anyway. Would you like to see what we're working on?"

Pleased that she'd apparently won him over, she immediately accepted, and for the next half hour was totally enthralled as he took her through the various stages of the experiment he was working on. Using a series of petri dishes, flat round plates with a small lip, he showed her how he injected a protein that had been produced by a cancer-causing gene into a dish of living cells.

"We call these cancer-causing genes 'oncogenes,' he explained, "and discovery of these little guys is probably the most important cancer breakthrough in years."

"Why is that?" Reya asked, fascinated.

"Because now we can start—and stop—certain types of cancer," Colin answered.

As Reya looked at him, wide-eyed, he shook his head. "It will be some time before we're able to do that in humans, but still, it's a start."

Rick went on to the next plate, showing her under the microscope that after several hours the cells he had injected earlier that day were beginning to divide wildly.

"Now they've become cancerous," he said, and laughed as Reya involuntarily reared back. "Don't worry, they're not going to jump out of the dish."

Feeling a little foolish, she followed him to the next step. "This is an antibody we've made to counteract that protein you saw me inject in the first dish," he told her, concentrating as he injected this substance into a set of diseased cells.

Watching carefully, Reya asked, "What will this do?"

He put a petri dish from another ongoing experiment under the microscope and directed her to look down at the stage. "What do you see?"

Frowning, Reya stared through the eyepieces for a few moments, trying to decide. At last she looked up and said uncertainly, "It looks like the first dish, before you injected the protein."

Rich beamed at her. "Exactly," he said, with the pleased air of a teacher receiving the correct response from a student.

She looked confusedly from the smiling Colin to Rick again. "Exactly... what?"

Colin laughed. "What Rick is trying to say in his inimitable way is that those cells look the same because they are. A few hours after injecting the anti-body, the uncontrolled growth has come to a halt. The cells have returned to normal."

"That's what you meant when you said you could start and stop cancer, isn't it?" she asked excitedly, grasping the principle at last.

Colin nodded. "But only a fundamental level, re-member," he warned.

Her eyes widened again. "Do you know what this means?"

Rick and Colin exchanged amused glances. "I think she's got it," Rick said, and then took pity on her when he saw how embarrassed she was. "Don't worry," he said kindly, patting her arm. "I work here every day, and I still feel the same way you do right now."

Reya felt even more dazed and awestruck as they continued to a second lab where she met Molly Lan-sing, another young biologist who headed a group ex-ploring the phenomenon known as "jumping genes."

As Reya looked at her in disbelief, Molly laughed and explained, "We've known about jumping genes—or transposable genetic elements, if you want to be technical—since the 1940s, when Barbara McClin-tock discovered it first in maize. Now we're trying to discover how some organisms, such as yeast, rou-tinely alter their genes in response to their environ-ment."

Reya glanced around the laboratory at the compli-cated equipment, the computer terminals, and the ribbons of graph paper that covered the walls. "It's incredible," she said admiringly. "Can you really do that?"

"If we can," Colin said, staring at her intently, "we'll have some idea how all life forms are regulated, how the gene for one trait knows when to make its product and when not to."

"Yes," Molly put in, suddenly a little grim. "And we'll be able to explain why dogs don't grow wings, or why cats have claws instead of webbed feet."

Reya heard the same outrage and frustration in Molly's voice that she'd heard in Rick's, and for the first time really understood their anger. Now that she had seen for herself some of the work they were doing here, she sympathized completely with their reactions to the newspaper articles, and she couldn't even blame Colin for his earlier abruptness. It was obvious to her now that whoever had written those articles hadn't the faintest idea what he was talking about, and worse, without researching his material, had committed the sin of resorting to sensationalism to grab his readers' attention.

She was quiet as they left the last lab, where another group headed by a young husband and wife team were working on gene splicing: recombining genes to study their functions. Deep in thought, she was too preoccupied to notice Colin glancing curiously at her as they walked back to her car.

Something had happened to her during the tour, and she realized with dismay that she was having a difficult time being objective, an attitude that was essential if she was to be effective here. But after meeting Colin's young scientists and seeing their work, she was struck with the importance of what they were doing. Geneticon wasn't just a scientific institute exploring the mysteries of biology. The people here were on the threshold of a vast new frontier, offering tantalizing glimpses into a world where disease would be a thing of the past. It was mind-boggling, unbelievable. Even reading about it last night, she'd had no real idea. . . .

"Is something wrong?"

She looked blankly up at Colin, still preoccupied with her thoughts. "Wrong? Why do you ask that?"

He shrugged. "You've been so quiet."

"I was just thinking . . ."

He smiled slightly. "About your strategy?"

This time she looked at him directly. "Am I going to get a chance to plan any?"

"Do you think you can do something about the situation?" he countered.

Her chin lifted. "If I can have access to whatever files and information I might need . . . yes."

The gauntlet thrown, she waited tensely while he glanced away from her, toward another section of the complex. "Geneticon is a big company," he said finally. "You've only seen part of it. Over there—" he gestured toward a group of buildings some distance away that he hadn't included in the tour "—is the division where we make bacterially produced insulin and vaccines. And over there—" he indicated another section "—we're working on the hybridization of various agricultural crops, all genetically engineered products. There's more to Geneticon than what you saw today, and I'm not sure you understand that."

Mentally blessing her foresight in staying up half the night to memorize the facts and figures she'd gathered on the company, she said, "I understand that in the past six months your biggest competitor in making vaccines has overtaken you."

He blinked in surprise. "How do you know that?"

"That's my job."

He frowned. "Go on."

"Well, I think from what I've reviewed of your marketing procedures, you could reverse that with a new strategy. I worked out some projections last night. I could send them to you if you like. And as far as your agricultural division is concerned—"

He shook his head, holding up a hand in surrender. "All right, I give up. You've obviously done your homework."

"Naturally," she said, as though it shouldn't be a surprise. "And if Clendenin takes this account—"

His eyes narrowed. "If?"

She looked directly at him again. "I can't help you if I don't have full cooperation, Mr. Hughes," she said evenly. "But of course that decision is up to you. Now, if you still prefer to handle this yourself..."

He shook his head. "I think," he said slowly, "that you're capable of handling just about anything. If you're willing to take Geneticon as an account after that business in the papers, I'm willing to give it a try."

They had reached her car. She wanted to dance around it in sheer joy, but she smiled demurely instead. Holding out her hand to seal the bargain, she said, "After what I've seen today, Mr. Hughes, we'll do more than that."

He smiled, too, that wonderful smile of his that lightened his face and swept the shadows from his dark eyes. Grasping her hand in his, he said, "In that case, why don't you call me Colin?"

CHAPTER THREE

REYA WAS STILL EUPHORIC the next morning as she drove to a breakfast meeting with the owners of Hayes' Emporium, a small department store chain with stores in Denver and Colorado Springs. It was another of the meetings she'd had to have Sally hastily reschedule, but it was worth it, after what had happened yesterday.

Still hardly able to believe that in the past two days she'd captured two big accounts, she felt like shouting the news to the whole world. It was the most exciting thing that had happened in her career since the day eight years ago when she'd walked into her first job as a research assistant. Now, if things went the way she planned, she'd soon be an account executive, and the dream she'd dreamed then, in that tiny cubicle of an office she'd shared with three other assistants, would come true. It seemed within her grasp now, for yesterday after she'd returned from Geneticon, she'd told Joseph Clendenin the exciting news, and he'd been very pleased.

"It's a big account, Reya," he'd said, gazing at her through those thick glasses with a twinkle in his eye. "Do you think you can handle it?"

"Absolutely."

He smiled at this show of confidence. "It will be a lot of work, what with the Weidmar Foods account, too."

"I'm prepared for that."

He sat back in his chair. "Yes," he said thoughtfully, "I believe you are. All right, Reya—it's all yours."

She'd practically floated out of his office and back to her own. It wasn't until Sally had mentioned Darren that she'd returned to earth with a thump.

"Oh, Reya, I knew you could do it!" Sally said, hugging her. "Just think, I'm working for an executive now!"

"Well, he didn't go that far...."

"Yes, but he will if you do well on this, Reya. And you will—I just know it. What did Darren say when you told him?"

Reya's smile faded. "I, uh, haven't had a chance to tell him yet."

"Oh, boy," Sally said, sighing. They'd been friends long enough for her to know how Darren felt about Reya's devotion to her job. "What are you going to do?"

"I don't know. He'll just have to understand, I guess."

Sally rolled her eyes. "I can see it now."

"Well, what else can I do?"

Shaking her head dolefully, Sally said, "Don't look at me. Darren is your problem, not mine. I wish you luck. I've got a feeling you're going to need it."

Thinking about that conversation as she drove down Colorado Boulevard this morning, Reya felt her elation disappear. What *was* she going to do about Darren? She had deliberately refused to think about his reaction when he heard the news. She had been so jubilant last night that she hadn't mentioned it to him when they'd spoken over the phone.

But she knew she couldn't avoid the subject forever. This problem Darren had with her working had to be dealt with, and soon. They'd been engaged almost a year, and every time Darren asked her to set a wedding date, she'd put him off with some excuse. She was running out of excuses, and Darren was starting to get impatient. She couldn't blame him, but she was still hesitant, and this was why.

Thoughtfully, she glanced down at her engagement ring, a diamond solitaire in a prong setting. She'd wanted a heavy band set with jade, and she still remembered how shocked Darren had been at the idea. An engagement ring meant a diamond to him, and that was that. He'd been so pleased with himself the night he'd presented her with the ring that she hadn't had the heart to say anything. Now she realized there were a lot of things she hadn't said these past few months, and she knew it was time she did.

Vowing that she'd ask Darren over for dinner tonight and talk to him then, she resolutely put the problem from her mind. Right now she had other things to think about, chief of which was convincing Delbert Hayes and his sons that they'd have to put an employees' lounge in each of their three stores if they expected to keep their clerks. Pulling into a parking spot at Writers' Manor, a favorite meeting place because the conference rooms were so spacious and the setting so pleasant, she grabbed her briefcase and purse and went inside.

The meeting lasted nearly three hours, and by the time she climbed into the Thunderbird again and headed downtown to the office, she was awash with innumerable cups of coffee, teary eyed with the smoke from Delbert Senior's fat cigars, and elated that she had at last wrested a sullen agreement from him about the employees' lounges. The next thing she had to do was get comparative costs for the construction, and she was still mulling over which companies to call for bids when she arrived at the agency. Lost in thought, she didn't notice at first that Sally wasn't at her desk. She went straight into her office and then halted in surprise to see Sid Beamer, head of the art department, sitting behind her desk, his feet propped comfortably on one of the drawers.

She liked Sid, a slight, blond man of thirty-five, with perpetually ink-stained fingers and an incredible talent for transforming ideas into pictures. They had developed a good working relationship, and had collaborated on many successful layouts. "What are you doing here?" she asked, and gestured good-naturedly for him to remove his feet from her desk.

Swinging his legs down, he stood and stretched. "I came to congratulate you," he replied and looked pointedly at the clock. "But obviously success has gone to your head. Since when do you waltz in at noon?"

She smiled. "It's not nearly that, and for your information, I had an early meeting." She wrinkled her nose. "With Delbert Hayes and his cigars. Can't you tell?"

"I thought you'd taken up smoking."

"Are you trying to tell me I should have gone home first and changed?"

He looked innocently at the ceiling. "Well, an account executive does have to maintain a certain image."

"That's a little premature. Mr. Clendenin is waiting to see how I handle the account."

"Which one—Weidmar or Geneticon?"

"Both," she admitted. "But Geneticon especially."

"Well, from the looks of it, it's going to be a challenge. Have you seen the paper today?"

The smile vanished from her face. "No, why?"

He pulled a rolled paper from his back pocket and held it up for her to see. "Here, read it and weep."

The front-page headline leaped out at her, and she groaned. "Where No Gene has been Before, and Shouldn't have Gone."

As Reya sank down onto the edge of the desk, gripping the paper, Sid said sympathetically, "It looks like you've got your work cut out for you, doesn't it?"

She hardly heard the remark; she was too busy reading the article. It was even worse than she had anticipated, and she grimaced when she finished. "I'm surprised we didn't hear the explosion from here."

"From Geneticon, you mean?"

"Who else?" she asked glumly, and handed the paper back to Sid.

"I wonder which 'highly placed' source the reporter is referring to," Sid murmured, glancing over the article again.

Reya stared at him, wondering why she hadn't asked herself that question before. Where *was* the reporter getting his information?

Colin had given her reports and records on all the ongoing experiments at Geneticon yesterday before she left, and she'd again spent half the night reading. He had warned her that the reports were confidential, and that normally he wouldn't have allowed any written material to leave the complex. She had been flattered that he'd trusted her so completely, but now she wondered if he had trusted someone else who was busily betraying him to the press. He had assured her that everyone who worked at Geneticon was loyal, and she had seen evidence of it herself. But the rumors had started somehow, somewhere, and inside Geneticon seemed the logical place to look. Dreading the thought of asking Colin about his security and screening procedures, she looked at Sid. "I hope you don't believe that rubbish," she said.

He pretended surprise. "You mean Geneticon really isn't out to create a master race?"

She glared at him. "Not funny."

"Oh, come on, Reya. Who's going to believe this? Everyone knows we're light-years away from doing something like that, assuming anyone would even want to try."

"I'm sure one day there will be someone who will. And in the meantime, people believe what they read. Colin will be furious about this, and I can't blame him."

"Colin?" Sid asked innocently.

Despite herself, Reya flushed. "Yes, Colin," she said, and reached for the phone. "Now, if you don't mind, I've got some work to do even if you don't."

Sid laughed, unperturbed. Saluting her with the paper as she glared at him, he turned around and bumped into Sally, who had just come rushing in. At her assistant's expression, Reya put down the receiver.

"What's wrong?"

"God, I thought you'd never get here!" Sally cried. "Where have you been?"

Reya tried to hide her alarm. "You knew I had an early meeting."

"Yes, but I didn't think it would last this long!" Sally wailed, and threw herself into the chair opposite the desk. "Geneticon's been calling all morning. First the secretary, and then someone named Richard Carlyle, and finally, Colin Hughes himself. He wants to talk to you right away."

Reya reached hastily for the phone again. "I was just going to call him—"

"No!" Sally said, shaking her head. "He wants to talk to you out there, at Geneticon. I told him you'd be there by noon."

Reya's eyes swung to the clock. Grimacing when she saw that she had twenty minutes to make the drive, she grabbed her purse and briefcase again. Sally followed her as she rushed out, and she paused briefly to look back at her assistant. "Did he say anything? How did he sound?"

Sally hesitated. "Mad," she finally admitted. "I'm sorry, Reya. I didn't know what else to tell him."

Reya jerked the door open. "If he calls again, tell him I'm on my way."

Fighting the urge to press the accelerator to the floorboard as soon as she got onto the highway, Reya took the little Thunderbird to the speed limit and held it there as she flew down the road, thinking furiously.

She hadn't planned on meeting Colin again until the end of the week; she'd hoped she would have that much time at least to map out a full campaign. Now she had to come up with something concrete before she got there, and the thought that she had only about twenty minutes to do it galvanized her. Examining and then rejecting alternatives as soon as they occurred to her, she finally realized there was only one thing they could do at this point. Praying that Colin would agree with her, she practically skidded to a stop before the tall wrought-iron gates, and this time didn't wait to be greeted politely by the disembodied voice. Slamming her hand down, she held it on the horn.

Mercifully the gates swung open almost at once, and she drove through, forcing herself to a slightly slower pace. She was not going to arrive in a spew of gravel and dash disheveled into his office, but all the same her steps were quick as she entered the building. The grim-faced secretary, even more grim than before, was waiting for her, and she barely had time to take a deep breath to steady herself before she was in Colin's office again.

He wasn't standing by the windows this time. He was seated behind his desk, and after seeing the expression on his face, she was surprised that the entire office hadn't burst into flame. She had never seen anyone look so enraged, and for an instant or two, she was so unnerved she couldn't say anything.

Then his glance met hers, and that was even worse. His eyes looked black with anger, and his voice actually shook as he stood and said, "*This* is how you're going to take care of Geneticon's account?"

Reya saw the newspaper spread out on his desk and brushed away the thought that he wasn't being fair. She'd only gotten the account yesterday, and he couldn't possibly blame her because another article had appeared in the *Tribune* this morning. Even if she'd had time to find out about it, she wouldn't have been able to prevent it. As much as she would have liked to at times, she couldn't control the press. All anyone in public relations could do was try to swing reporters over to the client's side, or at the least, convince them that the client deserved a fair hearing.

All these thoughts flashed through her mind in those first few seconds. But even if she hadn't been too proud to make excuses, she wouldn't have tried to rationalize. It wasn't a question of guilt or blame anyway; the important thing was to decide how to handle it now that the damage had been done. Taking another deep breath, she plunged in with her proposal.

"I think we should call an immediate press conference to refute these articles," she said. "We'll set it up for—"

"No!"

The single word was like a rifle shot, and Reya actually jumped. She stared at him in surprised dismay. "But—"

"I said, no press conference!"

Trying to remain calm, she made another attempt. "I know how you feel about the press—"

He cut across her words again, his voice harsh. "You don't have any idea how I feel about the press!"

She refused to let him intimidate her. "I know you're angry, and that you have a right to be, but—"

"I'm not going to stand up in front of a crowd of reporters and defend Geneticon against such outrageous lies!"

"You don't have to," she said quickly. "That's my job. I'll act as Geneticon's spokeswoman—"

"No!"

For an absurd instant, Reya felt like banging her fists against the top of the desk in sheer frustration, insisting that he listen to her, demanding to know why he was being so stubborn. Realizing that she was clenching her jaw so tightly it was beginning to ache, she tried to get herself under control by glancing around the room, away from those smoldering dark eyes.

She'd been so intent yesterday, focusing all her attention on Colin himself, that she hadn't noticed the office decor until now. As she looked around in an attempt to collect her thoughts, she was suddenly struck by the total absence of personal effects.

Despite the luxurious thick beige carpet on the floor and the obviously genuine walnut desk, the office could have belonged to anyone. There was a rust-colored couch at one end of the room, flanked by two matching chairs, and a walnut cabinet in one corner beside some shelves. Colin's desk with the two chairs in front completed the furnishings, and there were no accessories that might have given a clue to the occupant, not even a plant or two to provide color.

Most of her clients' offices had been personalized to some degree. She could get a sense of the person she was working with the instant she entered, by the family photographs on the desk or the pictures on the walls or even the artifacts placed carefully around the room. Auguste Weidmar had a collection of still lifes, which hadn't surprised her; his display of antique pocket knives in a glass case had. And Delbert Hayes of Hayes' Emporium, with his fat cigars and blustering manner, had astonished her with his curio cabinet filled with delicate jade and porcelain figurines.

But Colin's desk was bare of all but essentials: a beige telephone, a leather-bound blotter, an onyx pen stand. And the only picture on the wall was a technical representation of the DNA molecule, the double helix with its two entwined strands that contained the genetic code of life. It was a working office, clean and bare and functional, and gave absolutely no hint of the man who occupied it save for that single picture. It seemed obvious from that that Colin Hughes was obsessed with genetics, and as Reya glanced back to him, she thought that perhaps that was the most significant clue of all.

She tried again. "If you would just consider the idea..."

His jaw set. "No. It's out of the question."

"But you have to say something!"

The jaw tightened. "I don't have to say anything, Miss Merrill. That's your job."

"Then let me do it!"

There was a sudden, awful silence during which Reya tried vainly to control the color creeping up into her cheeks at her outburst, and in which Colin looked ready to explode again. Before he could order her out of his office, she had to make him understand how important it was to speak out. If they didn't refute those articles, she knew the tone would only get worse. She had seen it happen before, and the only way to stave off real disaster was by being as open as possible. They had to remove Geneticon as a target, and the most effective means of doing that was to provide information. Feeling a little desperate, she tried to explain that to him.

"Mr. Hughes, my business is educating the public to accept certain ideas or products in the best possible light, but I can't do that if my hands are tied. Geneticon is under attack right now, and there's no point in debating the injustice of that. The fact is that some reporter is trying to make a name for himself by sensationalizing this story, and the only way to stop him is by taking away his ammunition.''

"And you believe that a press conference is the way to do that."

It wasn't a question, and her reply was just as direct. "I do."

"Well, I don't. The most I'll agree to is a flat denial."

Reya wanted to accept the compromise; she knew she should be grateful he'd conceded her even that. But he hadn't hired her to adopt half measures, and she knew that once the public interest was aroused, a denial wasn't going to satisfy the growing curiosity about what was going on at Geneticon. She shook her head, once more braving his anger.

"I'm sorry, but that's not going to be enough. If you don't agree to an open forum, the press will be convinced that you really do have something to hide, and then we'll have a real fight on our hands."

With an angry exclamation, he turned abruptly away from her. His profile and the set of his wide shoulders were so stiff that she despaired. He had to see the logic of what she suggested, she thought, and wondered what she would do if he didn't. She held her breath as he finally turned back to her again.

"No," he said flatly. "No press conference. You'll have to think of something else."

She knew by his expression that it would be pointless to argue any further, but she was taut with anger as she whirled around and went to the door. Just what did he expect her to do when he stymied her at every turn? Maybe he'd do better with another agency, one that would unquestioningly obey without regard for what was best for Geneticon. Was that what he wanted? If it was, he'd hired the wrong person.

Her lips tight, she decided right then that she wasn't going to bow out so easily. He had hired her, and she was going to work on the account until he fired her. Because that's what he'd have to do. It had become even more of a challenge now, and she wasn't going to give up, not until she'd exhausted every possibility. And certainly not because he was too stubborn and pigheaded to listen to reason.

"Miss Merrill...Reya..." he said suddenly, just as she reached the door.

Still angry, hardly trusting herself to speak because she felt like shouting at him, she looked over her shoulder and said coolly, "Yes?"

He still looked angry himself. "I'm sorry," he said brusquely. "I have my reasons."

Taken aback by the apology, as curt as it was, she steeled herself against the shadows that had appeared in his eyes. "I'm sure you do," she replied. "Unfortunately that isn't going to alleviate the situation."

He flushed under his tan, but held her glance. "I know," he said, and then surprised her even more by adding, "I'll think about it. That's the most I can promise."

It wasn't enough, but it would have to do. Amazed that she'd gotten even that much of a concession from him, Reya drove slowly back to the office. It wasn't until she'd pulled into her space in the parking lot that she realized she hadn't thought of campaign strategy at all during the thirty-minute drive. To her annoyance, she'd been thinking of Colin himself, remembering how handsome he'd looked despite his fury, recalling that startling apology at the end. She'd been affected by that despite herself; it wasn't the words he had uttered, but the tone in which he had said them....

Am I attracted to him? she wondered as she got out of the car, and then immediately dismissed the idea as absurd. Oh, of course, he was a handsome man; she'd be a fool to deny that. And she supposed there would be plenty of women who would be attracted to those dark good looks, that lean face with the hollows under the cheekbones, and that aristocratic, high-bridged nose. His eyes alone were enough to set feminine hearts fluttering: so dark they appeared almost black at times, with those straight, black brows. And his lean body allowed him to wear clothes with such a casual grace that she knew, even if they hadn't been tailored, they would have looked as though they had been.

He did have an air about him, she had to admit that. He wore confidence and assurance as easily as he did his clothes. She hadn't noticed a wedding ring, but that didn't mean anything, and if he wasn't married, undoubtedly he'd have dozens of mistresses. A man like that would, she thought, and wondered why she felt so annoyed at the idea. It wasn't any of her business. The only thing she had to be concerned about was what she was going to do for Geneticon itself.

And that, she thought darkly, was another problem entirely. If she didn't come up with some ideas soon, she wouldn't have to worry about Geneticon; she would lose the account.

That wasn't going to happen, she vowed. From now on, if she wanted that promotion, she'd devote more thought to Geneticon than she did to its owner. On that resolve, Reya marched into the office and stopped at Sally's desk.

"I want all the information you can get me on Colin Hughes," she said. "Today."

Sally looked up from her typewriter. "Don't tell me—it didn't go well."

Reya looked grim. "About as well as you'd expect."

Sally sighed and reached for the phone. "I'll get on it right away."

Reya didn't know how Sally did it, but that afternoon she came in with a stack of typed papers. Seeing one of San Francisco's prominent newspapers mentioned at the top of nearly every page as she thumbed through, Reya looked up curiously.

"The *Chronicle*?"

Sally lifted her shoulders. "That article we have said that Colin Hughes was originally from California, so I called a friend of mine who works at San Francisco library. I knew you wanted this stuff right away, so I had her give it to me over the phone, but she's sending photocopies out today."

"You're a wonder, Sally. What would I do without you?"

Sally grinned. "Fortunately for you, you won't have to try. Do you want a summary, or do you want to read it yourself?"

She could see that Sally was eager to impart the news, and because she'd been so diligent, Reya couldn't deny her the opportunity. "Go ahead."

Sally immediately perched on the desk. "Well, according to the *Chronicle*, five years ago Colin Hughes owned a huge computer-component manufacturing company in Silicon Valley. That's near San Jose, not too far from—"

"I know where it is, Sally," Reya said dryly. "Go on."

"Well, the company was called Hughes TechCraft, and in addition to manufacturing computer parts, they'd patented several inventions that set the whole industry on its ear. I don't understand all that computer stuff, but apparently they had something to do with speeding up the process or something. Anyway, it doesn't matter, because after he sold the company, he held on to the patents, and those alone would have made him a wealthy man."

"If the company was doing so well, why did he sell?"

Sally's expression was mysterious. "No one else could figure that out either, at first. He just put the company up for sale one day, and that was that."

Reya tried to contain her impatience. "But he must have had a reason."

"Oh, he did." Obviously tempted to draw this out, Sally paused dramatically. "He managed to keep it a secret for a long time, but some reporter finally found out that his daughter was sick."

"His daughter!"

Launched into her story again, Sally didn't notice Reya's dismayed expression. "Yes, and that reporter also found out that Colin and his wife had taken the little girl everywhere for treatment, even to Europe. He guessed then that that was why Colin sold the company. He was too preoccupied with his daughter to care about anything else."

Reya had a sinking feeling. "She must have been very sick," she said faintly, somehow sure of what Sally was going to say.

"She was. They finally ended up at Stanford Medical Center. Colin stayed with her for weeks, until . . ."

There was a silence. Finally Reya said quietly, "He must have been devastated."

Sally looked indignant. "And do you know that reporter dogged them the whole time? It was almost as though the man had an obsession or something. He had to find out everything he could and publish it all, as though the family had no rights to their privacy. Well, he found out all right. Colin's daughter died of some rare and fatal form of congenital anemia."

Reya sat back, stunned, remembering suddenly that picture of the DNA molecule in Colin's office. She'd thought then that he was obsessed with genetics; now she understood why. And the news about his daughter also explained his deep antagonism toward the press. Cringing, she recalled how adamant she'd been about the press conference. If only she'd known!

"But that's not the worst of it," Sally said, interrupting her thoughts.

"There can't be more!"

"There is. Apparently Colin's wife was so distraught by their little girl's death that she...she killed herself."

Reya was so shocked she didn't know what to say. Sally saw her expression and asked quickly, "Are you all right?"

Reya hardly heard her. She was thinking of that shadowed expression she'd seen in Colin's eyes, the sadness and the pain that sometimes seemed to lurk so near the surface despite his control. Now she knew why. "Yes," she said faintly. "I'm fine. It's just such a...a sad story."

She couldn't concentrate after Sally had returned to the outer office; she just sat there staring vacantly into space. Finally her glance went to the phone, and she reached for it without thinking, intending to call Colin and tell him...

Tell him what? she wondered, dropping her hand abruptly to the desk. What could she say? That she knew he'd lost his wife and daughter, and that she understood now why Geneticon was so important to him? He'd think she'd lost her mind.

Wondering if she had, Reya told herself firmly that it wasn't any of her business. Colin Hughes was a client, nothing more. Her only concern was how best to represent Geneticon, and his private life was none of her affair.

But all the rest of that long afternoon, as she tried to concentrate on other matters, her thoughts kept returning to Colin and the look she had seen in his eyes hours before when he'd apologized to her. She hadn't thought so then, but the longer she pondered it, the more she was convinced that he'd been almost pleading with her to understand.

Then she told herself she was being ridiculous. Colin Hughes was undoubtedly the last man she'd ever met who would plead with anyone about anything. This wasn't a romantic story where the tragic hero turned to the sympathetic heroine because she understood how he had suffered; this was real life, and she wasn't a heroine at all. She was a working woman who would be out of a job if she didn't get something done, and with a sigh, she got back to work.

She was halfway home that night before she remembered she hadn't called Darren to ask him to dinner. It had completely slipped her mind, and she wondered what was wrong with her. Normally she didn't forget things like that. Everyone teased her, in fact, about her infallible memory.

Well, it hadn't been so infallible today, and those articles from the *Chronicle* were at fault. If she hadn't had the brilliant idea of asking Sally to dig up all she could about Colin Hughes, she wouldn't have been so distracted by what they'd found out. She could have remained in blissful ignorance and not given him another thought.

It was absurd, ridiculous, and she was annoyed with herself. If she couldn't control herself any better than this, she didn't deserve the Geneticon account. Tomorrow, she vowed, she'd have herself in hand. This preoccupation with Colin Hughes simply had to stop.

COLIN STOOD at his office window, gazing somberly at the mountains. The Rockies, still covered with snow even in April, were beautiful at any time of day, but especially at sunset, when the snow on the peaks turned to glittering gold. The sight normally soothed him, but it didn't tonight, and with a frustrated exclamation, he turned away.

His glance fell on the desk, and he frowned. It was covered with reports and charts and requests for new equipment that had come in during the day, and usually, he would have taken care of it all long before now. He always read the reports eagerly; he had no trouble making decisions about even the costliest of equipment. Tonight, he felt like sweeping it all into the wastebasket.

He'd been trying to concentrate all day, and yet every time he opened a new folder or ran a column of figures, he'd find himself pausing in the middle of it to think about Reya Merrill. It was maddening, infuriating, and the more he told himself he was going to forget about her, the more preoccupied he became. He couldn't stop thinking about those deep blue eyes of hers, or the way her dark hair fell like a lustrous curtain to her shoulders. He'd wanted to touch it this morning to see if it was as soft as it looked, and remembering the way her slender hips had moved under her slim skirt, he felt a pang.

Then he remembered the diamond engagement ring she was wearing, and he threw himself into the desk chair he'd just abandoned and pulled one of the reports toward him. He wasn't going to think about Reya; he was going to get some work done. He wouldn't leave the office until the desk was cleared, even if it took all night.

A few minutes later, after reading the same sentence five times, he realized that it might. What the hell was the matter with him?

Shoving the folder away, he stood up and began to pace. He couldn't imagine why Reya Merrill affected him so much, but the fact that she did disturbed him even more. Was it because she had blue eyes, like Claire?

But Claire's eyes had been cornflower blue, not the deep sapphire of Reya's, and her hair had been a soft blond, not Reya's deep brown, a color so dark it could have been sable. They weren't anything alike at all.

He paused abruptly, realizing for the first time that he'd actually been thinking of his wife without feeling that devastating sense of loss. The idea was so novel that he dropped down onto the arm of the rust-colored couch, hardly daring to believe it. He'd trained himself not to think about either his wife or his daughter because the pain had been so great that sometimes he'd thought he'd go out of his mind with it. It had been five years since Becky's illness and

Claire's suicide, but until a few moments ago, it was as though it had happened yesterday. Was he really getting over it? Was that terrible pain going to go away? The psychiatrist had said it would, but he hadn't believed it....

He still didn't, he thought, angrily getting up again to go back to the desk. He'd had moments before where he'd forgotten—almost. He'd forced himself to go out with several women since Claire, but they'd all been brief encounters that hadn't done anything but alleviate his loneliness for a night. Then the pain would return, more intense than before, until he felt like smashing something just to make it go away. He wasn't going to be fooled this time, not again.

Resolutely he pulled another folder toward him, a cost estimate of an upcoming project. His work was the only thing that kept him sane, and he willed himself to concentrate, running the figures in his head so that he wouldn't be distracted.

But still he saw a face in his mind, and he paused again. Because this time the face was framed by sable hair, and the eyes that looked back at him weren't a cornflower color at all, but a blue so deep he knew this time he might drown.

CHAPTER FOUR

REYA TOOK ONE LOOK at her assistant's face when she arrived at the office the next morning and felt even more exasperated than she had before. It was barely nine o'clock and already it hadn't been the best of days. She hadn't slept well last night and Darren was the reason why.

She knew she had to tell him about the Geneticon account sooner or later, and she'd finally decided after tossing and turning all night that it might as well be today. She had called him upon rising before she lost courage to ask him to lunch, and had been so tense about the whole situation that she hadn't even objected when he immediately suggested meeting at the Quorum, across from the state capitol. It was one of his favorite restaurants because it was a haunt of politicians, and normally she shunned the place. Today she didn't care. She just wanted to get this Geneticon business straightened out with him before he found out about it from somewhere else, but after she hung up, she began to feel resentful. It wasn't fair that she felt so reluctant to discuss her work with Darren. He was supposed to be proud of her success. Wasn't that what a relationship was all about?

Apparently it wasn't, at least in this case, and as she left her apartment on University Boulevard and drove into the office, she was annoyed. Her annoyance deepened the longer she thought about the situation, and by the time she arrived at the agency on Colfax Avenue in the heart of downtown Denver, she was in a foul mood that worsened the instant she saw Sally's expression. Something was wrong.

"What is it?" she asked, pausing by Sally's desk. "I know there wasn't another article about Geneticon in this morning's paper because I checked."

Sally stood, gathering the messages she'd taken since coming in. "The boss wants to see you," she said.

Reya held out her hand for the memos. Despite her effort to remain calm, her heart was beginning to pound. A summons to Joseph Clendenin's office wasn't unusual in itself; she wouldn't have given it a thought except for the strange expression in Sally's eyes. "All right. When?"

Sally glanced down, pretending some preoccupation with the things on her desk. "He said as soon as you came in."

Reya's pulse began to beat a little faster. "Did he say why?" she asked as casually as she could.

Sally shook her head. "No, but he didn't sound too pleased."

"That makes two of us," Reya muttered, and started toward her office to put away her things. "Buzz and tell him I'm on my way, will you?"

Joseph Clendenin's office was at the end of the hall, and as Reya walked toward the closed double doors, she tried to bring herself under control. She had to be professional about this. She suspected that he was going to ask her about the progress of the Geneticon account, and she had to think of something to tell him.

The only problem, she thought glumly, was that she had nothing to say.

She'd spent half of last night trying to come up with a strategy after Colin had made it clear he didn't want to give a press conference, but she'd finally given up and hoped that something would occur to her today. After that scene yesterday, she wondered if he would approve any idea that called for his working with the media, and yet if he didn't allow someone from Geneticon to act as spokesperson, her hands would be tied. She had to make him see that a flat denial of the allegations made so far would only make things worse, but she could just imagine what his reaction would be if she tried to make use of her contacts at the local radio and television stations.

She and Brian Goodwin of KRDA were good friends and had worked together in the past. She knew that if she could convince the station manager to give Colin an interview, Brian would be impartial and fair. But it wouldn't matter how fair Brian was if Colin refused to speak to him, and as Reya approached Joseph Clendenin's office, she felt even more discouraged than before. She'd hoped to get something settled before the boss asked for a report, but it seemed she wasn't going to have that luxury. Wincing at the memory of her arrogant display of self-confidence the other day, she went in. Across an expanse of gold carpet, Clendenin's secretary, Martha Kinsey, glanced up.

"Good morning, Reya," she said pleasantly. "Mr. Clendenin is waiting for you. Please go right in."

Martha had been with the agency for years, so long she was just as much a fixture as the owner himself. She was somewhere in her fifties, no one knew for sure just where, with short, neat, iron-gray hair and cool gray eyes and a well-kept figure. She could recall with unfailing accuracy details of accounts dating back nearly twenty years, and she had made the transition from typewriter to word processor with her usual intimidating efficiency. Reya had heard it said that Joseph Clendenin wouldn't be able to function without her, and she believed it. But as she summoned a smile for the secretary today, she wished that Martha wasn't so adept at hiding her feelings. No one ever knew what Martha was thinking, and at times like this, it would have been helpful to have at least a little hint about what was going on behind that door.

Knowing it would be futile to ask, she stifled a sigh, knocked lightly, and went in.

"Ah, Reya," Joseph Clendenin said, "here at last."

Was that a subtle rebuke for being late? As he set aside the newspaper he'd been reading and gestured for her to take a seat, Reya couldn't prevent a quick glance at the ornate clock on the wall behind the desk. Her guilty conscience was working overtime; it was still only a few minutes after nine. She sat down, and as she looked around, trying to compose herself, she couldn't help thinking how different this office was from Colin's. There were no beiges and rusts and earth tones here; the color scheme was gold and red with black accents, as bold and aggressive as the occupant himself. As her glance nervously came back to Clendenin, she privately took back everything she'd thought before about not feeling intimidated by him. Trying not to feel like a supplicant, she forced herself to say, "You wanted to see me?"

He sat back in the black leather wing chair. Reya had been reminded of a throne the first time she'd seen it, and the impression hadn't been altered since. It seemed even more appropriate today because she couldn't tell from his expression if he was displeased with her or not. Deciding that she hadn't given him anything to be pleased about, she tried to smile. Her face felt too stiff.

"I thought you might want to see me," he said, and gestured toward the paper he had set aside. Reya realized then that it was yesterday's edition of the *Tribune*, with the latest article about Geneticon prominently displayed. Trying not to flinch, she raised her eyes just as he leaned toward her. "This is your first account, after all," he said, "and I thought there might be some, er, problems you would like to discuss."

"Problems?" she repeated, trying to sound surprised. She wanted him to think that she was in complete control of the situation. "Why, no, not really. I was out at Geneticon yesterday, in fact, working on strategy with Col—with Mr. Hughes."

"I see."

She wasn't sure what that meant, and for an instant was tempted to abandon her pose and just blurt out the awful truth about what had happened when she'd gone to see Colin. But she couldn't confess to failure that quickly, not when Joseph Clendenin had just entrusted her with this account. She knew that if she admitted she needed help, she'd never get another chance at managing another account by herself. Her head came up. Her professional pride was at stake, she thought, not to mention her professional future. She had to make him think that everything was going well, that she was absolutely in charge.

With more confidence than she felt, she said, "I thought an antipublicity campaign to counter the effect of the damaging articles would be most effective.''

''An excellent idea,'' he said approvingly. ''Go on.''

She should have known he was going to ask her to elaborate, and the warmth she felt at the first part of his comment vanished abruptly. Feeling like a fool, she prayed that he wouldn't question her further when she said, somewhat lamely, ''Well, we're working on the details right now.''

''I see,'' he said again, and glanced at the newspaper with the headlines that seemed to scream at her. ''Do you mind my making a suggestion?'' he asked dryly.

Her cheeks reddened. ''Of course not.''

''I'd recommend that you don't take too long deciding on strategy. The tone of these articles about Geneticon is getting, shall we say, somewhat strident?''

We could definitely say that, Reya thought, and excused herself as quickly as possible. Relieved that she'd escaped so easily, she wanted to sag against the door as soon as she came out, but Martha was there, so she squared her shoulders and marched down the hall. Trying to take comfort in the fact that she still had an office of her own to go back to, she waited until she was behind her own desk to collapse.

''How'd it go?''

Reya was sitting with her head in her hands, trying to recover from that nerve-racking conversation when Sally hesitantly asked the question from the doorway. Dropping her hands, she straightened. She had managed to squirm her way out of trouble this morning, but she knew she couldn't be that evasive again. The next time Clendenin asked, he'd want to know the details about Geneticon's account, and if she couldn't give him something concrete, he'd take it away from her and handle it himself. She wasn't about to let that happen, not the first time he'd given her this responsibility. She'd find a way. All she had to do was to discover the right approach.

"It went better than I expected," she lied. "But I'd like an appointment with Colin Hughes today. Please call Geneticon and set one up."

She was almost at her desk when Reya remembered her fiancé. Calling Sally back again, she said, "I promised to have lunch with Darren, so see if you can work around that, all right?"

Sally looked skeptical. "What if Mr. Hughes says lunch is all he's got?"

Reya felt a fierce headache coming on. Why was nothing simple today? she wondered, and tried not to snap back a reply. "Do what you can. But if that's all the time he has, Darren will just have to understand."

Sally knew by her tone not to say anything to that. She went wordlessly out again, and Reya was just reaching for her briefcase when the intercom buzzed. "Mr. Hughes isn't in yet, Reya. His secretary doesn't know when to expect him."

Exasperated at the news, Reya couldn't help a sarcastic, "Today—or ever?"

Sally giggled. "Should I ask?"

"Don't you dare! Just . . . keep trying, I guess. He's got to come in sometime."

"You're the boss."

Was she? Reya wondered dismally. The way things were going, she doubted she'd be able to keep her present position, much less be promoted to account executive. Sighing, she rifled through the messages

Sally had given her earlier and started to work. It was senseless worrying about Colin and Geneticon until she could get hold of him, and in the meantime she had a thousand other things to do before lunch.

She never made it to lunch. Just as she was leaving the office for the brisk walk down Colfax to the restaurant, Sally buzzed on the intercom again. "It's Mr. Dunne of Sweet Dreams," Sally said, naming the owner of a chain of confectionery shops who was in the process of selling out to a conglomerate.

Reya glanced at the clock. If she stopped to take the call she would probably be late, and she didn't want to do anything to upset Darren today before she told him her latest news. Things were going to be tense enough. "Tell him I'll call him back."

"I don't know.... He sounds pretty upset."

Sighing, Reya put her purse down on the desk and picked up the phone. "Mr. Dunne?" she said pleasantly. "This is Reya Merrill. How are—"

"It's disastrous, the worst possible thing that could have happened!" Mr. Dunne's high-pitched voice cried in her ear. "You have to do something or I'll be ruined!"

She didn't want to deal with this, not today when she had so many other things on her mind. Herbert Dunne had been hard to please from the beginning, and everyone at the agency had agreed they'd be relieved when the sale of his sweet shops was complete and their job was finished. Suppressing a sigh, she sat down again.

"I'm sure it's not as bad as that," she said soothingly. "Can you tell me what the problem—"

"The problem is that Sugarland's executives are coming two weeks earlier than we planned!" Dunne cried. He sounded as though he was almost in tears. "We're never going to be ready, not with the presentation you planned! Oh, what are we going to do?"

"I think the first thing to do is—"

"Yes, yes, I know," he interrupted shrilly. "I've already called an emergency meeting of my executive officers and we're all here, waiting for you. I knew you'd want to come to my office right away."

She was dismayed at that. "Well, I—"

His voice rose even higher. "Are you saying you won't come?"

She closed her eyes, praying for patience. She thought of Darren and decided he'd just have to accept the fact that she had an emergency. "Of course I'll come," she said. "I just need a few minutes to clear up some things, and then I'll be right over."

He was too upset to thank her. "We'll be waiting," he said, and hung up.

As much as she wanted to, she couldn't waste any time being annoyed at this peremptory summons. The receiver still in her hand, she dialed Darren's private line, hoping he hadn't already left for the restaurant. She didn't want to imagine his reaction if he arrived and found a message saying she couldn't come after all. Drumming her fingers on the top of the desk, she listened as the phone rang for the third time and was just about to hang up when he answered.

"Darren, it's me," she said quickly.

"Where are you?"

"I'm still at the office. That's why I'm calling—"

"Are you calling to tell me you're going to be late?" he interrupted, immediately sounding exasperated.

"Well, I—"

"Do you know how much juggling I had to do to free this hour today? I'm up to my ears in research for that corporate takeover case, and we're meeting this afternoon!"

"I'm sorry, Darren, but this emergency just came up—"

"What emergency? What could be so important that you have to break our date?"

She took a deep breath, reminding herself to be patient. She hated it when he took this tone, as though his time were more precious than hers. "If you'll give me a chance, I'll explain."

"Oh, forget it," he said petulantly. "You were the one who wanted to have lunch today. I assumed you meant it when you said you had something important you wanted to talk to me about."

It seemed that every time she'd turned around this morning she'd been faced with yet another unsolvable problem, and Darren's attitude right now was the last straw. Even though she knew she should have chosen a better time, she couldn't stop herself from saying sharply, "I did have something I wanted to talk to you about."

He didn't care for her tone, either. "So, go ahead."

That did it. "All right," she said. "I didn't intend to discuss this over the phone, but since you ask, I thought you might like to know I got a new account the other day."

There was silence. She defiantly refused to break it. *Let him ask for a change,* she thought irately, and waited.

After a moment he said warily, "I thought we already had this conversation."

"Well, we're about to have it again," she informed him, and despite herself, took a deep breath. "The account is Geneticon."

There was another silence. She could almost hear him thinking furiously, see his frown becoming deeper. "Geneticon," he said finally. "That's the research center that's been in the papers lately, isn't it? The place where they're doing all those weird experiments."

"The experiments they're doing aren't 'weird'!"

"Well, what would you call them then? Aren't they trying to create a master race or something?"

"They most certainly are not!"

"How would you know?"

"Because I've been out there!"

His voice sharpened. "When?"

"Yesterday...the day before. What does it matter?" she asked impatiently. "The point is—"

"The point is that you have no business being out there in the first place! Damn it, Reya, how could you do this to me?"

Reya was so surprised that for a few seconds she didn't know what to say. "What are you talking about?" she sputtered finally. "I haven't done *anything* to you. I'm just doing my job!"

"And that includes making a fool out of me? How do you think this is going to look?"

She stiffened. "To whom?"

"To...to everyone!"

Her eyes narrowed. "You mean to the men in your law firm, don't you? That's who you're really concerned about, isn't it?"

"Well, of course it is," he said angrily. "And I think you should be, too! You *know* I'm working toward a partnership here. It doesn't take much imagination to picture what the reaction will be if anyone finds out my fiancée is involved with that...that reincarnation of Frankenstein's laboratory!"

"How dare you call it that!"

"That's what it is, isn't it?"

"It is not! What happened to your assertion that a good attorney always gets the facts before he makes a judgment?"

"I know what I read!"

"Then you should know that what you read in the papers isn't always the gospel truth!"

There was another of those silences. Reya could almost see him struggling for control, and if the circumstances had been less heated, she would have marveled that he'd lost command of himself as much as he had. This was the closest they'd come to an argument since they'd met, and she knew he had to be genuinely upset to have taken it this far. Even so, she couldn't allow herself to weaken and apologize. This difference of opinion was about more than Geneticon and they both knew it.

"I think," he said finally, "that we should end this conversation before we both say something we regret."

"I agree," she said, equally cool.

He wasn't finished. "And in the meantime, perhaps you can think about which means more to you—our relationship or this...this new account."

Her hand tightened on the receiver. "I don't think it's fair of you to ask me to make that choice, Darren. I wouldn't ask it of you."

"I'm not involved with Geneticon," he said coldly, and hung up.

"Damn it all!" she muttered, and was tempted to smash the phone down in exasperation. She couldn't believe she'd just had that conversation; it hadn't turned out at all as she'd planned. Now things were worse between them than before, and she knew he expected her to mull over the situation during the next few days and come to the conclusion that he was right. She'd done it before, she reminded herself, over other small differences of opinion. He had no reason to think that this time would be different.

Grabbing her briefcase again, she stood up. Well, this time was different, she thought defiantly. She wasn't going to give up a career opportunity like this just because Darren was afraid of what the men in his law firm might say. *Darren* was the one who was going to have to make the choice this time, and if he felt that their opinion was more important than hers, well . . .

But she didn't want to think about that yet. Gathering her things, she went out to Sally's office to ask for the Sweet Dreams file so she could go over it before her meeting with Herbert Dunne.

"Do you want me to get you some lunch?" Sally asked, handing her the folder.

Reya took the file, scanning it quickly. "No, I don't have time. I'll grab something on the way back." She looked up again. "Did you make my appointment with Colin Hughes?"

"His secretary hasn't called back yet. She said she would when he came into the office, so—"

Reya impatiently placed the folder in her briefcase. "Try again while I'm gone," she ordered. "I shouldn't be out of the office more than an hour or so, and unless something else goes wrong, my afternoon is free. I want to see him today."

"I'll try," Sally said with a sigh. And as Reya hurried out, she called, "Don't forget to get a sandwich or something!"

Reya waved her hand in acknowledgment without turning around, but she'd already forgotten about lunch by the time she reached her car. There were too many other things to think about, one of which was getting this meeting over with the hysterical Mr. Dunne so she could race back to the office to see if Sally had gotten through to Geneticon yet. If she hadn't, Reya vowed, she'd either call herself and keep on calling until Colin answered, or she'd go out there and camp on his doorstep. One way or another she was going to see him today. They had some things to straighten out.

COLIN JERKED OPEN THE DOOR of his office and strode inside, Richard Carlyle following close behind. They had just returned from lunch at another of Richard's fabled finds, and until a few minutes ago, everything had been fine. Then Richard had asked him about Reya Merrill, and he'd made the mistake of telling him what had happened yesterday. Richard hadn't wasted any time telling him what a fool he'd been, and Colin was still irritated when he threw himself into the chair behind his desk. To his annoyance, Richard sat down across from him.

"I told you I don't want to discuss it anymore," he growled as Richard opened his mouth. "You've had your say. Don't you have any work to do...in your *own* office?"

Richard wasn't intimidated. "This is more important," he said. "You still haven't told me why you—"

Colin jumped up again. "I don't have to explain anything to you," he said angrily.

"You do when Geneticon's future is at stake. Or don't you need a legal adviser anymore? I can always go back to private practice, you know."

Colin abruptly stopped his pacing. "Do you want to?" he demanded.

"I think the point is more whether you want me to," Richard said. "Now, are we going to talk about this or not?"

"We are not."

Richard didn't argue further. He rose and started toward the door. "Suit yourself, then."

"Wait!"

Richard waited.

"All right, all right," Colin said in exasperation. "But there's nothing to talk about. She wanted to hold a press conference and I said no. That's it."

"That's hardly 'it,'" Richard said, sounding irritated himself for the first time. They'd had these discussions about the press before, and he knew how difficult Colin could be. He admitted he had a good reason for his aversion, but there were limits, even to a friend's patience. "By telling Reya—and her name *is* Reya, you know—"

"I'm aware of that!"

"You are? I wasn't sure you were, since you keep calling her 'she.'"

Did he? Colin wondered, and knew he did. It was his way of keeping her at a distance mentally. Not about to admit that to Richard, he said impatiently, "What difference does it make what I call her? Why don't you just get to the point? Or do you have one?"

Ignoring the sarcasm, Richard said, "My point is that you have to cooperate with some of Reya's suggestions."

"Why?"

Richard looked nonplussed. "Why? Well, isn't that evident? If you don't, what point is there in having a public relations director?"

Colin threw himself into his chair again. "I don't know—you tell me. This was *your* brilliant idea, remember?"

It wasn't often that Richard lost his temper; it was rare that he even became angry. But that stubborn expression on Colin's face was the last straw. He'd tried to be tactful and diplomatic; he'd tried to spare Colin's feelings. But as he'd thought moments ago, there were limits, and he'd reached them now.

"I can't believe you're being so willfully obtuse about this!" he exploded. "Don't you understand what Reya can do for you—what she can do for Geneticon—if you just give her the chance?"

Colin shot to his feet again. "I won't have reporters nosing around again! They've done enough damage!"

Despite Colin's efforts, Richard heard the note of pain in his voice, and knew he wasn't thinking of the current situation, but of what had happened last time. But he couldn't weaken now; if he did, Colin's blindness about the press might cause him to lose Geneticon, and he knew that his friend would never recover from that blow, not after all he'd lost before. It would be the end of him, and Richard was not going to allow that to happen, not without a fight.

"It won't be like that," he said.

Colin's eyes blazed. "How do you know?"

"Because I know!" Richard shouted. "Now, damn it, Colin, you've indulged yourself enough in this childish revenge against the press! I know how you suffered before, and you had good reason to hate the media then. But this is *now*, and the situation is entirely different! You've got someone who is trained to deal with exactly this type of thing, and if you don't let her do her job, you deserve to lose everything!"

Out of breath, Richard stopped. He was appalled at what he'd said, all those terrible things. Then he stiffened. He'd meant every word. He was tired of being diplomatic. What Colin needed was a good right to the jaw. Metaphorically speaking, that was.

Colin was staring at him as though he couldn't believe what he was seeing. While Richard waited for the explosion, he went to the bar hidden in one of the bookcases and poured himself a glass of water. He was tempted to pour something stronger. Glass in hand, he turned back to the room. "Well?" Richard demanded aggressively. "Aren't you going to say anything?"

Colin shook his head. Richard was still so unnerved at what he'd done that he didn't see Colin's mouth twitch in the beginnings of a smile. "I'm not sure," Colin said. "Don't you think you've said enough for the both of us?"

Richard tossed back the rest of the water and slammed the glass on the bar for good measure. "I can go on if I have to," he said, bracing himself for the onslaught. "It's been a long time, but you know I can give as good as I get."

"Yes," Colin said solemnly. "I know that."

"We'll stay here all night if that's what it takes."

"I don't think that will be necessary," Colin said. "You made your point."

"Because if you think I'm going to give up... What did you say?"

"I said you made your point. I concede."

"I—" Richard stopped and looked at him suspiciously. "I don't know whether to believe you or not."

"Believe it, because you're right. Geneticon is more important than my feelings about the past."

Now that he'd won the argument, Richard was uncomfortable with the victory. "I didn't say that, exactly," he muttered.

Colin waved his hand. "It doesn't matter. The only thing that matters is Geneticon, and what... Reya... can do for us." His expression became rueful. "Any suggestions on how to extend the olive branch? In addition to everything else, I wasn't very pleasant to her the other day."

Trying to stifle his grin of triumph, Richard went to the door. "I'm sure you'll think of something," he said, and went out.

CHAPTER FIVE

IT WAS THREE O'CLOCK by the time Reya returned to her office. The session with Herbert Dunne and his people had gone on much longer than she had anticipated, but by the end of the marathon meeting she had finally succeeded in convincing everyone that the presentation would go ahead as planned. She didn't mention that to pull all this off she'd have to log extra hours; it wasn't really Dunne's concern. Driving tiredly back to the office, she didn't care how much time she had to devote if, when she was finished, Sweet Dreams became someone else's problem. Trying to calm the hysterical Mr. Dunne had been exhausting.

Sally was at her desk typing furiously when Reya arrived. She had to lean over the desk and touch her assistant on the shoulder to get her attention. Sally jumped, whirling around to exclaim, "Oh! It's you!"

Reya was amused. "Who did you think it was? Did you get that appointment for me with Mr. Hughes yet?"

"No, his secretary hasn't called back. I—"

The phone rang just then, and Reya gestured, indicating she could go ahead and answer it. She went into her own office and saw that the work she'd left in such a rush was still there, with more added in her absence, and with a sigh she sat down at her desk. She was just reaching for some artwork Sid had left when Sally appeared in the doorway.

"It's Mr. Hughes, Reya," she said.

Reya looked up in surprise. "That was fast."

"He called before I got a chance," Sally said, round eyed. "He's on the phone right now—him, not his secretary. Line one."

Reya reached for the phone before she lost courage. She hadn't expected Colin to call himself, and the fact that he had flustered her so much that the speech she had so carefully prepared about having to see him today completely slipped her mind. Unnerved, she retreated into formality, and winced after she lifted the receiver and said, "Good afternoon, Mr. Hughes. This is Reya Merrill. I'm glad you called—"

"I just got the message that you wanted to talk to me."

His voice was just as deep as she remembered it, but different, and at first she didn't know why. Then she realized he didn't sound antagonistic. Since the only reason she could think of was that he had decided against using the agency's services, she tried to brace herself. It was too nerve-racking to wait until he said something, so she plunged in and said briskly, "Yes, I was hoping to set up an appointment to see you today, but I suppose it's too late for that now. Would you possibly have time tomorrow? There are a few things I'd like to discuss."

"As would I," he said, alarming her even more. What things did *he* want to discuss with her? "But unfortunately tomorrow is a bad day for me."

"I see," she said, trying to control her voice. Did he plan to relieve her of the account before she even got started? "Well, then, if tomorrow isn't suitable, how about the day after?"

"How about tonight?"

"Tonight?"

"Yes. I thought we could meet for dinner."

A refusal immediately sprang to her lips, and she was about to make any excuse not to go when she realized how ridiculous that would sound. She'd just told him she was anxious to meet with him, and it wasn't as though the invitation was an outrageous proposal. She went to dinner with clients all the time.

But not with clients like Colin Hughes. She rejected the thought the instant it flashed into her mind. There was nothing different about Colin Hughes, she told herself firmly. He was just like any of her other accounts.

"Miss Merrill?"

She blinked. How long had she been sitting here, just staring into space? She made up her mind. "Dinner is fine, Mr. Hughes. Where shall we meet?"

There was the briefest of hesitations, just time enough for her to wonder if he had intended on picking her up at her apartment. She rejected that notion, too. This was a business dinner, nothing more. There was no reason to believe that he intended it to be a date. But then, despite her assertion, she felt a thrill when he said, "I enjoy Château Pyrenees. How about you?"

Château Pyrenees was one of Denver's finest, a restaurant housed in a wonderful stone château that Reya suspected might have been transported stone by stone directly from France. The superb cuisine rivaled the decor, and she'd heard that the waiters and waitresses actually wore tuxedos. She was flattered that he had chosen such a place, but it was out of the question. How could she discuss business there, surrounded by all that elegance?

"I'm afraid I haven't been there," she said. "But—"

He seemed not to notice her objection, or if he did, he ignored it. "Château Pyrenees it is, then. Shall I pick you up?"

She was dismayed by that, too. She seemed to have lost control of the conversation, and in an effort to remind him that this was a business meeting, she said firmly, "I think it would be better if we met there. What time would be convenient for you?"

He seemed amused at that. "Eight-thirty would be nice," he said. "Unless another time is better for you."

"No, eight-thirty is fine," she said, wondering how she'd gotten into this. Well, it was too late now. The instant he'd mentioned the name of the restaurant, she should have countered with someplace a little less . . . intimate. Annoyed with herself, she hung up and saw Sally still standing in the doorway. From the expression on her face, she'd obviously been listening to the entire conversation, and because she felt so foolish, her voice was more sharp than she intended. "Yes? What is it?"

Sally was so enthralled that she mistakenly took the question for an invitation. She came the rest of the way into the office and sat down on the edge of a chair. "Are you really going out with Colin Hughes?" she asked, her eyes even more round than before. "Where?"

Reya pretended a sudden interest in the jumbled folders on her desk. "Château Pyrenees. But it's a business dinner, nothing more," she said coolly.

"At Château Pyrenees?" Sally said disbelievingly. "That's one of the most romantic places in town! It's like going to a real château. Even the menu is entirely in French!"

"I'm not going there for the menu, remember? Mr. Hughes and I have important things to discuss."

"Well, good luck," Sally said doubtfully. "If it was me—"

"Well, it's not," Reya said abruptly. Sally was conjuring glamorous visions in her mind that she'd rather not think about. When she found herself wondering what Colin would look like in formal evening dress, she reached for the nearest folder on her desk. "Don't you have any work to do?" she asked. "Where are the figures on the Fenneman account? Or the press releases for Arbitron? I can't seem to find them here."

Sally reluctantly stood up. "You don't want to talk about it, do you?"

Reya looked up. "No."

Sally sighed. "All right. But I think you're making a big mistake."

"I'm beginning to think that my mistake was in accepting the Geneticon account in the first place," Reya said irritably. "Now, may I *please* have those things I asked for?"

"You're looking right at them," Sally said, and hastily skipped out, closing the door.

By sheer force of will, Reya stayed at the office until six that night. The afternoon had dragged on interminably, and she couldn't seem to concentrate no matter what she did. She told herself that she wasn't going to think about dinner until she got to the restaurant, but it seemed that was all she could think about. She vacillated back and forth, wondering at first if Colin's choice of a restaurant was significant, as Sally had implied. Then, with her face reddening, she told herself he'd probably chosen the restaurant because he couldn't imagine going anywhere else. Colin Hughes was wealthy and successful. A man like that wouldn't have suggested dinner at some greasy spoon, it was as simple as that.

Then why did she spend a great part of that afternoon wondering what to wear? When she found herself debating between evening pants or a dress for the twelfth time, she uttered an impatient exclamation. What difference did it make what she wore? She hadn't agreed to this dinner to impress him. She'd only consented because they couldn't seem to work out another time and she had to talk to him immediately about her plans for Geneticon.

At a restaurant like Château Pyrenees?

Muttering again, she decided enough was enough and went home to take a long bath. The traffic was heavy that afternoon, and as she inched along, she distracted herself from thoughts of Colin by remembering her first visit to Denver. She had found her apartment then, and liked it so much she hadn't looked for another since. It was near enough to the University of Denver so that if she ever found the energy or the time to take a night class or two, she wouldn't have far to drive, but the best part was that Washington Park was so close. She often took the work she brought home on weekends to the park, and when she'd been office-bound too long, she went around the fitness trail a time or two. She'd found a place she liked to work near one of the ponds, and never forgot to take the ducks something to eat when she went. Spoiled by other visitors, the birds expected a treat, and would pester her until she threw every last breadcrumb to them. The sight was so amusing that she often went there just to feed them.

Turning off the busy street when she reached her address, she parked the car under the carport and went through the courtyard with its fountain and profusion of vines. The greenery gave the courtyard an old-world look, and her apartment on the second floor reflected a blending of old and new. Darren had been scandalized at first by her eclectic mixture of periods and styles, but even though she loved hunting antiques, she preferred to use her finds as accents. Opening the door onto a living room that was decorated in the jade and mauve and cream colors taken from the fabric of her gull-arm sofa and love seat, she smiled. She loved her apartment. Whenever she came home, she always felt as though she'd entered a haven.

She glanced at the beautiful Country French coffee table that had taken hours of refinishing. Remembering that Darren had helped her refinish that table, she frowned and went into the bedroom. She didn't want to think about Darren, not right now.

Eight-thirty arrived both too quickly and not soon enough. The restaurant was softly lighted from the outside when she turned onto Arapahoe Road, and with the skyline behind, Château Pyrenees looked exactly like a French château. She didn't see Colin, so she quickly checked her makeup in the rearview mirror as the valet came to take her car.

She had taken time with her appearance tonight, trying to convince herself as she spent an hour getting

ready that such attention wasn't out of the ordinary.
She refused to recall when she had last taken so long
to do her hair and eyes, but when she saw the valet's
face light appreciatively as she stepped out of the car,
she knew the time had been worth it. She was also glad
she'd decided to wear black evening pants and a sap-
phire-beaded overblouse. The outfit made her feel elegant and sophisticated, and as she walked toward the
door, she hoped she'd continue to feel that way. She
knew from experience now how difficult a man Colin
could be, and the last thing she wanted tonight was to
create another scene.

The moment she entered the restaurant she forgot
about Colin and everything else. Awed by the sight of
a magnificent Spanish chandelier, she was staring at
it when she felt someone come up behind her. Thinking it was the maitre d', she turned with some comment, but whatever she'd been about to say died
unsaid. Colin was standing there, and he was so
handsome in his dark suit that he took her breath
away.

"I hope you haven't been waiting long," he said
with a smile that made her heart turn over.

The thought flashed through her mind that she'd
been waiting for him all her life. She was appalled.
What was happening to her? She wasn't even sure she
liked this man; what she'd thought just now was absolutely mad.

"I...uh...no," she stammered, trying desperately to pull herself together. It took a tremendous effort, but she managed to wrench her eyes away from
his face. The first thing she saw was that chandelier,
and she seized on that as a conversation topic with al-

most overwhemling relief. "In fact, I was just admiring this chandelier."

"It is beautiful, isn't it," he murmured.

Why did she have the feeling that they weren't talking about the same thing? She could feel him staring at her, and that unnerved her even more. She couldn't understand it. She'd been out with handsome men before. Why was Colin having such a devastating effect on her tonight? It must have been that quarrel she'd had with Darren, she told herself, and frowned.

"Is something wrong?"

She didn't dare look at him, not until she had herself under better control. "Wrong?" she repeated, and glanced quickly around. Spying the magnificent grand piano that was yet another part of the elegant appointments, she forgot her discomfiture. "That's Louis XVI, isn't it?" she exclaimed.

Colin followed the direction of her glance. "I believe it is," he said, sounding amused. "I didn't know you were an expert on antiques."

She did look at him then, relieved that for the moment, at least, they had found a safe subject. "Hardly an expert," she said wryly. "But it would be difficult to miss something like that. It looks like an original."

They were shown to their table then, and as Reya was seated, she reminded herself again that this was a business meeting. That fact was all too easy to forget, surrounded by all this grandeur, especially when a pianist appeared and classical music began wafting through the restaurant. While Colin ordered wine, Reya listened to what she knew was a Beethoven sonata, and reflected that the notes were even more beautiful because of the instrument upon which they were played. It was all so perfect, she thought, and she couldn't help remembering Sally's remark today about the château being romantic.

Well, she wasn't here to be seduced by soft lights and gentle music, she told herself. She was here to discuss Geneticon.

"I'm so glad we have this chance to talk," she said, deciding to broach the subject immediately so there would be no doubt about why they were here. "I've been thinking about Geneticon and what course of action we can take, and I'd like to—"

"Do you mind if we discuss business later?"

She was taken aback. "But I thought—"

"That when I asked you to dinner this would be a business meeting."

"Well, yes," she said uncomfortably, and didn't know what insane impulse made her add, "Isn't it?"

"Only if you insist."

"Well, of course...I mean..." She stammered to a halt, not sure what she meant.

He leaned forward. She didn't know why, but she unconsciously leaned back. It was almost as though she had to keep some distance between them, or...

Or what? she wondered uneasily, and didn't want to answer that question, either.

He must have noticed her withdrawal, for he sat back again himself. She felt like a fool. How could she have been so obvious? She was more sophisticated than that.

"I thought that by asking you to dinner tonight, we might start over again," he said finally. "I have to admit that I haven't been the most pleasant person to be around lately, but I shouldn't have taken it out on you."

She was touched by the apology. "I understand. I know this business with the newspapers has been difficult."

"Difficult? I'd put it in stronger terms."

"It seems strange that those articles suddenly started appearing in the paper," she said thoughtfully. "Do you have any idea why that is, or who might be responsible?"

His expression darkened and she thought for an instant she'd made a terrible mistake. He'd said he didn't want to talk business, but did that mean he didn't want to talk about Geneticon at all?

"No to both questions," he answered finally. She saw that he was angry, but she was relieved when she realized his anger wasn't directed at her. "Richard and I have been trying to find out, but so far...nothing."

"You haven't any clues at all?"

He shook his head. "No, I could understand it if there was some kind of trouble at Geneticon, but you've been through the labs, you've talked to some of my people. What did you think?"

Reya thought that all of the people she'd met at Geneticon seemed to be as fiercely loyal to Colin as they were protective of the work they were doing. Remembering Rick and Molly in particular, she shook her head in puzzlement. "I don't know. I can't imagine anyone I've met at Geneticon talking to the press, but obviously someone has. Or else that reporter managed to get access to important files."

"I doubt that. No one gets onto the grounds without an appointment during the day, and everything, even a memo, pertaining to ongoing experiments is locked away when the labs are empty. In addition to that, I have two security guards patrolling on shifts during the night, and the gate code is changed every day."

"It sounds like Fort Knox would be easier to break into," she said, slightly awed. "I hadn't realized your security system was so...impregnable."

His expression tightened. "No security system is, but I've done what I could to protect my people."

She looked at him curiously. It sounded to her as though he was more concerned with the experiments his people were performing, rather than the scientists themselves.

Colin saw her expression and smiled humorlessly. "I'm not really the monster the press has played me up to be," he said. "I do care about the people who work for me, you know."

Embarrassed, she said quickly, "I never thought you didn't."

He raised a skeptical eyebrow. "You're probably the only one in Denver, then."

"I'm sure that's not—"

He held up his hand. "It's not important. What is important is that Geneticon exists because of the scientists who work there. Without them, the center would be nothing. I would do anything to protect that, and I'm not ashamed to admit it."

She tried again. "I know how important Geneticon is to you—"

He leaned forward again. This time she didn't move away. She was too intent on his expression, on the look of hurt she saw in his eyes. "Do you?" he asked softly. "Do you know how important Geneticon is to me?"

She wanted to look away and couldn't. "Well, I—"

"Have you ever heard of Fanconi syndrome, Miss Merrill?" he asked.

"Fanconi syndrome?" she repeated, startled by the apparent change of subject. "No, I . . ."

His eyes took on a faraway look and she realized suddenly why he had asked. She didn't have to be told what he was talking about. Her mind flashed back to the articles Sally had given her about Colin's hopeless search for a cure for his small daughter. She remembered the lurid descriptions in the papers about his wife's subsequent suicide and wanted to stop him and couldn't. She could only listen helplessly as he went on.

"It sounds almost musical, doesn't it? As though it could be a dance. . . ." He shook his head abruptly, coming back from wherever he had gone to look directly at her. "But it's not a dance, and there's nothing musical about it. Fanconi syndrome is—" his voice shook for an instant, alarming her even more than the previous look in his eyes "—a rare, fatal childhood anemia, probably familial and hereditary, characterized by—"

He stopped abruptly, seeing the look of horror on her face. His own face became grim. "Well, it doesn't matter what it's characterized by," he said flatly. "The point is that it exists, and I'd give anything, *anything*," he repeated fiercely, "to find a cure for it and diseases like it."

She could no longer pretend she didn't know why he was so dedicated to finding the answers. "I hope you will," she said quietly. "It would be a wonderful tribute to your . . . family."

He looked at her quickly, his eyes bleak and fierce at the same time. "You know?"

Wishing she hadn't mentioned it, she nodded reluctantly. "The information came through a routine background check we did," she said, and unconsciously reached out and touched his arm. It felt like stone under her fingers, and she forced herself to meet his eyes as she continued, "Please believe me, Colin, I wasn't prying. But after reading about...about your daughter, I do understand...."

For just an instant he put his hand over hers. She wasn't sure whether it was her imagination or not that he squeezed her fingers, for in the next second he was reaching for his wineglass. Somewhere in the interim, the waiter had come with the wine. Colin must have approved it because both their glasses were filled, but she'd been so preoccupied she hadn't noticed. Feeling the need of a draught of courage as well, she took a sip from her own glass.

To her relief, that intense moment seemed to have passed. By the time Colin put his wineglass down again, he appeared to have recovered his composure, which was more than she could say for herself. It was an effort to pull herself together again. She wasn't sure what to say.

"I'm sorry," he said while she struggled to compose herself. "I do have a tendency to become... heated...about the subject of genetic engineering."

She took her cue from him. Despite his return to poise, he was obviously embarrassed, and she was only too glad not to pursue such a delicate subject. This was neither the time nor the place, she told herself, and tried to ignore the thought that she just didn't have the courage to continue the conversation about his family. So she said instead, "I can't blame you. It seems these days that people are divided into two camps—those determined to pursue genetic engineering, and those equally determined to have nothing to do with it.''

His jaw tightened in a movement she was beginning to know well. "I'm afraid I can't understand the latter group," he said coldly. "Anyone of intelligence realizes that genetic engineering is the promise of the future."

She wasn't about to argue that flat statement, so she said mildly, "Perhaps some people are afraid."

"Of what?" he scoffed.

Encouraged that he had at least asked, she said, "Well, of the loss of control, for one thing. Only a few people understand what these genetic developments mean, Colin. The rest have to rely on experts who themselves are often in the dark. Maybe people feel they're being dragged into a future they're not sure they understand or want."

He snorted. "Unfortunately for them, genetic engineering is a reality. It's not going to go away, and the only questions now are the purposes for which it's going to be used."

"I don't think those are the only questions, Colin," she said quietly. "There *are* legitimate concerns—"

"Such as?"

"Ethical considerations, for example," she said, glad that she'd been reading everything she could get her hands on about biotechnology. Even though she wasn't as versed as he was about the scientific aspect of the subject, she felt she knew enough to make a valid point. "Genetic engineering will make it possible to improve the human species, but who's going to decide which of us will be entitled to those improvements? Will it be confined to those who can pay? To those whose IQ is above an arbitrarily determined number? Perhaps it will be those who are more creative or more talented or more athletic. Who's going to decide that?''

Colin shifted uncomfortably in his chair. ''We're a long way from redesigning the human species,'' he said with a frown. ''Despite what the newspapers say.''

She wasn't finished. ''All right, leaving that aside for the moment, let's consider which of these future genetic improvements should have priority. Our culture values youth and beauty, but do we want a society comprised solely of beautiful young people? And who will decide what constitutes beauty? Someone who prefers blond hair and blue eyes, or someone who is partial to—''

He leaned forward, his expression intent. ''Let me ask you something, Reya. If you had the means to cure someone of some dread disease, would you use it?''

She flushed. ''Well, of course. But that's not what we're talking about.''

''It's exactly what we're talking about. We both know that there has been hysterical opposition to every major medical discovery from penicillin to the artificial heart—''

''And why do you think that is?''

''Ignorance,'' he said disgustedly.

''Exactly,'' she said, trying to keep the triumph from her voice. Everything she'd said so far had been designed to lead him to this point. She had him now, and even though he'd begun to glower again, she pressed on. ''You said yourself that those articles in the paper were filled with half-truths and suppositions and outright lies.''

He wasn't a stupid man; he obviously saw where she was going with this and glowered even more. "Yes, but—"

"And you just admitted that ignorance was the reason why."

"I meant—"

She knew she had only this chance to convince him, and she was determined to make the most of it. Ignoring the scowl he had developed now, she interrupted earnestly. "Those articles prove that it's time to start educating people about what you're doing at Geneticon. Once the public understands why genetic research is so important, all this sensational publicity will fade away. There will be no purpose to it, and the hysteria will die of its own accord."

He wasn't about to give up so easily. Before she could catch her breath, he demanded, "How can you be so sure?"

She looked directly at him. "Because that's my job."

He sat back, frowning so fiercely that she knew she had offended him. Enough to fire her? Her chin lifted. Well, fine. If he couldn't see the logic of her argument, she couldn't do anything for him anyway.

"Where did you learn to present an argument like that?" he asked, interrupting her thoughts.

Too embarrassed to notice the beginnings of a smile on his face, she said uncomfortably, "I was on the debating team at UCLA."

He laughed aloud. "I should have known. Captain, no doubt."

She had to laugh, too. "How did you guess?"

"After the way you just led me down the garden path, you have to ask?"

"I'm glad to see I haven't lost my touch," she said with a smile.

He didn't answer right away, and she realized that what she'd meant to be a joke suddenly didn't seem that way at all. He looked at her so intently that she felt her cheeks redden again. "I doubt you'll ever lose that," he said, still staring at her. "You're a remarkable woman, Reya . . . but I suspect that's not the first time you've heard that."

She had to keep it light. The urge to reach out and touch him was almost overwhelming, and she couldn't believe this was happening to her. Because she didn't want just to touch him; she wanted *him* to touch *her*, to hold her . . . to make love to her. She wanted to know how his arms would feel around her, how his lips would move on hers, what his body would feel like covering hers. Gazing into his eyes she knew that he was thinking the same thing, and she caught her breath.

This is crazy, she thought, and wanted to look away from him. The candlelight flickered on his lean face, and it seemed to her that all she could really see were his eyes and the candle's flame reflected in them. He hadn't moved and neither could she. It was as though some spell had overtaken them.

What was happening to her? She had never felt this way in her life. She knew if he had held out his hand she would have taken it, rising instantly from her chair, following wherever he led. She almost willed him to move, to hold out that hand and release her from this agonizing anticipation. Before he could, she wrenched her eyes away from his face and reached for her wineglass. To her horror, her hand was shaking.

"Reya . . ."

Somehow she had to get a grip on herself. She could feel his glance on her even though she was no longer looking at him, and she had to do something before she betrayed herself in a way she might regret.

"Thank you for the compliment," she said, "but the remarkable thing is that I succeeded in convincing you to have that press conference at Geneticon."

He shook his head. "I never agreed to that."

"But—"

Just then someone came up to their table. Reya looked up and when she saw who it was, she froze. Serena Jackson, a reporter and news anchor at KRDA-TV, was looking down at them, and from her expression Reya knew she was out for blood. Of all the times for a reporter to interrupt, Reya thought bleakly, this had to be the worst.

She and Serena knew each other, of course. Reya was acquainted with most of the local media people through her job. But even though she had tried to be friends with Serena, the woman had rebuffed her efforts. It was obvious that Serena wanted a network position, and because she was so ambitious, no one who knew her doubted she'd eventually get it. She was one of the most tenacious reporters in town, and now that Reya thought about it, she was surprised that Serena hadn't approached Colin before this. Usually she was the first with a scoop, and if by some chance she hadn't gotten there first, she wasn't above stepping over someone else to get an exclusive for the station. With her red hair and blue eyes, she would have been attractive if she hadn't been so hard—or so obsessed with her job.

Cursing at the chance that had brought Serena to this restaurant the same night she and Colin were here, Reya tried to summon a smile. "Hello, Serena."

Staring at Colin, who was obviously wondering who she was, Serena ignored Reya's greeting and stuck out her hand to him. "Serena Jackson, Mr. Hughes," she said. "I'm with KRDA, and I'd like to ask you a few questions."

Colin had politely begun to stand in acknowledgment of the introduction, but the instant he heard the call letters for the local station, he sat down again. That cold look had returned to his eyes and Reya cringed when he said, "Ask what you like. I've no intention of answering anything."

"This isn't the time, Serena," Reya said hastily.

Serena glanced briefly at her. "When *will* be the time?" she asked coolly before looking back at Colin. "Or perhaps Mr. Hughes is content to let everyone believe that what Jim Naughton says in the *Tribune* is true."

It wasn't a question, and Reya immediately recognized what Serena was trying to do. It was her style to needle someone into saying more than he or she intended; that was one of the ways she had so often obtained her exclusive scoops. By mentioning Jim Naughton, the reporter who was bylining the current newspaper articles on Geneticon, Serena obviously hoped to convince Colin that she knew more than she actually did. But Reya knew that Jim detested Serena and wouldn't have given her the time of day if she'd asked. Serena was on a fishing trip and Reya had no intention of letting her catch anything.

"You know you can't believe everything you read in the papers, Serena," she said lightly, aware that Colin was glowering again. So far he hadn't said anything, and she prayed it would stay that way. All a reporter like Serena would need was one ill-advised word and she'd run with it. "And if you're interested, we'll have some information soon."

The reporter's blue eyes raked her. "And are you the spokeswoman for Geneticon now?" she asked sarcastically.

"Yes, I—"

"Can't the owner speak for himself?"

Reya closed her eyes, anticipating the imminent explosion. She didn't have long to wait. Colin erupted right on schedule, throwing down his napkin and standing. He almost towered over Serena, who was no small woman herself, but to her credit she didn't flinch. Reya knew it cost her an effort. Colin looked infuriated.

"The owner could speak for himself if there was anything to say," Colin said coldly. "But I don't need to defend Geneticon, and I certainly don't have to explain anything to people who are either too stupid or too incompetent to understand the work we're doing there. Good night, Miss Jackson, and in the future, if you don't have the good manners not to interrupt a private conversation, at least have the decency to confine your comments to a goodbye!"

Serena took the hint. Whirling around, she left, but not without a backward glance. Reya saw the fury in her eyes and knew they were in trouble. Uneasily, she looked at Colin and saw to her dismay that he was now glaring at her.

"And *those* are the type of people you want me to invite to Geneticon?" he demanded angrily. Reaching into his pocket, he pulled out a couple of bills and threw them onto the table to pay for the wine.

"Are you ready?"

She had no choice but to rise from the table herself. But as they were waiting for their cars to be brought around, she turned to him. "I'm sorry that had to happen. Serena isn't known for her tact."

"I'm sorry too," he said, his voice tight.

"I hope this doesn't mean that you've decided not to hold that press conference," she said anxiously.

He looked at her as though she'd taken leave of all her senses. "This is no time for jokes," he said harshly.

"I wasn't joking! I mean it, Colin. It's more important now than ever!"

Her car was here. The valet was holding the door and Colin grabbed her under the elbow and practically propelled her over to it. She didn't want to get in, but she was afraid that if she didn't, he might pick her up bodily and put her inside. She slid behind the wheel and looked pleadingly up at him. "At least think about it—"

He slammed her car door. His eyes were as black as a winter night and just as cold when he said, "I don't have to think about it. The day I invite reporters to Geneticon is the day I close the place down forever!"

Without waiting for a response, he turned and went to the Porsche parked behind her. She was still sitting there, frozen, when the sports car roared past her, disappearing, like her career, into the night.

CHAPTER SIX

IT WASN'T A SURPRISE to Reya that she didn't sleep well after that scene at the restaurant, and after tossing and turning for the second night in a row, she was exhausted when she dragged herself out of bed the next morning. Trudging into the bathroom while the coffee perked, she looked at herself in the mirror and grimaced. There were circles under her eyes, and even her hair, always shiny and healthy looking, seemed to hang limply around her face. Sighing, she took a shower and then dressed in a gray suit to match her mood.

Still depressed when she finished her makeup, she went into the kitchen to make some toast. Switching on the small television set on the counter to listen to the morning news while she poured a cup of coffee, she heard Geneticon being mentioned, and looked up in time to see Serena Jackson on the screen. The coffee spilled and she almost burned her hand as she listened in dismay to the reporter who had been so furious with Colin last night. It hadn't taken Serena long to get her revenge.

"...research center that's been in the news lately. The preceding statement is a direct quote from Geneticon's owner, Colin Hughes, as given to this reporter last night...."

As Reya groaned, Serena paused dramatically. The camera zoomed in on her face, and she had never looked so sincere. "Station KRDA joins with other responsible members of the media who are anxious to uncover the truth about what really is going on at Geneticon," she said. "Are the rumors about Frankenstein's laboratory unfounded? This reporter, and I'm sure many of Denver's concerned citizens, would like to know."

Reya didn't wait to hear the rest of the newscast. Reaching over the counter, she turned off the TV just as the bread popped up from the toaster. She looked at the two pieces of toast in distaste before shoving them into a paper bag for the birds at the park. She had completely lost her appetite.

Drumming her fingers on the counter, she wondered how she was going to handle this. She knew that even if by some miracle Joseph Clendenin hadn't watched Serena's newscast, someone would be sure to tell him about it, and she wanted to have some answers ready for him by the time she got to the office. The only problem was what to say. How could she come up with a brilliant solution to this latest crisis when her client refused to let her do anything at all?

Damn him, she thought irately. This was all Colin's fault. If he had followed her advice in the first place, none of this would have happened. Why had he even hired a public relations director if he hadn't any intention of listening to her advice? Annoyed, she collected her things and drove downtown. She hadn't decided what approach to take by the time she arrived, but the instant she saw Sally's face, she knew she was in trouble again.

"What are you doing here?" Sally cried as soon as she saw her. "I thought you'd be out at Geneticon!"

Reya rested her heavy briefcase on top of Sally's desk. "You mean because of Serena's newscast this morning?" she asked wearily.

"No, because of the picketing that's going on out there!"

Reya looked at her sharply. "What picketing?"

"You haven't heard? Don't you listen to the radio?"

She usually did but not this morning. She hadn't wanted any more surprises as she drove into work; she'd needed the silence to try to think her way out of this dilemma. "No, I—"

"Oh, I can't believe you didn't know!" Sally cried. "There are all sorts of people out there, with signs..." She shuddered. "The most horrible things..."

Reya didn't have to ask; she could imagine. "Cancel whatever I've got this morning," she said quickly. "I'm going out there right now."

"Oh, Reya, be careful!"

Reya had already started out. She halted briefly. "Don't tell me there's been violence!"

Sally was wringing her hands. "Not yet, but—"

"If anyone asks," Reya said, knowing Sally would understand she meant Joseph Clendenin, "that's where I'll be. I'll try to get back as soon as I can, but don't expect me until...well, just don't expect me today."

"Good luck!"

She'd need it, Reya thought grimly, flinging herself into the Thunderbird and racing out of the lot. She held the car right to the speed limit during the drive. She could feel herself tensing even more as she turned off the highway onto the road that led to Geneticon, and she was some distance away when she saw the crowd milling around. She was too far to read the signs they were carrying, but she could hear the angry voices and her mouth tightened grimly. She had no idea what she would do if they didn't let her through, but somehow she had to get inside. What Colin was doing about this, she didn't dare imagine.

To her relief, there was one lone patrol car parked by the gate when she cautiously approached. A uniformed officer was leaning against it, idly watching the restless crowd, and Reya felt irrationally angry with him. Why was he just standing there? Couldn't he see how explosive the situation was? Would he just continue to stand calmly by if the protesters stormed the gate? Eyes narrowed, she watched as he shoved away from his car and came up to hers.

"I'm sorry, Miss, you'll have to move your car."

She was even angrier at that. Barely suppressing a sarcastic remark about being glad to do so if he could move these people out of the way, she held on to her temper. "My name is Reya Merrill," she said between her teeth, "and I'd like to get inside."

He actually had the gall to grin. "So would all these other people," he said. "But you'll all have to wait."

She had no intention of waiting. "I'm afraid you don't understand—"

The grin disappeared. "Look, lady—"

"Don't 'lady' me, officer!" she said sharply, and remembered the identification badge Colin had given her before she left the last time. Jerking it out of her purse, she showed it to him. "Does this convince you that I belong inside?"

He scratched his head. "Well, I don't know. You could have gotten this from anywhere, and I'm not supposed to let anyone in. Orders are orders, you know."

She noticed then that some of the protesters had become curious about what was going on and had drifted her way. Before she knew what was happening, her car was surrounded and she could see angry faces all around her, peering in the windows. One of them grabbed her identification badge from the policeman's hand and shouted, "Hey, this chick works here!"

"No, I . . ." she started to say, and then to her horror realized the car was moving. They were rocking it back and forth, chanting something about Geneticon. She wasn't sure what it was; she was too terrified. What was happening? What were they going to do to her?

"Officer!" she cried.

He was still by the window. Shoving his face inside, he said, "I'm going to open the gates. As soon as you see the high sign, gun the car and get inside, all right?"

Too frightened to speak, she nodded, and for a horrified instant couldn't remember whether she had turned the engine off or not. She prayed that she hadn't, for her hands were shaking so badly she doubted she could drive, much less find the key. Riveting her eyes on the policeman, she waited in agony as the chanting continued all around her and the car rocked more dangerously. At last the policeman jerked his head at her and she gunned the engine. She was terrified that she'd run someone down if she started forward, but to her relief everyone around the car jumped back. Holding the steering wheel in a death grip, she raced through the gates. She was still shaking by the time she pulled up to the building that housed Colin's office, and it was a few seconds before she could compose herself enough to get out of the car.

"Miss Merrill!" Colin's secretary leaped up from her chair when she saw Reya. "How did you get in here?

Reya managed a weak smile. "I stormed the gates."

"You what? Oh, dear! I think you'd better sit down. You're white as a sheet!"

"Thank you, but I...I'd like to see Colin, if I may."

The secretary looked distressed, and Reya was dismayed. She hadn't imagined that Colin wouldn't be here, and after all she'd been through just to get inside, she felt like bursting into tears. "Don't tell me he's not here!"

"No, no—he's here!" the secretary said quickly. "It's just that he's meeting with Mr. Carlyle, and said he didn't want to be disturbed."

"But I—"

The woman saw her expression and took pity on her. "I think under the circumstances..."

Squaring her shoulders, the secretary marched to the closed office door. She knocked sharply twice, and at a growled, "What is it *now*?" opened the door. "Miss Merrill is here," she said primly, and stood aside to usher Reya in.

"Reya!"

Both men leaped to their feet when Reya appeared, but it was Richard Carlyle who sprang forward to help her to a chair. "Are you all right? How did you get in here?"

Reya grimaced as she sat down. Grateful that Richard was here so she wouldn't have to deal with Colin alone, she said, "It wasn't easy."

"But the crowd—"

She shuddered. "They're still there."

"Damn it all anyway!" Colin exploded. He'd been standing behind his desk; now he came around to the front of it. "Why in hell did you try to come here? You should have seen that crowd was dangerous!"

She did look at him then. "I thought I should take the chance," she said evenly.

He looked angry and concerned and worried at the same time. "Why?" he demanded.

"Because it's my job, that's why!" she cried, losing patience. If she hadn't been through such a terrifying experience just now, she would have been more composed. She'd intended to be. She'd told herself all the way over that she would approach this problem with him calmly and rationally and that they would work something out. But now she shot out of her chair and faced him with her fists clenched. "Why do you think I came?" she cried. "Because I hadn't seen an ugly mob scene before and was curious? Because I thought it would be fun to have my car rocked back and forth, practically off its wheels? Just why do you think I came, Colin? It certainly wasn't for my health!"

She gasped to a stop, appalled at what she'd said, but not sorry. She was willing to do whatever she could for him, and she had just proved it by coming here today. But she couldn't do anything if he continued to block her at every turn, and they might as well get that straightened out once and for all.

"It's my job," she repeated, before he could say anything, "but it seems to me you don't want me to do it. And if that's the case, I guess the only option I have is to resign."

"No!" Richard exclaimed.

She looked at him. "I'm sorry, but—"

"I never said you couldn't do your job," Colin growled.

She felt a stirring of hope.

"But no press conferences," he said flatly.

Her hope died. "Then we have nothing to talk about," she said. "I thought we agreed that educating the public was the only way to put these rumors to rest, but if you won't let me be Geneticon's spokeswoman—"

"No one speaks for Geneticon but me!"

She was losing patience again. She'd already lost her job, so she hardly cared. "Oh, yes," she said sarcastically. "And a splendid job you did of it last night!"

Richard stepped forward. "She's got a point, Colin."

Colin glared at him. "You, too?"

"Somebody's got to make you listen to reason," Richard said, "unless you want to do this all by yourself. As Reya said, you're doing a damned good job."

Colin flushed angrily, but this time he held on to his temper. "I take it you agree with Reya about the press conference," he said tightly.

"I do."

Colin's jaw tightened. Both Richard and Reya waited in silence while he struggled with the problem. Reya glanced covertly at Richard and tried to be encouraged by his slight nod, but she wasn't certain what Colin would say until he actually said it. "All right," he said grudgingly. "But I want to know what you're going to say."

She could feel a broad grin trying to spread across her face, but somehow she managed to keep her expression solemn. It wasn't a moment for celebration . . . yet.

"I'll say whatever you want me to say," she told him. "The only reason I'll be acting as your spokeswoman is because I'm trained to deal with the press."

"And I'm not, right?"

She did smile slightly at that. He sounded so indignant that she couldn't prevent it. "Well, let's just say that perhaps your talents are more . . . administrative," she said tactfully.

Richard grinned, and even Colin had to smile. "I take it that means you don't want me to say anything at all."

Reya hesitated, and Richard chuckled, relieved that the crisis had passed. "That's what she means, Colin."

"I thought so. Can I at least be there to see how it goes?"

"Well . . ." she said tentatively.

Richard said it for her. "But only if you stay in the background," he warned. "If you promise that, I'm sure everything will be fine. Won't it, Reya?"

Relieved, she smiled again, too. "Yes, I'm sure it will be," she said confidently, and didn't remember until much later that old saying about pride going before a fall.

REYA SUGGESTED calling the press conference for that afternoon. Now that Colin had agreed, she wanted to commit themselves as quickly as possible, before he changed his mind. After notifying the media, Reya spent the next few hours being grilled about what she was going to say. By the time the reporters had gathered in the cafeteria, which had been set up for the conference with a makeshift dais, even Colin had to agree that Reya could either answer, or field, any question the press had to ask.

"Now, remember," she said as the three of them were leaving Colin's office for the short trek to the cafeteria, "let me do the talking. That's what you hired me for."

Colin waved a dismissive hand. He had consented to this procedure, but he obviously still didn't like it. Richard saw his expression and tried to assure her. "Don't worry. I'll be sitting there with him. If he tries to do anything other than smile, I'll put him in a hammerlock."

Since Richard looked about as capable of that as she did, Reya had to laugh. Trying not to feel nervous, she left Colin and Richard in the hall and entered the cafeteria. The instant she did, the buzz of conversation stopped. She was too keyed up as she approached the dais to recognize more than a few people in the crowd of reporters, but she did see Tom Johnson of the *Denver Post*, and Rudy Sabin of the *Rocky Mountain News*, two of Denver's major papers. Jim Naughton of the *Tribune*, the reporter whose articles had fueled the present controversy, was there as well, and Reya looked hastily away from him right into Serena Jackson's avid eyes. The anchorwoman from KRDA-TV stared aggressively back at her and Reya nodded coolly as she took her place behind the podium. She glanced around the room before she began speaking, and thought uneasily that she could have heard a pin drop.

"Good afternoon, ladies and gentlemen," she said, and listened carefully to the way her voice carried through the room. She had learned the hard way during her first press conference that she had to sound sincere and in complete control no matter how nervous she felt. Reporters who made a living interviewing others would hear any hesitation or uncertainty and pursue it relentlessly. She wasn't about to let that happen today. To avoid more unfavorable publicity, she had to convince everyone here that Geneticon had absolutely nothing to hide. Satisfied that she sounded relaxed and confident, she saw that Richard and Colin had slipped in a rear door and were standing at the back of the room. Praying that they would remain unnoticed, she went on.

"As some of you know, my name is Reya Merrill, and I'd like to take this opportunity to welcome you to Geneticon. I've been designated as the company spokeswoman today, so—"

"Where's Colin Hughes?" Jim Naughton demanded. "Why isn't he going to talk to us?"

She had expected an early attack from Naughton, who was known for his aggressive and hostile manner, and she was ready with her answer. "As you're no doubt aware, Jim," she said smoothly, "Geneticon is a huge company, requiring constant supervision and attention to detail. Mr Hughes sends his regrets, but was unavoidably detained."

Serena Jackson decided to get into the act. "Why is that?" she asked nastily. "Is he supervising one of those questionable experiments Jim's been writing about lately?"

Reya managed to hold her smile. "I plan to address the issue of Geneticon's ongoing experiments in a moment or two, Serena, but first I'd like to give you all some background on Geneticon itself, which is a company specializing in genetic research—genetic engineering, if you will. It might be helpful at this point to define that term. In its broadest sense, genetic engineering is the attempt to modify the structure, the transmission, or the effects of genes, which themselves are the ultimate directors of heredity."

She saw recorders whirling and pencils busily writing and stopped to take a sip of water. "Would anyone like me to repeat that?" she asked, and smiled at the representative from KRMA, Denver's educational television station, when she raised a hand. She repeated the definition for her, and the others in the audience too proud to ask, and then went on.

"There have been reams of paper and millions of words written about genetic engineering," she said, "with the result that today many people regard the subject as threatening at best—"

"You can say that again," someone muttered. There was a general chorus of agreement that Reya decided to ignore.

"And so," she said determinedly, "because Geneticon is anxious to soothe some of these irrational, and in some cases hysterical, fears, we have called this press conference."

"To try to pull the wool over our eyes, you mean," someone threw out.

"To try to set the record straight," she said evenly. "In the future, applications of genetic knowledge will lead to the prevention and alleviation of birth defects and other genetic disorders. It will conquer heart disease and cancer, and even provide the means to abolish hunger. Those are just some of the goals of genetic engineering.''

"Yeah, and what about the other goals?" a gruff male voice demanded. "The legless astronauts who'll fit better in space capsules, or men designed with gills so they can live in the ocean?"

Before she could answer, someone else jumped up. "Yeah, and what about cyborgs, or the mass production of babies in test tubes?"

"Or what about another Nazi society, where the 'unfit' are eliminated?"

The questions were getting louder and more aggressive, led by Jim Naughton and Serena Jackson, who had leaped to their feet, too. Reya didn't dare look in Colin's direction. She just hoped that Richard would keep his promise and drag him out of the room if necessary.

"If you'll all please take your seats," she began, and had to raise her voice to be heard. She realized with dismay that she had to get control of the situation right now before things got even more out of hand. "Please! I'd like to—"

"All right, that's enough!" The new voice came from the back of the room, slicing effortlessly through the hubbub and reducing everyone to silence.

"Thank you," Reya said, knowing in advance that Colin wasn't going to return control to her, but praying he would all the same. "I think we can go on now—"

"You're not going on with anything!" Colin looked at her for a second, and even across the big room she could see how furious he was. His jaw was clenched so tightly that the muscles stood out in ridges along his jawbone, and his eyes practically shot sparks.

"I think—"

He refused to listen to her. Looking away before she could say more, his glance contemptuously raked the entire room. "Geneticon invited you here in good faith," he said, his voice shaking with rage, "but you people don't want to hear the truth, you just came to see how much damage you could do! Well, I've got better things to do than stand here and listen to a group of cretins who wouldn't know a gene if it stood up and waved, so you can all get out. As far as I'm concerned, this press conference is over!"

Reya closed her eyes. Everyone in the room had turned curiously around and she could hear excited voices raised when those reporters who had either seen Colin's picture or knew who he was recognized him.

"Hey, that's Colin Hughes...."

"It's the owner of Geneticon!"

"Let's have *him* answer some questions...."

Colin's expression turned from thunderous to murderous. "I have no intention of answering any questions!" he snarled. "You've already demonstrated you don't want to listen, so I'm not going to waste my time."

Dismayed, Reya watched Jim Naughton shouldering his way to the front of the crowd facing the irate Colin. Richard caught her eye just then and shook his head helplessly. She gestured, trying to indicate that this wasn't his fault. She had seen him say something to Colin right before his outburst, but she'd had the sinking feeling even before Colin exploded that whatever Richard said to him was going to be useless. Too late, she realized she shouldn't have allowed Colin anywhere near this room. Despite his promise to let her act as spokewoman, she should have known he wouldn't have been able to keep quiet when Geneti-con, or the work they were doing here, was being attacked.

"So you don't think there's an ethical question to address here, is that right, Mr. Hughes?" Jim Naughton asked just then.

Colin looked at him. If the reporter had been a less aggressive, belligerent man, he would have shriveled at that look, but he stood his ground, his chin actually thrust out as he held a tape recorder practically under Colin's nose.

"The only question," Colin replied furiously, "is how quickly you can leave before you're thrown off the property."

Reya wanted to sink down behind the podium and crawl out of the room, praying that no one would notice her ignominious departure. But this press conference had been her idea and she had to follow it through. Clearing her throat, she said, "If I could have your attention..."

No one even looked at her. They were all watching Serena pushing her way forward to stand beside Jim Naughton. In a voice that carried easily throughout the room and scraped along Reya's nerves like nails on a blackboard, she asked clearly, "Then you're not concerned if experiments such as yours lead to atrocities we've come to associate with a Nazi-like society, Mr. Hughes?"

Colin's hands actually clenched, and Richard hastily gripped his sleeve. Colin drew himself up to his full height, which at two inches over six feet, was considerable. "No," he said coldly. "I am not concerned."

Reya closed her eyes briefly again. "I think what Mr. Hughes means—"

But Tom Johnson of the *Post* had already stepped forward, pen poised. "Then you don't feel Geneticon has any moral or ethical responsibility to—"

"The only responsibility I have is to see that my people provide me with valid results!" Colin snapped. "What society does with them is not my concern!"

"But what about all the things that can go wrong? Wouldn't it be wiser to wait, to make sure we understand all the ramifications—"

Colin glared at the speaker, an anxious-looking man who continually glanced around as if for reassurance. "There are always consequences to any discovery," he said scornfully.

Serena spoke up again. "Yeah, like fire eventually leading to the development of atom bombs!"

"Or the discovery of antibiotics that have saved millions of lives over the past thirty years!" Colin shot back. "Would you have denied all those people a chance to live because resistant bacterial strains might develop, or because someone, somewhere, someday, might dream of an application for germ warfare? How do you decide ethical *responsibility* then?"

"Well, I . . ."

Colin looked around, his expression becoming even more derisive. Frozen behind the podium, Reya couldn't imagine what else Colin might say, but it was obvious that he intended to say more, and she tried frantically to think of something that would forestall him. She was too late. With a gesture of disgust that left no doubt in anyone's mind just what he thought of them, Colin turned and started for the door. Once there he paused to look back at the silent room. It seemed to Reya that he deliberately avoided her eyes, but she couldn't be sure. She was trying too hard to brace herself for the last blow.

"A moment ago, you mentioned something about the discovery of fire, Miss Jackson," he said, his glance coming to rest at last on the female reporter. His voice was deadly. "After listening to all of you today, I've no doubt that if you had been there when lightning struck that first tree, you would have gathered together to douse the resulting fire because someone might have been burned."

Pandemonium broke out at that, but even though several reporters rushed after him, Colin had already disappeared down the hallway. As the rest of the crowd dashed after their colleagues, Reya nearly shouted herself hoarse trying to get their attention. When the last echoing footstep died seconds later, she and Richard were alone in the big room.

"Oh, Richard!" she said, and to her horror, her voice caught. She had to pry her fingers away from their death grip on the podium, and as she fumbled for a chair, she told herself fiercely that she was not going to cry. Clutching her hands tightly in her lap so she wouldn't be tempted to cover her face with them and burst into tears, she watched as Richard came up to her. His face was pale, too, when he sank into the chair beside her, and for a moment neither of them said anything. Finally he sighed.

"Well, it could have been worse, I guess," he ventured.

She looked at him disbelievingly. "How?"

"Well, if they'd asked him what he thought about the press," Richard said ruefully, "things might *really* have gotten out of hand."

Reya saw the wry look in his eyes and didn't know whether to laugh or cry.

CHAPTER SEVEN

THE RESULTS of the press conference were even more disastrous than Reya had predicted. Awakening the next morning to find a renewed furor that made the previous problem seem like child's play, she wanted to crawl back into bed again and pull the covers over her head.

"Geneticon Denies Responsibility!" bawled the headlines of the *Denver Post*.

"Owner Colin Hughes Says Ethics Not a Consideration!" whooped the *Rocky Mountain News*.

"Valid Results Only Concern!" screamed the *Tribune*.

And in an editorial on the morning news, Serena Jackson smugly summarized, "Colin Hughes summoned reporters yesterday to a press conference to inform them that neither they, nor the general public, have the intelligence or the wit to comprehend a science so esoteric as genetic engineering...."

Reya threw the newspapers into the wastebasket and turned off the television. She debated briefly about calling in sick, which wouldn't have been far from the truth, she thought bleakly, but decided against it. Everyone at the office would know she was just trying to avoid the inevitable meeting with Joseph Clendenin, and since he'd been known to visit an ailing employee on occasion, she had to grit her teeth and get it over with. Wondering if she should wear black, she dressed and was just starting out the door when the phone rang. Groaning, she wondered if the harrassment was starting already. She'd been so depressed at the way things had turned out that she'd taken the phone off the hook last night when she got home. The last thing she'd needed was to field questions from some reporter hunting the rest of the story, but as she listened to the third ring this morning, she knew she couldn't avoid it forever. Sighing, she answered.

"At last!" Darren exclaimed when he heard her voice. "Damn it, Reya—do you know I've been trying to call you all night? What the hell's been wrong with your phone?"

The last person she'd expected to call was Darren, and when she remembered the last time they had talked, her voice was cool. "Nothing was wrong with the phone. I took it off the hook."

"Well, I'm not surprised, judging from the headlines in the papers today. After seeing this, I hope you've learned your lesson."

"What lesson is that?"

"Don't be coy," he said sharply. "You know very well I'm talking about your involvement with . . . with that place."

"You can say the name, Darren. It's not going to contaminate you. That 'place' is called Geneticon."

"I know what it's called! And after this latest debacle, so will everyone else in the country!"

She was beginning to be irritated. "That has nothing to do with you."

"Does it with you? Have you resigned that account yet?"

"No."

"Damn it, Reya. I thought we discussed this!"

"We did."

"Then why haven't you resigned?"

That was a good question: why hadn't she? It was more obvious now than it had been before that Colin felt he could handle Geneticon and its problems by himself. After the way he'd behaved at the press conference yesterday, it was clear he didn't want her help, however badly he might need it. Why *didn't* she just quit? She was risking everything—her job, her career, even her fiancé—to keep this account, and for what?

"Try to have patience with him, Reya," Richard had said quietly to her yesterday before she left. "He's been through a lot these past few years. Sometimes I wonder if he'll ever get over it."

"Is that why you stay?" she'd asked, needing his reassurance, his assertion that she was doing the right thing by staying herself.

Richard had nodded somberly. "I wish you'd known Colin before...before his wife and child died," he said wistfully. "He's changed so much since then, become a completely different man. I guess I stick around hoping that we'll get him back again some-day. I see flashes of it now and then, but..."

She'd seen flashes of it, too, she remembered, the first day she'd met both men in Colin's office. Recalling how surprised she'd been at Colin's lightning change of mood that day, she could understand Richard's wistfulness. Colin *had* been different then, and maybe that was why she wanted to stay, too. She wanted to see those shadows disappear from his eyes, to hear that marvelous laughter of his, to see that sensuous mouth curve into a genuine smile. But even

more than that, she wanted—"*. . . listening to me?*"
Darren's voice demanded harshly. "I asked you why
you haven't resigned from that account!"

She'd had enough of this. "Because I haven't been
asked to resign, for one thing."

"After all that's happened, you need an invitation? For heaven's sake, Reya, can't you see what this
is doing to your reputation?"

"To *your* reputation, you mean!" she said sharply,
annoyed by those daydreams about Colin. What difference did it make to her whether he was the same
man he'd been before or not? He was supposed to be
just a client to her; she certainly shouldn't be thinking romantic thoughts about him.

Then why did she keep seeing his face in her mind?
As humiliating as it was to admit it, last night she
hadn't been thinking of herself and what that disastrous press conference might do to her career; she'd
been thinking about Colin. Where he was, what he
was doing . . . what he was thinking about. The desire
to talk to him had been so strong that she'd gone so far
as to look up his home number. It wasn't listed, and
she put the book away again, not sure whether she was
relieved or not that she hadn't been able to call. What
would she have said? That she should have handled
those reporters more deftly, that she shouldn't have
allowed that press conference to get out of hand? But
they both knew that, just as she knew he'd be impatient with her apologies. He wanted action, not wail-
ing about why things had gone so wrong.

Darren was obviously stung by her last remark. She
came out of her reverie to hear him say, ". . . put it like
that, I *am* concerned about my reputation! I have

every right to be! We did talk about this, Reya, and I thought we agreed—"

"*We* didn't agree on anything," she said icily. "*You* simply assumed that I would give in to you, just as I always do."

"If that were true," he said curtly, "we would be married by now, and you would have forgotten all this nonsense about a career of your own!"

She was barely holding on to her temper. "Is that what you think my work is—nonsense?"

He obviously didn't hear the warning note in her voice, for he replied just as sharply, "There's only room for one career in a marriage, Reya. We've discussed that, too."

She could feel her whole body becoming flushed with anger. "What happens if I believe that career should be mine?"

There was a pause. She used it to try to control herself. She felt like smashing down the phone, but she had to hear his answer. She knew their entire relationship balanced on what he said next.

"*Do* you feel like that?" he asked finally.

She wanted to say that she wasn't that narrow-minded, but she swallowed the hasty words just in time. "No," she said evenly. "I feel that both partners in a marriage have the right to feel satisfied and productive, Darren, and if that means trying to work around two careers, adjustments just have to be made—on both sides. *That's* how I feel."

There was another pause. Finally he said, "In that case, I'm afraid we're faced with an irreconcilable difference."

She almost laughed. An irreconcilable difference. It sounded like one of those stuffy phrases he used in a courtroom, reducing an important difference of opinion to an intellectual exercise stripped of all emotion. How like him, she thought, and wondered what had made her think they could have had an enduring marriage if they disagreed so completely on such a basic issue.

"I see," she said.

Darren misinterpreted her. "Well, I'm glad that's settled," he said in relief. "I have to admit, you really had me going there for a minute, Reya. I was actually beginning to believe you were serious!"

"I *am* serious," she said slowly.

"I . . . what?"

The idea had been growing at the back of her mind during the entire conversation. She realized now that it had been there long before; she just hadn't wanted to admit it. She hadn't wanted to hurt him; she hadn't wanted to believe that they just couldn't work things out. But after today she knew they would never agree. Darren would never understand that her work was just as important to her as his was to him. He'd never take an interest in what she was doing because he simply didn't believe it had any significance.

But even if they could have compromised on a solution about her career, she knew that Darren would continue to regard it at best as a . . . nuisance. He'd still expect her to be a traditional wife in every other way, and she knew she could never be that. House and home and husband were important to her, but not at the price of her own self-respect. To her, marriage was a partnership with responsibilities shared equally, where both partners were free to express themselves. She knew that Darren would never understand that, either.

"I'm sorry, Darren," she said quietly, "I didn't want to tell you this over the phone, but there doesn't seem to be a better time. Our engagement was a mistake. I . . . I can't marry you, after all."

When he didn't reply, Reya wondered absurdly if he'd dropped the phone. She couldn't have let go of the receiver herself; her fingers were clamped around it so tightly her hand ached. "Darren . . . ?"

His voice was harsh when he finally answered. "What is it? Is it another man?"

"Of course not!" she denied vehemently, and then was horrified when another face flashed into her mind. Why in the world was she thinking of Colin Hughes at a time like this? He had nothing to do with her decision, absolutely nothing!

"It's Colin Hughes, isn't it?" Darren asked, almost as if he had read her thoughts. His voice turned even more bitter than before. "He's swept you off your feet, hasn't he?"

If she hadn't been so appalled at the turn of the conversation, she would have laughed at the old-fashioned phrase. Swept her off her feet? Hardly. The only thing Colin Hughes had done for her was make a fool out of her and place her job—not to mention her career—in jeopardy. Sweeping her off her feet would have been a welcome substitution.

No, she didn't mean that, either, she thought distractedly, and forced her attention back to Darren. "I don't know why you think Colin Hughes has anything to do with this—"

"You've been spending a lot of time with him, haven't you?"

"As a matter of fact, I haven't," she said. "But even if I had, that has nothing to do with it."

"Oh, come on, Reya. You've just insulted my manhood, don't insult my intelligence, as well! I know who Colin Hughes is. Everybody in the country does now, thanks to you! I've seen what he looks like—dark and brooding, with a tragic past. All the perfect ingredients to make women swoon!''

"That's the most ridiculous thing I've ever heard! If you knew him you'd realize how foolish you sound.''

"I don't want to know him! As far as I'm concerned, he's responsible for your change of heart.''

"I don't believe this!'' she cried. "I'm telling you, he has nothing to do with my breaking our engagement! You're the reason, Darren, you and your attitude toward my work. I just can't be the kind of woman who stays home ironing handkerchiefs until her husband arrives, but that's apparently the kind of wife you want me to be. I'm sorry, Darren. I hope you understand.''

"No, I don't understand,'' Darren said angrily. "But I'll tell you one thing, Reya...if I ever get a chance to get even with that man, I'll do it. That's a promise.''

She couldn't believe what she was hearing. Darren seeking revenge? Just for a moment, she felt a sharp stab of uneasiness at the thought, then she resolutely dismissed it. It was just talk, she assured herself. Darren was hurt and angry; he didn't mean what he'd just said.

"Darren—'' she began pleadingly. She didn't want to leave it like this, not after the good things they'd shared.

He interrupted. "There is one thing you can do for me.''

"What?" She was eager to do anything because she felt so guilty, so sorry that she'd been forced to hurt him like this.

"You can send back that engagement ring," he said coldly. "It's worth quite a bit of money, and I might as well get a return on my investment."

She was so shocked that at first she didn't know what to say. The thought flashed through her mind that she wasn't under any obligation to return the ring, and for a second or two she was tempted to tell him that. Then she tightened her lips. If a financial investment was all he could think about at this point, he was welcome to the ring. She'd never liked the damned thing anyway.

"Fine," she said through her teeth. "You'll have it back today."

"Send it by courier, will you?" he asked, maddening her even further. "I wouldn't want it to get lost."

She couldn't help herself. "Why?" she asked irately. "Isn't it insured?"

"As a matter of fact, it is. But I—"

"Goodbye, Darren," she said, and managed to hang up the phone before she burst into furious tears.

Unfortunately she didn't have time to luxuriate in a crying spell, no matter how she felt. Until she was told differently, she still had a job to go to, appointments to keep, meetings to hold. Heading the list was Joseph Clendenin. After the furor in the papers and on television this morning, she knew he'd want to see her. And this time, she thought, she'd better have some answers.

Thirty minutes later, makeup retouched and ring finger conspicuously bare, she drove to the office. Without waiting for the summons, she went inside and directly up to Joseph Clendenin's secretary, Martha. Sixty seconds after that, she was sitting in one of the barrel chairs facing her boss. To her relief, he hadn't started to glower . . . yet.

"I wanted to fill you in on some of the details about the Geneticon account," she began, more confidently than she felt.

Joseph Clendenin sat back in his chair. Although the top of his desk was spotlessly clean, she was sure that he'd read the articles in the papers and had seen Serena Jackson's newscast this morning. His next words confirmed her suspicions. "I think we're all getting a few more details than we need, with all this uproar in the media. Don't tell me there's more on the way."

She flushed. "I realize that press conference didn't go well . . ."

He raised an eyebrow.

"But I still think it was a good idea. Or at least it would have been," she amended, trying not to glower a little herself, "if I had been allowed to speak for Geneticon, as we'd agreed."

Clendenin made a tent with his fingers and rested his chin on them, regarding her thoughtfully. "You mean, if Colin Hughes hadn't upstaged you."

She could feel herself flushing again, but she was not going to give in to embarrassment. Nor was she going to offer apologies or excuses. She couldn't change what had happened yesterday; the only thing she could do was go on—and muzzle Colin Hughes the next time he got within a mile of a reporter.

"I admit that made my job more difficult," she said, unconsciously lifting her chin. "But since it's obvious that Mr. Hughes has a...problem...dealing with the press, I've decided on a new approach...."

She outlined her ideas about filming some educational commercials, and talking to Brian Goodwin, station manager at KRDA, where Serena Jackson worked. Brian was fair, and even though Serena was on his staff, she was sure she could convince him to devote some time to Geneticon's side of the story. It would enhance the station's image, and deflect some of the bad publicity from Geneticon at the same time. After that...

Joseph Clendenin held up his hand. "You've obviously devoted a lot of thought to this new strategy," he said.

Thinking that she'd hardly been able to devote a thought to anything else, Reya nodded.

He looked at her thoughtfully while she waited in suspense. Finally he waved his hand. "All right, then," he said. "For the time being, you're still in charge of this account. Keep me posted, please."

Assuring him that she would definitely do that, she practically skipped out of the office. Martha actually smiled at her as she went by, and she was still euphoric that afternoon after presiding over two meetings and endless phone calls with clients. Then she remembered the envelope in her purse, and her expression became grim. She buzzed Sally to come into her office and when her assistant appeared, handed her the envelope. "Send this by courier please...today."

It was too much to expect that Sally wouldn't be curious. She'd started out of Reya's office carrying the envelope, but the instant she saw Darren's name on the front, she whirled around. Her eyes dropped to Reya's hand, and then up to her face again. "This isn't what I think it is, is it?" she asked.

Reya knew it was futile to lie. Sally would have to know the truth sooner or later. "It is," she said briefly.

Sally blew out a breath. "Wow. What happened?"

Reya looked up from what she was pretending to write. "It's not very complicated. Let's just say we didn't see eye to eye."

"About Geneticon?"

"Among other things."

Sally nodded. "Your job, for one, right?"

Reya's mouth tightened. "Yes. As Darren put it, we had an irreconcilable difference of opinion."

Sally's eyes widened again. "He said that?"

"His very words."

"Wow."

Reya pretended to scribble busily again. "Now that you know the whole story—"

"So why are you sending him back your engagement ring?" Sally demanded. "According to Ann Landers, it belongs to you!"

Amused at Sally's indignant tone, Reya looked up. "Would *you* keep it?"

"A ring like that?" Sally exclaimed. "Are you kidding? I wouldn't have given it back even if he'd asked for it!"

"He did ask for it," Reya said flatly. "So please, just get rid of it, will you?"

Sally was about to say something more, but at the look on Reya's face, she turned and started out. She paused at the door. "You're taking it better than I would," she said. "If that had happened to me, I'd be in tears. Is there anything I can do?"

Reya was grateful for the offer, but she shook her head. "No, thanks. This is something I have to deal with myself."

"It's almost quitting time. We could go out for a drink or something."

Reya shook her head again. "No, I'm okay—really," she said with a smile. "I think I'll just have an early dinner and take a long bath and go to bed. It's been a long day."

"You're sure?"

"I'm sure."

But she didn't get a chance to do any of the things she'd planned. She hadn't been home five minutes before the doorbell rang, and when she saw who her visitor was, everything else slipped her mind.

COLIN WAS STANDING in front of his huge office window, staring broodingly out at the mountains when Richard knocked and came in. Without turning around, he muttered, "If you're here to read me the riot act about that damned press conference yesterday—don't. I already know what a mess I made of it. I don't need you to tell me."

"I wasn't going to say a thing," Richard said, taking a chair.

Colin did turn around then. "That's a first. Usually you can't wait to put your oar in."

"Not this time," Richard said calmly. "If I'd made as big a fool of myself as you did, I wouldn't need anyone to tell *me*. I'd know."

"Well, thanks for that vote of confidence. Don't you think I feel badly enough about it already?"

"I don't know. Do you?"

Scowling, Colin threw himself into the desk chair. "You know I do."

"What are you going to do about it?"

"What can I do? It's too late now."

Richard looked directly at him. "It's not too late to apologize to Reya."

His mouth tight, Colin glanced away.

"You did promise to let her speak for the company, you know," Richard pointed out mildly.

"I couldn't help it!" Colin erupted. "Didn't you hear the questions those people were asking? The whole thing was an insult to everyone working here, to everyone in the field of genetics! I couldn't just stand by and ignore the inference that we were engaged in some kind of witchcraft, could I?"

"You could have let Reya handle it, as arranged," Richard said, unimpressed by Colin's impassioned speech. "She was doing just fine until you interfered."

"But she—" Colin began hotly, and then stopped, looking even more embarrassed.

Richard wasn't about to let him off so easily. "But she what?" he pressed. "She didn't get red in the face and beat her fists against the podium and call every reporter in the room an idiot? No, pardon me. I believe the term you used was cretin, wasn't it?"

Colin's face was red beneath its tan. "Don't remind me."

Richard pretended not to hear. "And she didn't proclaim for all the world to hear that Geneticon is not overly concerned with moral or ethical responsibility, did she?"

Colin's face was crimson now. "I didn't mean it that way and you know it."

"I know it, but I doubt that anyone else in that room—including Reya, I might add—knows it. You were very convincing, my friend. I'm sure by now everyone over the age of six who's heard about that press conference is convinced that Geneticon is engaged in voodoo as well as black magic. And just think! We have you to thank for that."

Colin flung himself out of his chair again. "All right! You don't have to beat it to death. I admitted I made a fool of myself. What more do you want?"

"It's not a question of what I want, Colin. It's what you should do to make it right."

"And what, exactly is that?"

Richard examined his nails. "I think you should decide that."

Colin gritted his teeth. "Well, what a surprise. I was sure you'd have an opinion on that, too. You do on everything else!"

Richard rose with dignity from the chair. "Decisions are your department," he said. "But if you want my advice, the first thing you'd better do is find out if Reya is still willing to keep Geneticon as an account."

"You don't think she is?"

Richard saw the look of dismay flash across Colin's face and drove home his point. "Would you be, after this? She's very good at what she does, Colin— if she's allowed to do it. You might think about that . . . while you're considering how you're going to apologize."

Colin uttered an exasperated sound as Richard went out and closed the door behind him, but as soon as his friend had gone, he threw himself into his chair again. Since he'd stalked out of that disastrous press conference yesterday, he'd thought about nothing but how he was going to apologize to Reya. He'd picked up the phone a dozen times to call her, but each time he'd slammed the receiver down again. Now he was convinced that he couldn't apologize to her over the phone, but that left meeting her face-to-face, and he wasn't sure he wanted to do that, either.

He couldn't get her out of his mind. He kept seeing her behind that podium, the proud lift of her head, the flash of those incredible blue eyes. He'd been so enthralled with her during the opening minutes of the press conference that he hadn't really been paying any attention to what was being said. All he could think about was how beautiful she was and how much he wanted her.

Then she had raised her hand to make a point, and he saw that damned engagement ring again. He'd felt an irrational rage against the man who had given it to her because he'd had the good fortune to find her first, then he'd been appalled at himself. What was he thinking about? Geneticon took all his time, his energy. It was the focus and pivot of his life. He had nothing left for a relationship; he'd proved that with those other women these past five years. Everyone and everything came second to Geneticon and the work being done here, and he couldn't let himself forget that purpose even for an instant. Not when he had vowed that Becky... and Claire... hadn't died in vain.

That was when he'd jerked his eyes away from Reya and realized what kind of questions those reporters were asking. He'd lost his temper and made a shambles of the whole conference then, and when he remembered the look on Reya's face just before he walked out, he winced. She hadn't been able to hide her shock, and he would never forget the accusation in those sapphire eyes. He'd broken his promise to stay out of it and let her handle the reporters, and when it was too late, he would have given anything to make things right again.

Anything? he thought uncomfortably, alone in his office with the sun going down and the complex so quiet around him. If he really meant that, now was his chance. Before he could change his mind he grabbed his coat and left.

REYA OPENED THE DOOR, half-expecting Darren. When she saw Colin standing there, a scowl on his face and a huge bouquet of carnations in his hand, she was so shocked she didn't know what to say. Colin seemed equally at a loss for words, and for a few seconds they both just stood there staring at each other. Finally, with a tremendous effort, she remembered her manners.

"Would you like to come in?"

He hesitated. "Is it safe?"

Despite herself, she felt like smiling. "Well . . . that depends."

He seemed disconcerted. "On what?"

She gestured toward the flowers. "On whether those are for me or not."

He seemed to have forgotten he was holding the carnations. She almost laughed when he looked blankly down at the bouquet then back to her again. "I thought these might be better than a white flag," he said, and handed them to her.

"How thoughtful." The spicy scent filled her nostrils, and as she stepped aside to let him in, she added, "How did you know that carnations are my favorite flowers?"

He'd gone in the living room directly ahead. Glancing around appreciatively, he turned back to her. "I thought they might be," he said. "They suit you somehow."

"Thank you."

He hesitated again. "I also came with an apology," he said uncomfortably, and gestured. "Just in case the flowers didn't work."

"I see," she said, and buried her nose in the bouquet so he wouldn't see her smile. She couldn't help thinking how nice it was to see him uncomfortable for a change, since she was usually the one who felt off balance with him.

"You're not going to make this easy for me, are you?" he said, and took a deep breath. "All right. I apologize. I shouldn't have taken over the press conference like that, and I'm sorry. It was a stupid, senseless thing to do, and I've probably made things worse than they were before...." He paused and glared at her. "You can stop me anytime, you know."

"I know. But you were doing so well I hated to interrupt," she teased, and then had to laugh at the look on his face. "Why don't you sit down while I put these in water? I'll only be a minute."

To her dismay, he ignored her suggestion and followed her into the kitchen instead. She'd hoped to have a few minutes alone before she had to go back out to the living room; she needed the time to catch her breath. His unexpected appearance had completely unnerved her. She could hardly believe that he had come in person to apologize, and his thoughtful gesture with the flowers rattled her even more.

Finding a vase at last in a cupboard where it had been in front of her eyes all the time, she told herself

fiercely that she had to regain her composure or he'd
think she was an idiot. Even his presence in the kitchen
was disturbing, and she turned shakily with the vase
to put it under the faucet.

"Here, let me," Colin said, and reached out to take
the heavy cyrstal from her.

Their hands touched, and suddenly the atmosphere
changed. Reya felt the thrill of that simple contact
throughout her body, and for a second or two, she
didn't dare even look at him for fear something in her
expression would betray her. Then she felt his hand
tremble atop hers, and she slowly raised her eyes. Her
breath caught. The look on his face was unmistak-
able. She saw the desire, and her heart began to
pound. She couldn't look away. She knew her cheeks
were flushed; her whole body felt flushed. They were
so close she could feel his breath fan her face, so close
all she could see were his eyes, filled with the same
longing she felt herself.

He jerked his glance away from her face, down to
her hand. "You're not wearing your engagement
ring," he said suddenly, his voice loud in the vibrat-
ing silence.

She looked at her hand, too. He had put down the
vase and taken her hand in his, and when he raised his
eyes to her face again, she somehow managed to force
the words between her trembling lips. "I broke my
engagement to Darren Enderly this morning...."

His eyes held hers. Reya felt as though she could
hardly breathe. "I'm sorry," he murmured, and didn't
look sorry at all.

"Yes," she said softly. Her heart was pounding so
hard she thought it would leap out of her chest. Her
ears were ringing, and she knew that if he didn't kiss

her she was going to faint. He wanted to kiss her; she could see it in his face, feel it in the trembling of his hand, sense it in the tightening of his body. Unconsciously, she leaned toward him, her lips parted, *willing* him to take her in his arms.

Slowly, as though some powerful force beyond his control was making him do it, he lowered his head. It seemed an eternity before his lips touched hers, but the instant they did, she was swept up in a sensation that so overwhelmed her she forgot everything else. Even though he was barely touching her, she could feel the power of his desire behind that light kiss, and her lips trembled under his. Unconsciously, she pressed herself against him.

Abruptly, he straightened. The naked longing she had seen seconds before vanished from his face as though it had never been, and she looked at him in dismay when he said harshly. "I'm sorry. I shouldn't have come here. It was a mistake, like so many I've made lately."

He didn't wait for her reply, but turned and started out of the kitchen. He was almost at the front door by the time she overcame her shock and ran after him. "Colin...wait! I don't understand...."

He looked at her, and again his eyes burned, but not with passion. "There's nothing to understand," he said flatly. "I came to apologize for my behavior yesterday, and I hope you have accepted my apology. It won't happen again, I promise you."

"But—"

He reached the door. "Good night, Reya. I'll be in touch."

She couldn't even say goodbye. The door closed behind him with such finality that she could only stare at it, and when her trembling legs refused to hold her, she sank down onto the couch. She hadn't been mistaken. She had seen the same desire in Colin's eyes that she felt herself; she had felt the same longing in his body. But he had rejected her at the last, and she knew why. He was still trapped in the past, and she knew now there was nothing she could to to change that. Finally, after a long time, she rose stiffly and went miserably to bed.

CHAPTER EIGHT

REYA PRESENTED HERSELF at precisely ten the next morning at the downtown offices of Auguste Weidmar, owner and president of Weidmar Foods. She had resolved during a restless night that work went on despite her personal feelings. This meeting with Weidmar was the first since he'd signed with the agency, and she was determined to make a lasting impression. Resolutely putting Colin and Geneticon and everything else out of her mind, she had dressed carefully, donning a royal blue suit with a simple white crepe blouse. She'd even chosen pearl earrings and medium-heeled blue pumps, and if no one noticed the circles under her eyes or the tired lines around her mouth, she knew she looked the picture of professional respectability. Her manner was precise and direct as she began setting up the easel to make her presentation, but inside she was excited. She and Sid had worked hard on the artwork for the new label, and she was proud of it. Taking the pointer, she turned to the easel and began.

"Now, this first design is—"

"Excuse me, Miss Merrill," Auguste Weidmar interrupted.

She turned politely toward the white-haired man who sat at the head of a shining conference table that could easily have seated thirty. There were only three at the table today: Auguste and his two sons, Virgil and Tybalt, as white-haired as their father, and just as attentive to him as she was. It had been obvious to her from the beginning that even though his sons held executive titles, it was really the patriarch himself who ran the company.

She looked directly at him. "Yes, Mr. Weidmar?" she said pleasantly.

Weidmar's bushy white brows drew together. "Before you get started with that, I'd like to know what your agency is doing about that research place out on Highway 36—that Generacom, or Genterico. . . ."

One of the sons—she never could tell which was which—leaned forward. "I believe the name is Geneticon, Father."

Auguste barely gave him a glance. "Whatever," he said dismissively, and looked at Reya again. "Well, young lady?"

Reya hated to be called that; it seemed demeaning, as though she was a little girl who had wandered into this meeting by mistake and would be taken out again as soon as her nanny came for her. But this wasn't the time to get annoyed at the term, more important things were at stake here than her feelings. Alarm bells had rung in her mind at Weidmar's abrupt question, and she answered cautiously. "I'm not sure I under stand what you mean, Mr. Weidmar."

The white brows became one. "There's no sense beating about the bush, is there, young lady? I believe in speaking my mind, so I'll just say it right out. Is your agency still handling that Gentericom place?"

Reya opened her mouth to answer, but before she could get out a word, he went on. "Because if you are,

I want to say that I don't like it. No sir, I don't like it at all." He paused. "Do you get my meaning?"

"Well, I—"

The other son leaned forward. "What Father means, Miss Merrill, is—"

"She knows what I mean," Auguste interrupted impatiently. "You don't have to spell it out for her, Virgil."

Virgil flushed.

"Thank you, Virgil," Reya said quickly, taking pity on the man. Sometimes it was hard to believe both Auguste's sons were in their sixties; when their father was around, they still acted like schoolboys. Glancing away from the red-faced Virgil and the smirking Tybalt, she looked at Auguste again. The Geneticon account wasn't any of his business and they both knew it. But because he was an important client himself, she was forced to watch what she was about to say.

"I'm sorry you feel that way about Geneticon, Mr. Weidmar," she said carefully. "Especially when the current publicity has been so one-sided. Perhaps if you—"

Auguste raised his hand, silencing her. "Don't you go trying to tell me that I should listen to the other side, young lady. I don't want to listen to anything that man has to say. For my money, he's on par with those snake oil salesmen I saw in my youth. All talk and doin' evil things behind your back."

She was shocked and couldn't help showing it. "Well, I hardly think—"

He interrupted her again. "What *you* think isn't important, is it?" he said complacently. "It's what *I* think that counts." He waved a hand. "So you go on with your presentation, Miss Merrill, but just remember what I said, and we'll get along just fine.''

Reya was so furious by the time she left Weidmar's offices that she was nearly grinding her teeth. She'd managed somehow to get through the presentation; she'd even sounded as though she'd enjoyed it. But she'd been seething inside, and she couldn't wait until it was over and she could escape. Every time she looked at that fat toad of a man sitting so arrogantly at the head of the table, she wanted to tell him exactly what she thought of him. Only her training prevented her from doing so, but when she was finally able to leave, she was exhausted from the effort at hiding her tumultuous emotions.

And for what? she wondered as she threw her oversized portfolio and easel into the car. Ramming the key into the ignition, she was so angry she nearly flooded the engine. For what? Did Colin Hughes appreciate what she was doing? No. Did he even realize how far out on a limb she was going for him? No. Did he even care? No!

Oh, there was no doubt in her mind what Auguste Weidmar had meant today. He hadn't even bothered to disguise his threat. The implication was crystal clear: drop Geneticon as an account, or lose Weidmar Foods. It was as simple as that.

She put the car angrily into gear and started back to the office. Well, it wasn't quite that simple. She had an obligation to Colin, too. She couldn't just drop him because Weidmar was nervous about the current publicity surrounding Geneticon and thought it might somehow reflect badly on him. If she'd had any courage at all, she would have told the old man that one had nothing to do with the other.

Why hadn't she found the courage to tell him that? All she'd had to do was thank him for his suggestion and at the same time suavely let him know that the agency had no present plans to eliminate Geneticon from their client roster. He would have fumed at that, but what could he have done?

He could have called Joseph Clendenin himself, that's what, she thought, and knew that was really why she hadn't said anything in her defense. She hadn't wanted to take the chance of losing both accounts, and if she had argued with Weidmar, he would have gone over her head. All she needed at this point was for her boss to start hearing from her other accounts that this business with Geneticon was disturbing them; she knew what Clendenin would say to that. If he didn't order her to resign from Geneticon, he'd undoubtedly take over the account himself, and she would have proved nothing except that she didn't know how to handle either Weidmar Foods *or* Colin Hughes.

So she hadn't said anything, and now she despised herself. She'd acted just like Virgil and Tybalt, yesing the old man all over the place. What was the matter with her? Didn't she have any backbone at all?

She didn't know what she had today; that was part of the problem. Colin had so confused her last night that she felt in complete disarray. The day of the press conference had been horrible, one of the worst days she'd ever spent in her life, and Colin's sudden appearance on her doorstep last night hadn't helped. He'd only succeeded in making her feel more off balance than she had before.

Oh, why had it all become so complicated? She didn't want to be attracted to Colin Hughes, yet she was, and she couldn't seem to do anything about it. Every time she thought about him she felt weak; every time she was with him, it was even worse. She couldn't keep her mind on business, and now everything was in a worse muddle than it had been before. She'd been so unnerved by what had almost happened last night that she hadn't even asked Colin about the new approach for Geneticon, and now she didn't know what to do.

Yes, she did. She might have acted like an empty-headed adolescent last night, but this was a new day, and it wasn't going to go by without her and Colin getting things settled about Geneticon. She'd waited long enough. After that disastrous press conference they had to do something immediately, and if they couldn't agree on an approach today, she was going to resign from the account.

Marching into the agency, she told Sally, "Get me Colin Hughes, please," and then paced in her office until the intercom buzzed.

"Yes?"

"I'm sorry, Reya, but his secretary says he's not in the office."

"When will he be?"

"She doesn't know."

Picturing Colin's secretary, Reya doubted that there was anything that woman didn't know about the movements of her boss. Her mouth tightened. "Is she still on the phone?"

"No, I—"

"Call her back. I want to talk to her."

Seconds later, the intercom buzzed again. "Line two, Reya," Sally said. "And she sounds annoyed."

Not as annoyed as she's going to be, Reya thought sternly, and picked up the phone. She remembered seeing the name plaque on the woman's desk and said pleasantly, "Ms Tyndall? This is Reya Merrill, at the Clendenin Agency."

"I'm sorry, Miss Merrill, but I already told your secretary that Mr. Hughes is out of the office."

"Yes, I know you did," Reya said. "But I don't think you're aware how important it is that I speak with Mr. Hughes today. Do you have any idea when he plans to—"

"No, I'm afraid I don't."

"But he will be back today, won't—"

"I'm sorry, I can't give out that information."

Reya could feel her face getting red with anger. Why was this woman being so stubborn? All she had to do was answer a simple question. After all, it wasn't as though she was a reporter trying to steal classified files from Colin's office! Getting a grip on her temper, she said, "It really is imperative that I get in touch with Mr. Hughes. If you could just give me a number where I can reach him...."

"I'm *sorry*, Miss Merrill," the secretary said primly. "I thought I made it clear that Mr. Hughes does not want to be disturbed."

"But—"

"Good day, Miss Merrill," tne woman concluded and to Reya's exasperation, hung up.

Reya hung up, too, muttering an imprecation. Drumming her fingers on the top of the desk, she debated what to do now. If that Tyndall woman hadn't been so obstinate, she might have let it go for a day, but now she was determined to talk to Colin if she had to search the entire state to find him. They were going to settle this one way or another before the day was over, and that was that.

Punching the intercom button again, she said, "Sally, Richard Carlyle is a lawyer who works for Geneticon. See if you can get him, will you? If he's not there, maybe he has a private office."

This time it took Sally longer to find the number, but at last she buzzed through. Richard was in his office at Geneticon, and Reya snatched up the phone. "Richard?"

"Reya! What a nice suprise. You caught me just as I was leaving."

Reya couldn't help herself. "What is this, a mass exodus from Geneticon today? Isn't anybody going to stay and mind the store?"

Richard seemed puzzled. "What do you mean?"

"I've been trying to get through to Colin, but his secretary insists he isn't there, and she absolutely refuses to tell me where he is or when he's going to be in the office."

There was a silence.

"Richard?"

"Yes . . . I'm still here."

"Do you know where he is?"

"Well, I—"

She was struck with a sudden horrible thought. "Has something happened to him?"

"Oh, no!" Richard said hastily. "Don't think that!"

Relief made her sharp-tongued. She had imagined Colin lying still and white in a hospital bed somewhere and was ashamed of herself for jumping to conclusions. "What am I supposed to think? Colin's gone and nobody will tell me where he is. You're all acting as though I'm the enemy, when all I want to do is help!"

There was another silence. She wanted to break it with an apology for snapping at him, but she kept quiet. It really was imperative that she talk to Colin today, and if Richard knew how to get in touch with him, she was going to make him tell her. She heard him sigh.

"All right," he said. "But he's going to be angry with me for telling you this."

"And I'll be angry if you don't," she said. "Please, Richard. It really is important. I wouldn't bother you if it wasn't."

"I know," he said, and sighed again. "All right, he's at the Double Ott."

She blinked, sure she hadn't heard right. "The what?"

"The Double Ott. It's a...a sort of a ranch, near Colorado Springs. Colin goes there sometimes when he wants to be alone."

She couldn't have been more surprised if he'd said that Colin had flown off to Tibet to commune with a monk. "When you say a ranch," she began cautiously, "do you mean...with horses and cows and things?"

Richard laughed. "Something like that. It's in the mountains, near the Garden of the Gods, with a gorgeous view of Pikes Peak. It's beautiful, especially at this time of year."

"I'm sure," she said, imagining snakes and mosquitoes and God knows what other crawly things.

He laughed again at her tone. "No, really. I can give you directions, if you like."

She was appalled. "Don't they have a phone?"

"Well, yes. But it doesn't always work."

"Then how—" she began, and stopped. It didn't matter. She wasn't going to bother him there anyway. Heaven only knew what he was doing out there in the back of beyond, at a place with an incomprehensible name where the phone only worked when it felt like it, and she wasn't going to try to find out. "Never mind," she amended. "Just tell me when he's going to get back."

There was another of those ominous silences.

"Richard? He *is* coming back, isn't he?"

"Well...usually when he goes to the ranch he stays awhile, Reya."

She was holding on to her self-control by a thread. "How long a while?"

He hesitated. "Well, it could be a few days."

"Days?"

"Or he could be back sooner. I'm sorry, Reya. I just don't know. You know Colin and how unpredictable he is...."

"But how could he go off at a time like this?" she cried. "I can't believe it!"

"All this business with Geneticon has been a terrible strain on him," Richard said quietly. "You don't understand...."

She did understand, that was the problem. She knew how much Geneticon meant to Colin, and she was willing to do anything she could to help. But she couldn't do it alone, and she was furious that he had left without even telling her. What was she supposed to do now? Sit and twiddle her thumbs until he decided to saunter back from wherever it was he'd gone?

Gritting her teeth, she said as calmly as she was able, "I've changed my mind. I'd appreciate it if you'd give me the phone number of that place—" her voice hardened "—and the directions, too. Just in case."

"Do you think you'll go up there?" Richard asked tentatively.

There was nothing tentative about her answer. "Absolutely not! But I want the directions just in case I have to send the state police to find him. God knows what's going to happen while he's off enjoying himself, and I want to be able to get in touch with him somehow!"

SHE DIDN'T DECIDE TO GO until the next morning. It was Saturday, and the weekend stretched emptily before her by ten o'clock. Despite her efforts to sleep in, she'd awakened early, and after that there was nothing to do but get up and clean the apartment. Then she'd done the laundry and the bills and balanced her bank statement, and after she'd restlessly circled the apartment for the dozenth time, she exclaimed angrily.

"You might as well go," she said to herself. "You know you're dying to anyway!"

Thirty minutes later, resolutely telling herself that she was doing the only thing possible under the circumstances if she wanted to talk to Colin, she was on her way down Interstate 25. It was a beautiful day, bright and clear, and soon Denver was behind her. It was a nice change to be away from the city, even for a short time, and she hummed along with the radio until she glanced at the overnight bag she'd put on the seat beside her.

Now that she'd brought it, she felt silly. Richard had told her that the drive was only an hour and a half or so. She could be there by lunchtime, and then back at her apartment before dinner. She supposed it hadn't been necessary to bring a change of clothes, but if she'd misunderstood Richard and this ranch was really a posh resort, she'd feel even more foolish with only jeans to wear.

She was angry with herself for even debating about it. What difference did it make? Whether she brought the bag or not, she didn't intend to stay the night, and if she left it in the car, no one would even know. The important thing was that she was going to talk to Colin today so that she could be ready to put her new scheme in motion first thing Monday. That was the only thing that mattered; seeing Colin was secondary.

Was it? She looked at the bag again and glanced away, glad she was alone in the car because she was embarrassed. Maybe she'd really brought the case because she hoped he'd ask her to stay. What would she say to that if he did?

Exclaiming angrily, she wondered what she was worried about. After what had happened—or rather, *not* happened—the other night, she was beginning to think she'd fabricated that entire episode in her apartment. It was obvious from his hasty exit that she'd allowed her imagination to run wild. It seemed now that she'd just wanted to believe he was attracted to her because she was so taken with him. But he had never given her a hint that he found her desirable. He hadn't said or done anything to make her think he wanted any kind of relationship that wasn't professional.

Her shoulders slumped. Sometimes she doubted he wanted even that, and when she saw her turnoff coming up, she wondered if she should just drive right on by, turn around and go home again. Now that she'd come all this way, she couldn't imagine why she had bothered. If he didn't care enough about Geneticon to stay in town, she shouldn't have to chase him down. Mouth tight, she almost drove past the turnoff.

Almost.

The Double Ott Ranch was a complete surprise... and a delight. She'd been prepared for anything from a luxury resort to a log cabin huddled against the mountains, but when she drove under the archway with the 00 logo and saw the yard just ahead, she couldn't help smiling. The place looked just like a movie set. There was a farmhouse boasting a wide veranda with chintz curtains at the windows, corrals for horses, a huge two-story barn and an assortment of trucks and tractors and other ranch equipment. There were even chickens scrabbling in the dirt and an old dog lying under the porch who cocked one eye, sniffed once, and then went back to sleep.

Parking the car in front of what had to be a genuine hitching post, she climbed the wooden steps to the front porch, and then saw the tiny sign affixed to the front door. It indicated the office was around to the side, but when she went there, that seemed empty, too. Wondering what to do now, she was about to start down the steps again when she heard a "Hallo there!"

Startled, she looked around and saw Tom Mix standing in the doorway of the cavernous barn. Of course it wasn't the real Tom Mix, but she recognized the chaps and the hat and that stance from an old cowboy movie she had seen. Entranced, she waved. He waved back.

"...do fer ya?"

The dog who had ignored her before suddenly decided to remember he was guarding the place, and the rest of the cowboy's sentence was lost in a warbling howl as the old animal got to his feet. He came lumbering toward her, and before she knew what was happening, the animal had jumped up and placed his paws on her shoulders. To her horror, she felt herself falling backward, and they both crashed to the ground just as the cowboy came running up.

"Here, you—Fergus! You git back from there, ya hear?"

To her relief, the cowboy hauled the dog off her, and then reached to help her up. "I'm sorry, ma'am," he said anxiously, brushing her off. "He didn't hurt ya, did he?"

Gingerly, she felt her hip. "Only my dignity, I'm afraid," she said with a laugh. It seemed like a miracle, given the size of the dog, but she wasn't hurt. "Does he always greet visitors like that?"

"Only the ones he likes," the man said, and scowled at the dog, who sat down and wagged his tail, raising clouds of dust. "You go on now, Fergus, afore you git us both in trouble."

The dog, which Reya guessed was some kind of hound, looked so woebegone that she had to laugh. "It's all right. Don't send him away. I wasn't hurt, just startled."

Touching the brim of his hat, the cowboy said, "M'name's Charlie, ma'am. Charlie Scroggin. What can I do fer ya?"

Reya smiled again. "I'm Reya Merrill....Reya. I was looking for somebody, but I think I might have the wrong address. Do you...do you know where I could find Colin Hughes?"

"Colin?" he said, to her surprise. "Why, shure. He's out with a party right now."

"A party?"

Charlie grinned. "This here's a pack station, ma'am. Colin took out a group of campers yesterday. They were only one-nighters, so they'll be back this afternoon. You're welcome to wait, if you've a mind."

"Well, yes, I would like to wait," she said, trying to recover from her surprise. What did he mean—a pack station? Was he talking about a dude ranch? Glancing around, she saw the small individual cabins dotted through the trees. Everything looked so rustic that she couldn't imagine Colin staying in one of them, much less going out with a group of people to camp overnight. Then she realized just what Charlie had said, and she looked at him in astonishment again. "You said that Colin took out a group. Does that mean that he's a guide?"

Charlie laughed. He looked to be in his fifties, but it was hard to tell because of his weathered face and the crow's feet around his eyes. His skin was tanned what she suspected was a permanent brown, and he was as lean as a whippet. Remembering how rough and callused his hands had been when he'd helped her up, she knew that he'd worked hard all his life, and probably around horses. His bowed legs under the leather chaps seemed proof of that.

"He's a guide, all right," Charlie said, answering her question with another laugh. His faded blue eyes twinkled under the ten-gallon hat. "Knows these mountains purty good now, e'en if he is a tenderfoot." He winked. "Course you're not gonna tell him I said that, are ya? He'd skin me alive."

Reya's lips twitched. "I wouldn't dream of telling him," she said solemnly.

"Well, I gotta get back to work. You can wait in the house if ya like. Or—" the eyes twinkled again "—you can come out to the barn and watch me clean tack. We can swap stories while we're waitin'."

But during the next two hours Reya did more than watch Charlie clean tack while they exchanged stories. Her hands became shiny with saddle soap, and she learned more about Colin that afternoon than she ever would have reading dozens of newspaper accounts. She'd told herself that nothing Colin did would surprise her, but the time spent with Charlie had been full of surprises, not the least of which was learning that Colin was the owner of the Double Ott. He'd bought this ranch five years ago when he'd first come to Denver, and had converted it from near bankruptcy to paying its own way, rescuing Charlie and his wife Matilda at the same time.

"We were near desperate," Charlie confessed. "Just couldn't make ends meet, no matter how we tried. Put the place up for sale finally. Figured we was just gettin' too old. Then Colin came and bought the place and tol' us 'bout his idear for takin' people out in the mountains the old way. Thought it'd give those city slickers a kick, to be cowboys for a day...."

"We still run cattle," he went on while she looked at him in amazement, "but the real operation's the pack station now. We open in late March, dependin' on the weather, a'course, and go right through till October or thereabouts runnin' groups in an' out. Some for only a day or so, others for weeks."

"I hadn't realized there were so many people who...who liked this sort of thing," Reya said, rubbing saddle soap into the reins of a bridle, as Charlie had showed her.

Charlie laughed. "We got people comin' out our ears! Don't have enough room to 'commodate 'em all!

And purty soon we're gonna be open all winter, too. There's good skiin' hereabouts, so they say. But we'll have sleigh rides, too and . . . oh, heck, all sortsa other things. It'll be a year-round operation then!''

''It seems to be quite an operation now,'' she said admiringly, and then looked around for the jar of saddle soap she seemed to have misplaced. ''Now, where—''

''Is this what you're looking for?''

She would have recognized his voice anywhere. Her heart began to pound, and she slowly raised her eyes to see Colin holding out the jar of saddle soap. Or at least she thought it was Colin. This man in faded jeans and a dusty plaid cowboy shirt and chaps like Charlie's was someone she had never seen before. He bore no resemblance to the withdrawn and reserved owner of Geneticon. That man wore suits and ties and hand-made shoes, and his hair was always carefully combed. This man's hair was hidden beneath his battered Stetson, and the hand that held the jar out to her wasn't immaculate and manicured, but calloused and rough from handling reins.

She wasn't sure what to say. Now that the moment had come, her mind was a complete blank. He looked so different that she felt off balance again, wondering too late if she should have come. Because she had known the instant she saw him that she hadn't driven all this way to talk business. Some compulsion she hadn't really understood had led her here, and as she looked up into that handsome face, she suddenly knew the reason. She wanted to be sure she hadn't imagined that moment in her apartment the other night. If she had, she could deal with it—she'd have to. But if she hadn't, she wanted to know that, too. She was risking everything—her job, her career—for him, and she had to know why.

Colin's eyes were in shadow under the brim of the Stetson as he reached down to pull her to her feet. His fingers closed around hers, and when she felt the roughness of his hand against her palm, she knew she hadn't imagined the calluses. Had she imagined everything else?

Then he took off his hat and his eyes were no longer in shadow. "Hello," he said softly. "Welcome to the Double Ott."

She hadn't been mistaken after all.

CHAPTER NINE

HOURS LATER, Reya was sitting on a log in front of a campfire, the night air cold on her back and the flames of the fire warming her face. Sighing in contentment, she wrapped her hands around her tin coffee mug and watched Colin stoke up the fire.

"If anyone had told me yesterday that I'd be sitting here tonight, I'd have thought they were crazy," she said.

Colin lifted the enamel coffeepot from the flat rock at the edge of the coals and filled both their cups. "I'd have thought the same thing," he said with a smile. "Somehow this place doesn't quite seem to suit your, er, image."

She looked at him over the rim of her cup. "I thought the same thing about you"

This was the first time they had really had a chance to talk alone since he'd come in from the camping trip. First Colin had had to get his campers off their horses and the animals themselves rubbed down and put away; then Charlie's wife, Matilda, who had been working steadily in the big farm kitchen, had called them all to a gargantuan dinner. There had been potato salad and baked beans and homemade bread, with the biggest steaks Reya had ever seen cooked over an outdoor barbecue pit. All wrong if you were con-

cerned about calories and a balanced diet, but fun
once in a while. Reya had helped with everything and
had enjoyed herself thoroughly, even if she protested
at the size of the steak Colin had lifted with a crane
onto her plate.

They had all eaten on long tables outside under the
stars and trees, and the party-like atmosphere had
prevented any private conversation. Those who had
been out on the pack trip were still excited about their
adventure, and Colin had been constantly consulted
about everything from the bobcat they had seen on the
trail to the saddle sores the expedition had left behind. He bore it all good-naturedly, while Reya
watched in surprise. She hadn't imagined he could be
like this, and sometimes when he responded to a joke
or sally with one of his own, she knew she was looking at him in openmouthed astonishment. He was so
different here from the man she knew in the city.
Which was the real Colin?

Wondering if she was going to find out now that
everyone else had wearily drifted off to their cabins
and to bed, she sipped her coffee and watched him
covertly. Sparks leaped up to disappear into the night
as he added another log to the fire, and somewhere
behind her an owl hooted, calling for its mate. That
and the snapping of the flames were the only sounds.
The stars were brilliant above, and the flickering
campfire tinted Colin's face an even deeper bronze. At
that moment he looked exactly like pictures she had
seen of cowboys on the range: strong, secure in themselves and the job they were doing...content with
being alone. Disturbed by that last thought, she shivered and glanced away.

"Are you cold?"

He sat beside her and touched the light jacket she wore. It was all she'd brought. When she'd packed this morning, she never dreamed she'd be sitting outside by a campfire late tonight. Trying to ignore the fact that their arms were touching and that her heart had begun to beat a little faster, she shook her head. "No, I'm fine," she said, and despite herself, shivered again. Now that they were alone, she didn't know what to say.

"Here...."

He took off his fleece-lined denim jacket and put it around her shoulders before she could protest, "But what about you?"

He shrugged. "The night air up here doesn't bother me. I'm used to it."

"I should be, too," she said smiling. "But even after several years in New York, and now two in Colorado, I suppose I'm still just a California girl at heart."

"Is that where you're from—California?"

She heard the guarded tone come into his voice and kept hers light. She knew he'd lived in California with his wife and daughter, and she didn't want to spoil the evening by calling up painful memories. "Southern California, born and bred," she answered with another smile.

He raised an eyebrow. "Ah, one of the famous Valley Girls."

"Wrong valley," she laughed. "I grew up in Arcadia, then I went to college in Los Angeles. I never even left the state until I graduated, and that was to go to New York."

"Where you found fame and fortune, no doubt," he said, teasing her.

Remembering that last humiliating scene in Jeffrey Dayton's office at Dayton and Associates right before he fired her, she winced. "Well, I found a job, at least," she said, still trying to keep it light.

"One you obviously didn't like," he commented.

She looked at him sharply, wondering if he knew about her background. It wouldn't surprise her; after today, she doubted that anything he did would. "Why do you say that?"

"The expression on your face just now. You looked like you'd swallowed some bad medicine."

She tried to smile. "Well, it was—one of those 'learning experiences,' if you know what I mean."

"I do indeed. Don't we all have those from time to time?"

"Yes," she said gloomily. "It's supposed to be character building."

"Well, if that's the case, I should have a sterling character by now," he said dryly. "I wonder what happened."

Her lips twitched. "Maybe it doesn't work with everybody."

He looked at her indignantly before he turned to prod the fire again. After a moment, his voice low, he said, "Was that what your engagement was—a learning experience?" He glanced quickly at her again, then just as quickly away. "I'm sorry. I shouldn't have asked."

"No, that's all right," she said hesitantly. "I guess in a way it was. It took me a long time to figure out that the only things Darren and I had in common were a liking for antiques and a genuine love of music."

He'd been hunched down by the fire, now he turned on his heels to look at her. "You like music?"

She glanced at him in surprise. "Doesn't everybody?"

He smiled. "I guess it depends. If you're a teenager—"

She smiled, too. "If you're a teenager, you don't listen to music, you listen to noise."

They both laughed at that, then he asked, "Warm enough?"

"Oh, yes," she said, snuggling down into his jacket. It was yards too big for her, and she wasn't sure whether she was more warmed by it or by the fact that he had given it to her. The scent of him filled her nostrils, and she breathed deeply. Even up here in the mountains, she could smell that fragrance she associated with him, a masculine combination of spice and something else that made her blood race. Hastily she said, "I envy you, owning a place like this. But it's so strange...."

"Is it? Why?"

"Well, it's just that you seem to lead two lives," she said hesitantly. "One in the future with Geneticon, and this one, here in the past."

He came to sit beside her again. "I hadn't thought of it that way, but I guess you're right."

Even though he wasn't touching her now, she was so aware of him that her skin tingled. Quickly, she looked away from him, into the fire. She could sense him watching her, and because his stare made her nervous, she reached for the coffeepot to fill her cup again.

He took it from her, and their hands touched. She pulled hers away. She wanted no repetition of the other night, when she'd made a fool of herself by misinterpreting him at her apartment. She had to keep the conversation going. "What made you decide to buy a ranch, of all things?" she asked hastily. "Or did you always have a secret desire to be a cowboy?"

"I'm not sure what my intention was," he said, placing the coffeepot next to the fire again. "I didn't intend to get involved with a working cattle ranch, that's for sure. But when I heard this place was for sale, and I saw it . . ." He shrugged.

"Well, I can see why you fell in love with it. It's beautiful here."

"It is, isn't it?" He leaned back, looking up through the canopy of trees to the brightness of the stars before he brought his glance down to her again. Casually, he placed his hand over hers. "I'll show you around tomorrow," he said, as though it had already been agreed she was going to stay.

She felt breathless at that casual gesture. Glancing down at his hand atop hers, at the strong fingers and the square palm, she wanted to turn her hand up and lace her fingers with his. She didn't dare. If she did that, she'd want more than just the touch of his hand on hers.... She was so aware of him now that every muscle in her body was taut. She wanted him. She wanted him more than she had ever wanted any man in her life.

But not this way...not because she was carried away by a romantic campfire and the realization that they were all alone, with just the mountains and the owls for company. She sensed that he wanted her, too. She could feel it in the slight quivering of his fingers; she knew she'd see it in his eyes if she dared look up. But she'd never been the kind who embraced casual sex, and she decided that's what it would be—for him, at least. He wasn't ready for more. He was too caught up in the past, too filled with his own sense of purpose to care about anything—or anyone—else in his life. She had seen that the other night at her apartment, and she wasn't about to forget it.

"What do you say, Reya?" he asked. "You haven't seen anything until you've seen this area on horseback."

"Oh, well, I . . . horseback?" She jerked her attention back to what he was saying. "You're not serious!"

He smiled. "You don't ride?"

"Not since I was a child, on the ponies at the park!"

"Then it's about time you got acquainted with the joys of being in a saddle again."

"But—"

"It's either that or hiking on foot."

"Can't we just take the car?"

He laughed at her expression. "Where's your pioneer spirit? Come on. You'll enjoy it."

She doubted that. She had seen some of the campers limping around tonight; she hadn't missed the gingerly way they sat down. They hadn't been kidding about the saddle sores, but suddenly she didn't care. She might not be able to walk for a week after riding with Colin tomorrow, but it would be worth it, just to be with him when he was like this; she had never seen him so relaxed. And the time would be fleeting enough as it was. Tomorrow was Sunday, and sooner or later, they both had to face the problems they'd left behind.

But not tonight, she thought, and said, "All right, I'll go. But on one condition. . . ."

"Let me guess. You'd prefer not to ride Ol' Thunder and Lightning, right?"

She gave a mock shudder. "I don't even want to *see* Ol' Thunder and Lightning. Don't you have a nice, gentle old horse called Daisy or Tulip or something?"

Colin smiled wickedly. "We'll see what we can find."

She didn't trust that smile. "Just remember, I wasn't born in the saddle like you."

He looked even more amused. "I was a tenderfoot, too, not too long ago."

Relieved that her moment of weakness about him seemed to have passed, or at least that she had herself under better control, she was able to laugh. "You didn't look like it this afternoon when you came in," she teased. "I would have sworn you were an old hand."

"Not me. Ask Charlie. If you could have seen me five years ago—"

He stopped abruptly, the laughter fading from his eyes. She saw the change in his expression and knew he was thinking of that traumatic time before he came to Denver. She tried to think of something to say, but the only remarks that occurred to her seemed either too frivolous or not frivolous enough. Nothing seemed right to break the awkward silence that had fallen, and so finally she decided to say nothing at all. Trying to give him time to compose himself, she stared into her coffee cup.

"I'm sorry," he said finally.

"You don't have to apologize. I understand."

There was another short silence. "I don't think you do."

She looked up at him. "Do you want me to?" she asked softly.

He looked away. "I don't know. It was a long time ago...."

"Not long enough perhaps."

He glanced quickly at her again, then down to the ground. "No. You're right. Not long enough."

"Sometimes it never is," she said, her voice taking on a faraway quality of remembrance. "I can recall vividly the night the police came to tell us that my brother had been killed in a car accident. That was almost twelve years ago, but I remember where I was standing when my parents opened the door. I remember what I was wearing, and what they said. They didn't have to tell me, I already knew—even before Mom and Dad opened the door." She looked at him. "I was eighteen then, so was Randy. We were twins."

Colin stared at her. "I'm...I'm sorry," he said, his voice low. "I didn't realize..."

She summoned a small smile. "You couldn't know, not many people do. It's not something I talk about."

His glance became even more intent. "Why did you now?"

She hesitated, wondering if she should tell him the truth. "Because we've both suffered a loss," she said quietly, "and I wanted you to know I understand. We didn't have to deal with the publicity you did, Colin, but it was horrible enough. Sometimes I thought I'd never get over Randy's death...sometimes I'm not sure I have. So you see? I do know how you feel. And I'm sorry."

He glanced away again. "Sorry," he said, unable to hide his bitterness. "Everybody's always sorry, but it doesn't make a damn bit of difference, does it?"

She didn't blame him for his bitterness; she'd felt the same way herself during those nightmare days after Randy had died. Friends, relatives, even mere acquaintances, had come to offer sympathy and condolences, but none of it had brought her brother back. She remembered wanting to scream at them all just to leave her alone.

Thrusting the memories away, she said, "No. It doesn't make any difference. But at least you're trying to do something to help, Colin."

"You mean Geneticon."

"Yes."

His eyes looked defeated. "Sometimes I wonder—" He shook his head. "Never mind. Is that why you came up here today, Reya? To talk about Geneticon?"

She was disconcerted by the abrupt change of subject. "Yes, of course," she said quickly, and avoided his eyes. "Why else? I had to ask your opinion about—"

"You could have done that over the phone."

"Yes, but...but Richard said the phone here didn't always work."

"So you decided to come up here in person, just in case."

She couldn't sit there any longer with him looking at her like that. She didn't know if it was her imagination or not, but it seemed there was a speculative expression in his eyes that hadn't been there before, and she jumped up. "Why all the questions?" she asked, turning away from him. "Look, if I disturbed you by coming here, I'm sorry. But I thought it was important that we talk."

He got to his feet, too. She could feel him behind her and she tensed. Even so, she nearly jumped when he put his hands on her shoulders. She was powerless to resist when he slowly turned her to face him.

"You did disturb me by coming here," he said, his voice harsh. "But not in the way you think."

She made the mistake of looking up at him. His eyes burned fiercely. "I didn't mean—"

"Yes," he said, and his hands trembled on her shoulders. "You did."

He drew her toward him then, slowly, agonizingly, until their bodies were just inches away. He was so tall she had to tilt her head back to look at him.

One of his hands went to the back of her head, burying itself in her hair; the other to her waist. She could feel his arm shaking as he pulled her into him, but by then she was trembling so badly herself she hardly noticed. Inch by inch, his head came down until their lips touched.

She had known passion before, and desire and want and need. But just like the other night when Colin had kissed her, she was so instantly swept away by emotion that nothing else mattered. An earthquake could have rattled the ground and she wouldn't have noticed; a lightning bolt could have split the tree next to her and she wouldn't have heard. The instant Colin's lips touched hers, she thought of nothing but him. She had longed for this moment, fantasized about it, dreamed that it would happen again. But nothing in her imagination had prepared her for the exquisite reality of being in his arms with his mouth hungrily seeking hers, not tentatively, as it had the other night, but with a man's full passion, demanding a response from her. She gave it to him with all the force of her being. Wrapping her arms around his neck, she never wanted to let him go.

They broke apart finally, both gasping, dazed with what had happened to them. She could feel him trembling again, but with a new emotion, and she was alarmed. "Colin!"

He released her, turning abruptly back to the fire, which had smoldered down to low embers. The faint light shone on his face, and she could see his expression was bleak. She reached out and grasped his arm. "Colin . . . ?"

She felt his arm tense under her fingers and she became even more dismayed. What was happening? Why was he acting like this?

He hunched down by the fire, using a stick to poke at the coals. "I'm sorry," he muttered. "I don't know why I did that. I shouldn't have."

"Why not?"

Her quiet question seemed to agitate him even more. He flung the stick away almost violently and stood again. "Because there's no point," he said, and glanced away. "I . . . I don't want to get involved. I've tried before, Reya, and it just didn't work. I can't give you what you want—what you need. It just isn't in me anymore."

She couldn't help herself. Some last bit of common sense was shrieking at her to leave it alone, to turn around and walk away. He'd given her the perfect excuse; she should take it. It was madness to get involved with this man she didn't understand and probably never would, and yet . . .

"Why don't you let me be the judge of that?" she asked softly.

Still refusing to look at her, he made an angry gesture with his head. "You don't understand."

She walked up to him. "I understand this," she said, and reached up to pull his head down to hers.

His kiss this time was almost savage, his mouth hard on hers, his tongue thrusting between her teeth. She responded just as fiercely, holding him tightly, feeling his erection grow even through their clothing. She was so aroused herself that if he'd desired, they could have made love right there, in the open night, in front of the fire, for all the world to see. She didn't care; all she wanted was him. The tension that had existed between them almost from the first moment they'd met exploded now, and they clutched at each other, swaying with the fire of their emotions. Uttering a groan, Colin pulled back yet again. His eyes were fierce and bleak at the same time.

"You don't know what you're getting into," he said hoarsely.

She smiled shakily. "Neither do you."

"This is crazy...."

She clung to him. "I know. I don't care."

He groaned again and buried his face in her hair. "I don't, either," he whispered, and suddenly making up his mind, reached down and literally swept her off her feet. Holding her in his arms, he started toward the house.

Charlie and his wife Matilda had left the front door open for them, and a light burning in the hall. Colin shut the door behind them with a well-placed kick, and started immediately up the stairs.

"Put me down," Reya whispered. "I can walk."

He held her even more tightly to him. "Not on your life," he said. "Now that I've got you, I'm not going to let you go."

The master bedroom was at the end of the second-floor hallway, and he shoved the door open with his shoulder, striding across the room to deposit her on the four-poster. "Stay right there," he commanded, and went quickly to the fireplace to build a fire. He had it going in a matter of seconds, and as the flames leaped up to make flickering shadows on the old-fashioned flowered wallpapered walls, he turned back to her. She hadn't moved; she was too entranced. The moon seemed to float just outside one of the dormer windows. The combination of the moonlight streaming in and the gold light from the fire made the room seem enchanted, and the sight of Colin standing there staring at her took her breath away. Unconsciously she raised her arms and beckoned to him.

He came to her at once, drawing her up from the bed to hold her close. They kissed, just touching lips at first, then as passion rose, more hungrily. She was still wearing two jackets: her light one, and his denim. He pulled them off and flung both to the foor, his fingers confident and sure as they came back to find the buttons of her blouse. Mouth clinging to hers, he unbuttoned them one by agonizing one, taking his time so that she yearned to finish the task for him. She wanted to feel his skin against hers, and when he finally pulled the blouse from her shoulders and reached for the wispy lace bra she wore, she couldn't wait any longer. His Western-style shirt had snaps, and she ripped them open, practically tearing the shirt from his body.

He laughed softly, tilting her head up to his. Her eyes were brilliant with desire as she looked at him, and the laugh died in his throat and became a moan. He pulled her to him again.

"God, you're beautiful," he murmured, stroking her back. His mouth moved to her throat and he kissed the wildly beating pulse there. She arched up against him and he cupped one firm breast in his hand, bending his head to tease the nipple with his tongue.

She was never sure how they got the rest of their clothing off; she didn't care. By the time they came together, skin against skin, the sensation was so exquisite she just wanted to lie there. He felt the same way. Wrapping her in his arms, he held her tightly and they watched until the fire died to low embers.

Reya looked up when Colin finally stirred. "Where are you going?" she asked in alarm.

He laughed softly. "To build up the fire."

She smiled and moved seductively against him. "Why don't we do it from here?"

He laughed again. "I'll be right back."

She couldn't keep her eyes off him as he rolled out of bed and walked across the room to the fireplace. He had a wonderful body with those long, lean legs and broad shoulders and tight buttocks; she could have watched him forever. Kneeling, he added more wood to the fire, and she was fascinated by the play of muscles in his strong arms. Then he stood and turned toward her and she was fascinated by something else. Sighing as he came toward her, she thought he was truly a beautiful man.

She discovered then that he was a beautiful lover, as well. She was prepared for him to be experienced...expert in the art of making love, but she wasn't prepared for the fury of desire he aroused in her. He was a gentle lover, considerate and passionate at the same time, and she thought fleetingly once that she had never made love like this, where one magic

moment led to another, and then another, until finally hands and tongues and legs and arms weren't
enough. She wanted all of him. She wanted to feel him
inside her, to draw him deeper and deeper within, until the moan she heard was torn from his throat, not
hers, until the cry for release burst from his lips instead of hers.

"You're beautiful, Reya," he murmured, staring
down into eyes dark with desire. His fingers brushed
her tangled hair back from her flushed face. "So
beautiful. I never thought I'd feel like this again."

"I never thought I'd feel like this at all," she whispered, and drew his head down to hers again. Opening her mouth, she took his tongue inside. He groaned
and rolled on top of her, both hands beneath her,
holding her to him with the same desperation she felt.
The shadows leaped along the walls, caressing their
naked, writhing bodies, but they didn't notice. It
wasn't the heat from the fire that caused the perspi-
ration on their bodies, and when she guided him inside her and raised her hips to meet him, he moaned
and buried his face in her hair.

She could feel herself being swept away with every
thrust. He was driving into her, deeper and deeper
with each answering rise of her hips, and she ran her
hands up and down that strong back, pulling him
down, down, into her, arching her back to present her
aching breasts. He bent his head, sucking first on one
swollen nipple, then the other, kneading the soft flesh
with his hand. Their bodies were slippery with sweat.
She felt the hard muscles of his legs and arms, the flat
belly tight against hers. She couldn't hold back any
longer, and the rhythm of her hips increased until he
pulled his head back and groaned. Through the sting-

ing sweat running down her face, she saw the muscles of his neck corded with effort, and she pulled him down again. "Colin...!"

His cry matched hers, and the pleasure seemed to mount and mount and mount until she thought she would die from it, and still it went on. She heard another cry and didn't realize it had been torn from her throat as he drove into her for the last time. Her body wasn't her own; it had become ethereal, a being that could fly.

Then Colin laughed softly, and she came reluctantly back to earth.

"Lord," he gasped, and collapsed beside her.

CHAPTER TEN

COLIN DIDN'T GIVE HER A CHANCE to luxuriate in bed the next morning. They had made love twice more after that first cataclysmic event, finally falling asleep in each other's arms long after the fire had died to mere embers and the moon had sunk low. It seemed as though she'd barely drifted off when she felt him stir, and when she reluctantly opened her eyes, he was starting to dress. He saw her looking blearily at him and laughed.

"Time to get up," he said, his eyes twinkling. "We're supposed to go for a ride, remember?"

She groaned and snuggled deeper under the covers. "I don't remember agreeing to go at the crack of dawn."

He laughed again and reached for his shirt. "Come on, lazybones. We'll have breakfast before we leave."

"Breakfast!" The thought nauseated her, and she pulled the blankets over her head. The room was freezing, and she had no intention of crawling out of this warm cocoon until noon at least.

"I'll give you to the count of three to get up," Colin said, laughter in his voice. "One . . ."

She peeped over the fold of blankets. "Wait a minute. What happens if—"

"Two . . ."

"This isn't fair!"

"Three!"

An evil grin on his face, he reached for the blankets. She scrambled to a sitting position, holding the covers protectively to her. "Don't you dare!"

"You can't stay in bed all day."

This time it was her turn to grin. "Why not?"

His eyes glinted. "That's a good question. Give me time, and I'll think of an answer."

She flipped back a corner of the blankets. "It might be easier to think of one in here."

He smiled and began taking off his shirt again. "You know, you might be right."

"I know I am," she said, and laughed softly as he crawled in beside her. Teasingly, she drew away for a moment. "What will Charlie think if we stay here all day?" she murmured, her eyes sparkling.

"Charlie minds his own business," he said, and reached hungrily for her.

Reya surprised herself with the fury of her response. She'd thought after last night that nothing could approximate that glorious feeling of making love with Colin, but it seemed she'd been wrong. The instant his mouth came down on hers, she was lost. Passion rose so quickly inside her that she felt on fire, and she returned his kisses so fiercely that if there had been time, she would have marveled at the nakedness of her desire for him. It was as though she couldn't get enough of him, and when he rolled over, pulling her on top of him, she knew he felt the same way about her. That aroused her even more, and she dropped her head to kiss him again. Clamping her legs around him, she moved against him until he was nearly frantic with desire.

"Reya..." he groaned. His hands moved all over her body, touching, caressing, seeking those sensitive areas he had found the night before, until she nearly pleaded with him to end the agonizing anticipation. When he rolled over on top of her, she was ready for him with opened thighs, and a second later when he entered her, she felt as though she was being transported to new heights.

"Colin!" she cried, and her slender body arched under his. The pleasure mounted, pulsing through her in waves that finally tossed her back onto shore, spent and exhausted. Colin lay beside her, gasping for breath. Their eyes met and they smiled a secret smile. She reached out to push a damp lock of hair back from his face, and her hand fell limply to his chest. They slept.

It was nearly ten o'clock before she awoke, and she lay there for a moment, just luxuriating in the aftermath of that glorious lovemaking. Uttering a contented sigh, she turned over and reached for Colin, but his side of the bed was empty. Her eyes flew open and she sat up.

"Colin?"

The house was so quiet around her that she thought she was alone, but then through the open window she heard a snatch of conversation and leaped out of bed. Hiding behind the curtain, she looked out. It was a glorious day, but what she could see of the yard below was empty. Even the overnight guests were nowhere in sight, and she wondered where everyone was. Biting her lip, she turned away and noticed her overnight bag placed conspicuously on the dresser. Colin must have fetched it while she was asleep, and she silently blessed him for his thoughtfulness. Twenty minutes later, showered and wearing jeans and a cotton shirt, she went tentatively downstairs. She heard voices from the direction of the kitchen and went there.

"Well, well!" Colin teased when she pushed open the swinging door. "I thought you were going to sleep the whole day away."

She saw his grin and tried not to smile in return. She wasn't sure how much Matilda knew, or guessed, but she didn't want to offend her, so she said, "It must be the mountain air. I can't remember ever sleeping this long. Good morning, Matilda."

Matilda was just taking some cookies from the big oven. She was a big woman, round and comfortable looking, with a wide smile and merry blue eyes. Reya had liked her instantly when they were introduced last night, and though she wouldn't have dreamed of saying anything, she was amused when that nursery rhyme about Jack Spratt and his wife had leaped into her head. It could have been written with Charlie and Matilda Scroggin in mind.

"Good morning," Matilda replied, and glared in mock annoyance at Colin, who'd snatched several cookies off the sheet she was holding. "Don't you pay any mind to Colin now. He's always up with the chickens. Would you like some breakfast?"

Colin grinned around a mouthful of cookie. "Don't you mean lunch?"

Reya gave him a quelling glance before she looked at Matilda. "Just coffee, please," she said. "But I'll get it myself."

Matilda raised a hand. "You sit right down. You're a guest here, and I'll be glad to get it for you."

Reya obeyed, watching as Matilda bustled around pouring coffee into a large mug, taking a plate down and piling half a dozen homemade biscuits onto it, adding a small crock of butter and one of jam, and presenting it all with a flourish in front of her. "If there's anything else..."

Reya looked at the array of food and had to laugh. "I think this will be just fine, Matilda. Thanks."

"You're sure now...."

Reya glanced in amusement at Colin, who winked back. "Yes, I'm sure."

Matilda smiled broadly back. Stacking another plate six inches high with cookies, she said, "You help yourself. I'll just take these out to Charlie." She grinned at the two of them. "Poor man. He hasn't eaten a thing since breakfast four hours ago."

"Better watch out, Matty," Colin said dryly, "or he'll starve to death before your eyes."

"Humph," Matilda said, and went out, a gleam in her eyes.

The screen door banged behind her, leaving Reya and Colin alone. For the first time since entering the kitchen, Reya felt uncomfortable. She sensed Colin looking at her, but for some reason she couldn't meet his eyes. It was almost hard to believe, sitting here in this sunny kitchen, with the cracked linoleum and the scuffed Formica counters, that they had experienced such fiery passion upstairs, and she wasn't sure what to say to him, or how to act.

He didn't make it any easier for her, leaning against the counter like that, sipping coffee, his long legs crossed at the ankle. He was wearing jeans again this morning, the denim so worn that it was a soft silver, and he had changed to another plaid Western-style shirt, this one in shades of turquoise that set off his tan beautifully. He'd rolled up the long sleeves to his forearms, and he was wearing boots. Remembering his usual attire at Geneticon, the hand-tailored suits and shirts, the French silk ties, she wondered which image she preferred. He looked equally at home in either wardrobe, outrageously handsome in both. Thinking of their lovemaking, she could feel her cheeks reddening and looked quickly away from him, down at the biscuit she had been nervously buttering. She put it aside. She didn't want it. The activity had just given her hands something to do.

"Why are you staring at me like that?" she asked.

"Was I? I guess I was thinking—"

"About what?"

He put the coffee cup down and reached for her hand. "Come on. Let's go for a walk."

"A walk?" she repeated, determined to keep the atmosphere light. Just looking at him made her feel dizzy, and she wasn't sure she liked the feeling. She'd never felt this way about a man before, and she was beginning to realize how dangerous it was to feel this way about Colin. She'd forgotten in the heat of the moment last night his assertion about not wanting to get involved, but she remembered it now. Was that why he wanted to take a walk? Was he going to tell her that last night had been a mistake?

Wondering if it had been, she allowed him to pull her up from the table. Cursing the fact that even this casual gesture could make her knees weak, she tried to get control of herself and the situation by joking, "I thought we were going for a ride this morning. Did my obvious reluctance make you change your mind?"

To her dismay, his reply was almost absentminded.
"I thought you'd prefer a walk," he said. "But if
you'd rather—"

"No, no," she said hastily. His mind was clearly on
something else, and she didn't want to think she knew
what it was. Trying to smile, she said, "Lead on. A
walk is just fine."

"We won't go far. There's something I'd like to talk
to you about."

"What?"

But he shook his head, preferring to keep it a surprise. Wondering how many other surprises were in
store for her, she followed as he struck off toward a
path through the trees. A creek bubbled beside them,
and the day was fresh with the scent of pines, brilliant
with the blue of the sky. She would have been awed by
this beauty at another time, but today she hardly noticed it; she was too concerned with what he was going
to say. Finally, after they'd gone a short distance from
the house, she couldn't stand it any longer. They were
walking side by side on the path, and she stopped in
the shade of some trees.

"Colin, what's wrong?"

He'd been looking ahead, to a glimpse of Pikes
Peak that could just be seen through all the foliage. He
turned, and when he saw her looking at him, it was as
though he couldn't stop himself. Before she realized
what he intended, he had taken her by the shoulders.
More puzzled than startled, she started to say something, but when she saw his expression, the words
died. There was no mistaking the look on his face, and
her heart began to pound. The same longing she felt
was evident in his dark eyes, and without realizing it,
she pressed against him. Slowly, as though compelled

by some powerful force over which he had no control, he lowered his head to hers. Their lips were only inches apart when he suddenly stopped, and she looked at him in dismay when he uttered a curse under his breath and moved away.

Dazed by what had almost happened, she clutched his sleeve. "Colin, what is it? What's wrong? Tell me!"

He turned to look at her, and suddenly she knew. "You're sorry," she said. "That's it. You're sorry about last night. I should have known...."

He reached for her again. "I'm not sorry!" he said fiercely. "Never think that."

She forced herself to look at him. "What, then?"

He released her so suddenly that she almost staggered back, but he didn't seem to notice. There was a flat rock near the bank of the stream, half shaded by the trees, and he gestured to it. "Let's sit down."

She didn't want to sit down; she wanted to know what was wrong. Then, just as abruptly, she decided she didn't want to know what it was, after all. If he regretted last night's intimacy, she didn't want to hear it. She didn't want to be let down gently; she didn't want to be let down at all. Wishing that she hadn't asked, she followed him reluctantly and sat beside him.

"Colin?" she asked tentatively when the silence had dragged on too long.

He'd been sitting with his legs drawn up and his arms crossed over his knees. He straightened, one leg out in front of him, the other bent at the knee. The creek widened at this juncture, swirling around the rock they were sitting on, broadening to form a pond. He looked down at the water and sighed.

"I'm sorry," he said unhappily. "I...it's really got nothing to do with you."

She wanted to reach out and touch his arm, but the expression on his face prevented her. "I see," she said uncertainly, even though she didn't see at all. "Well, I'm glad of that. I thought you regretted last night."

He glanced briefly at her, then across the pond again. "It does make things more difficult, doesn't it?"

She didn't like the sound of that. "Does it?" she asked. "You mean because of Geneticon?"

He shifted position, leaning forward to balance an elbow on his knee. "Geneticon, and other things."

She didn't like the trend of the conversation, and her voice sharpened slightly. "What other things? Colin, I don't know what you're talking about!"

He glanced at her again, then got to his feet. His back to her, he said, "I know I'm not making much sense...."

She scrambled to her feet, too. "You're not making *any* sense," she said, and grasped his arm, forcing him to face her. She looked up into his eyes and saw the unhappiness there, and knew. "You're having second thoughts, aren't you?" she asked quietly.

He tried to glance away, but she wouldn't let him. Her fingers tightened on his arm, and he muttered, "Damn it, I didn't want this morning to be like this."

She was certain, then, but she couldn't allow herself to feel hurt, not yet. This was her own fault, she reminded herself. She'd known from the beginning that it would end like this. But still, it hurt. She'd hoped...

She wouldn't let herself think of that, either. She'd been a fool to hope for anything beyond one magical night, and she'd had that, and more. "Look," she said. "No regrets, all right? We're both adults. Let's just walk away from it and pretend it never happened."

His eyes darkened, and now he looked angry. "You can do that?" he demanded. "After last night, you can do that?"

"If I have to," she lied, and then paused deliberately. "Do I?"

"Reya—" he began then stopped abruptly.

The look on his face was all the answer she needed. She was so mortified she had to escape before she made a fool of herself by bursting into tears. She'd known there was no future in this relationship; he'd said as much himself last night. It hadn't mattered, she'd still gone ahead. She'd been so hungry for him that she hadn't thought of anything else, certainly not paying the piper this morning. So there was no reason to feel so hurt, so betrayed. She should have anticipated this; if she'd been thinking at all, she would have. It was no more than she expected, no less than she deserved. Eyes brimming with tears, she started down the path again, her only thought to get back to the ranch, find her car and drive away, never to see him again.

"Reya, wait!"

She couldn't stop; if she did, he'd see that the tears were spilling over, about to drown her. Her throat was so choked she couldn't answer. Shaking her head wildly, she continued down the path.

"Reya!"

He caught up to her before she'd gone a dozen yards. Grabbing her arm, he whirled her around to face him. She brushed away her tears with the back of her hand and raised her chin defiantly. "I don't think we need to say any more," she said stiffly. "You've made yourself crystal clear."

His eyes darkened again. "You don't understand—"

"I understand all too well!" she cried, and jerked her arm furiously away from him. Her fingers itched to slap him as hard as she could across the face for putting her through this additional embarrassment, but she jammed both hands into her jean pockets instead. She wasn't about to make a bigger fool of herself by creating an even uglier scene, but she couldn't help saying angrily, "You were right, Colin. This relationship doesn't have a future. I'm beginning to doubt that our professional relationship—such as it is—has one, either. Now as far as I'm concerned, this personal...interlude...is over. The decision about any business arrangement is up to you."

They were both breathing hard from anger, and as they stood there and glared at each other, a hawk soaring high above them suddenly shrieked its displeasure. It seemed the perfect accompaniment to their charged emotions, and they both glanced up involuntarily. Then they looked at each other again and Colin started to say something. Before he could complete the first word, they were interrupted again.

"Colin!" someone shouted from a distance. "Hey, Colin! You out there?"

They had only gone several hundred yards from the house, and Charlie's voice rang clearly in the still mountain air. Reya wondered fleetingly if he had heard their furious argument just as clearly, and was embarrassed again.

"Someone's calling you," she said coolly, and started in the direction of the house.

"Colin!" Charlie shouted a third time.

"All right, all right!" Colin shouted back. "Hold your horses. I'm coming!"

Stiff with anger and hurt pride, they both marched back to the house, she in front, Colin right behind her. She walked briskly, determined not to let him catch up with her. She didn't want to take the chance that he might inadvertently touch her. She knew she wouldn't be able to bear it if he did, and they carefully avoided looking at each other when they finally emerged from the trees into the front yard. Charlie was standing on the porch, and when he saw them, he looked relieved.

"There you are! Say, Richard's on the phone, and he says it's an emergency."

They couldn't prevent a quick glance at each other at that, and she knew they were both thinking the same thing: Geneticon. Something must have happened to make Richard call the ranch on a weekend, and when Reya realized that neither of them had given a thought to the Sunday paper, she felt the first premonition of disaster. Following Colin as he sprang up the front steps and into the house, she wondered what mischief Serena and her friends had been up to now. One look at Colin's face when she entered the kitchen and saw him on the phone, and she suspected the worst.

"...do you mean, something's happened?" Colin was saying. "What is it?" He saw Reya's questioning glance and shook his head. Obviously Richard hadn't told him anything yet. She leaned against the table, intently watching his expression. "No, I'm not going

to wait until I get back! Tell me now, damn it! *What?*"
he shouted, his face suffused. "When?"

Reya had started to sit down; the fury on Colin's
face propelled her to her feet again. She wondered if
he was going to rip the phone right out of the wall.
"What is it?" she asked, unable to stand the suspense.

Colin shook his head again, obviously trying to
control himself long enough to listen to what Richard
was telling him. "Was anyone hurt?" he asked.

Reya looked up in alarm. Colin's knuckles were
white as he clutched the phone; he didn't even see her
frantic gestures to tell her what was going on. She
sagged against the table in relief when he finally said,
"Well, thank God for that." But she tensed again
when he added, "I'm leaving right now. I want everything to stay as you found it until I get there." His
voice shook with rage. "Somebody's going to pay for
this—I swear it."

He slammed the phone down again and stood there,
his fists clenched. His back was to her, and she was
even more alarmed at the stiff set of his shoulders, the
way his head was bowed. He looked like a tiger she
had seen once, poised to attack. Her own voice shook
when she said, "What is it, Colin? What's happened?"

He turned to her, his expression so fierce that she
nearly shrank back. "Geneticon's been vandalized."

She couldn't have been more shocked if he'd said it
had burned to the ground. "Vandalized! But what—
how...?" She realized she was stammering and tried
to get a grip on herself. "Was there much damage?"

A muscle sprang out on his jaw. "I don't know.
Richard is still trying to find out."

"But what about the security guard?"

Colin started to brush by her. Without turning around, he said, "He was knocked out."

She was horrified. "Is he going to be all right?"

Colin paused briefly at the doorway. "Yes. Fortunately for whoever is responsible, he wasn't seriously hurt. If he had been..."

He didn't have to finish the sentence. Reya actually shivered at the menace in Colin's voice, and she watched wordlessly as he straight-armed the swinging door and went through. The door crashed against the wall, and Reya swallowed. She had seen Colin angry before, but she had never seen him this furious. She could almost pity whomever was responsible for vandalizing Geneticon. She knew Colin wouldn't rest until the individuals responsible were punished. Shuddering at the thought, she hurried after him.

He'd just grabbed his jacket and was starting out the front door, and she didn't stop to think. "Colin, wait. I want to go with you."

He didn't even pause. "What about your car?"

She'd forgotten her car. Feeling foolish, she said, "All right, then, I'll follow you."

He did turn then, his eyes fierce. "Suit yourself," he said, and slammed out the front door.

She wasn't sure what he meant, and she didn't get a chance to ask. By the time she'd collected her things and hurriedly explained the situation to Charlie and Matilda, Colin was long gone. She never did catch up to him during that seemingly endless drive back to Geneticon, but with every mile, her doubts increased.

"Suit yourself." What did that mean? One minute she thought he'd just said that because he was too upset to know what he was saying; the next she was sure he'd meant that he didn't care whether she followed or not because she was no longer working for him. Which was it? She tortured herself with questions, and she still wasn't sure of the answers when she finally turned off the highway toward Geneticon. By then it didn't matter. She was still some distance from the brick fence and the high iron gates that surrounded the research center when she saw some of the graffiti that had been spray-painted on the walls. The words "Nazi" and "Voodoo" leaped out at her, and she uttered a dismayed exclamation. Then she saw Colin's bottle-green Porsche amid a crowd of reporters who had gathered to record the event, and knew the situation couldn't be worse. Now she didn't care what he had intended by his remark. She could just imagine what he was saying to the press, and she drove faster. Colin needed her whether he realized it or not.

Questions were flying at Colin from all directions when Reya braked to a quick stop beside the Porsche. Colin himself was standing by the gates, gesturing furiously when she tumbled hastily out of the Thunderbird, and she thought then that she might be too late. This impromptu press conference was already full steam ahead, and judging from the look on Colin's face, the damage had been done. Everyone was so busy scribbling and recording and taking pictures that no one even noticed her approach.

"Do you have any idea who did this, Mr. Hughes?" one reporter shouted, his voice rising above the others.

Colin glared at him. "If I did, the individuals responsible would be in custody right now," he said menacingly. "Or worse."

Everyone gleefully wrote that down, and Reya closed her eyes. She wanted to get to Colin, but the crowd was blocking her way and no one would let her through despite her pleas. One reporter actually turned to her and hissed, "Take your turn like the rest of us, lady!"

"But I—"

She didn't get a chance to finish her sentence; another reporter had pushed his way to the front of the crowd. Shoving a microphone under Colin's nose, he said, "I take it this means that you're going to make a public statement about what's going on here, Mr. Hughes."

The look Colin gave him should have turned him to stone. "What makes you think that?"

The reporter was new at the game; he faltered. "Well, I thought—"

Colin's voice was frigid. "You thought wrong."

Reya knew she couldn't let this go on. Ignoring the protests, she pushed her way through the crowd and finally reached Colin's side. She didn't dare look at him; she was afraid of what she would see. Praying that he would let her handle this, she said, "If I could have your attention for a moment . . . ?"

To her relief, the muttering reluctantly died down. "Now," she said clearly, "what Mr. Hughes means is that Geneticon will have a statement for you by tomorrow at the latest."

There was a renewed roar of protest, questions flying at her like arrows. She held up her hand and waited until the outcry died down again. "I'm sure you can appreciate how shocked we all are at Geneticon by this . . . this vandalism," she said, and didn't

care that her disgust colored her voice. "But I assure
you—"

"Yeah, well, there must have been a reason, right?"
someone yelled.

Beside her, Colin stirred. Hastily, Reya put her hand
on his arm. Before he could shake her off and say
something catastrophic himself, she looked the reporter directly in the eye and said quietly, "There's
always a reason for vandalism, isn't there, Jim? Ignorance comes to mind—"

"So does truth!" someone else shouted.

This time she couldn't hold Colin back. But instead of attacking the crowd of reporters, as she had
expected, he grabbed her arm and pulled her off to the
side.

"*These* are the people you claim can be educated
about what Geneticon is doing?" he demanded angrily. "I must have been out of my mind to let you
even try!"

Thankfully the reporters were muttering among
themselves, trying to decide what to do since it didn't
seem they were going to get much of a story today;
they didn't hear what Colin had said. "Don't give
them any more ammunition than they already have,"
she said, keeping her voice down. She could just
imagine what they would make of a quarrel between
her and Colin, and she glanced quickly at the milling
crowd before she added pleadingly, "Just let me handle this, all right?"

She was still clutching his sleeve; he pulled his arm
away. "Forget it," he said. "There's nothing to handle. As far as I'm concerned the police can take care
of the whole thing." His expression darkened danger-

ously. "Including getting these rabble-rousers off my land!"

"But you have to let me say something!"

"Why? What good will it do? They'll just think what they want, just like they always do. In fact...oh, the hell with it! There's no point!"

"There is!" she insisted. "If you'd just let me—"

The look he gave her was almost savage. "I think you've done enough damage, Miss Merrill," he said. "In fact, I'm beginning to think that hiring a public relations firm was a mistake."

She was suddenly so furious that she didn't care what she said. She'd done everything she could to convince him that she could handle this situation if only he would let her do it. But he'd obstructed her at every turn; he'd stubbornly refused to let her do her job. Well, fine! If that was the way he felt, he could manage the whole thing himself!

"You know," she said, her voice quivering with rage, "I think you're right. You don't need a publicity director. You get more publicity than you'll ever need just by being yourself. As soon as I can get to the office, I'll be happy to tear up your contract, because I assure you that as of this moment, the Clendenin Agency is no longer representing either you or Geneticon. Is that satisfactory?"

That muscle had bunched along his jaw again. "It is," he snapped.

"Fine!" she snapped back. "In that case, I wish you luck, because you're going to need it."

She turned around and marched back to her car, ignoring the questions and curious looks thrown her way. The reporters were unhappy that she was leaving without giving them anything to report, but she didn't care; she was unhappy herself at the moment. In fact, she was trying desperately not to cry. Bursting into tears before she got away would be the final blow to her pride, and she would not give Colin the satisfaction. The last glimpse she had of him was in the rearview mirror. He was standing there, watching her drive away, and she refused to believe that the expression on his face was one of uncertainty. . . and regret.

CHAPTER ELEVEN

REYA DIDN'T HAVE TO ANTICIPATE a summons to Joseph Clendenin's office the next morning; he was waiting for her when she arrived at work. She knew he would be, even before Sally jumped up and pulled her aside.

"For heaven's sake, what *happened* at Geneticon yesterday?" Sally asked anxiously.

"You don't want to know," Reya said with a brief shake of her head. She felt tired and haggard and she knew she looked it.

Sally looked quickly at the closed door of Reya's office and back again. "He's in there."

Reya sighed. "I thought he might be."

"Have you seen the papers?"

Reya grimaced. She had indeed. The remark Colin had made about justice for the individuals responsible had been taken out of context in one newspaper, blown completely out of proportion in another, and flagrantly misquoted in a third. All accounts made him sound like a modern-day vigilante, or worse. She'd been dismayed, but not really surprised, to discover that sympathy was almost running in favor of the vandals. The consensus seemed to be that since Colin refused to issue any statement, he really did have something to hide, and that the graffiti had been a way of pointing that out. She'd been angry when she read that; even angrier when she listened to Serena Jackson's account of the incident on the morning news. By the time Serena finished, one would have thought that the vandals had been the victims of Geneticon, and not the other way around. Reya had been so infuriated that she had started to call the station to protest. She had the receiver in her hand before she remembered that she was no longer working on behalf of Colin and Geneticon; it was none of her business.

"Yes, I saw the papers," she answered Sally, "and the morning news. It's worse than I expected."

"What are you going to do?"

"I've already done it," she said, and with Sally staring after her in surprise, entered her office. As Sally had warned her, Joseph Clendenin was already there, sitting in the chair by the desk. He was drinking a cup of coffee, and because his back was to her, she couldn't see his expression. Well, it didn't matter. She'd already decided to tell him the truth. She'd come to that conclusion sometime between two and three this morning, after she'd practically worn a hole in her carpet from pacing back and forth. She was still jittery from all those cups of coffee, and the worst thing about it was that her phone hadn't rung all night.

Had she really expected it to?

Yes, she thought dismally. In spite of everything, she had. She'd hoped Colin would call and they could get this straightened out. But he hadn't, and as the hours dragged on, she couldn't make herself call him. She'd spent the entire night in a turmoil, and by early morning, she was so confused about her feelings that she didn't know what they were. She knew they'd both spoken rashly in the heat of the moment, but even if she could have put aside her pride to apologize, she doubted he'd accept it. Personal considerations aside, they never had agreed on the proper approach to take regarding Geneticon, and she suspected he was relieved that she had quit before he was forced to fire her.

Was he equally relieved that their personal relationship had disintegrated, as well? She hardly had to ask herself that question, not after their conversation yesterday at the ranch. He'd made it abundantly clear that he regretted the time they'd spent together, and last night, when the hours dragged by without his call, she'd tried to tell herself that she regretted it, too. Her behavior had been utterly unprofessional, and when she thought about it in that light, she was mortified. She'd never had any relationship with a client that wasn't completely business, and the idea that she'd broken her own cardinal rule about not getting involved with clients was humiliating. She was glad she wouldn't have to see him again. It would only remind her of how foolish she'd been.

But that didn't make it any easier to explain what had happened to Joseph Clendenin, and he was obviously waiting for an explanation. Deciding she might as well plunge right in before she could change her mind, she closed the office door and said, "Good morning, Mr. Clendenin. I imagine you're here because of this latest crisis at Geneticon. Well, you'll be happy to know that Mr. Hughes and I discussed the situation yesterday—"

She'd gone too far. He looked at her curiously as she came around the desk and sat down in her chair. "Yesterday?"

She cursed her slip of the tongue. She didn't want to admit how she'd so fortuitously arrived at Geneticon the day before, it would only make things more complicated. Hoping he wouldn't ask for an explanation, she said, "Yes, I was there. Along with about a dozen reporters—"

She halted abruptly, suddenly wondering how the press had found out about the vandalism so quickly. Richard had only discovered it himself that morning, and she and Colin had arrived little more than an hour later. She couldn't believe that the media had been camping on Geneticon's doorstep in the hope of getting a story, but how had they found out? It wasn't as though the research center was in the heart of town, after all; it was some distance from Denver.

Had Richard called the papers? She dismissed that thought as soon as it occurred to her. She knew Richard wouldn't dream of adding to Geneticon's troubles. No, it couldn't have been Richard.

Then she realized that someone must have found out at the hospital. The injured security guard had been taken to Denver General for examination. Some enterprising member of the press must have been on hand and reported it to the wire services. That was the obvious explanation, she thought, and then was annoyed at herself for wondering about it. It wasn't any of her concern anymore, she reminded herself, and turned her attention back to her boss.

"I don't know how the press found out so quickly," she said, "but it doesn't really matter now—"

He stood up so suddenly that she was startled into silence. Watching in dismay as his face reddened and he took off his glasses, she knew she was in trouble. He always did this right before he launched one of his dreaded attacks, and she knew he was about to launch one now when he drew himself up to his considerable height. "What do you mean, it doesn't matter now?" he demanded, towering over her. "Do you have any idea what this latest debacle is going to cost us?"

She had to fight the urge to stand up herself, even though he was on the other side of the desk. "Well, I—"

"But of course you do," he interrupted. "You're not stupid, are you, Miss Merrill? Perhaps somewhat misguided at this point, but not stupid. You wouldn't be working here if you were, though at the moment, that, too, is in question."

She felt a stab of panic at that, and tried to tamp it down. It wouldn't help her case to become hysterical, and she tried to speak calmly. "If you would just listen—"

He leaned forward, placing both hands on top of the desk to balance himself. "I'm all ears, Miss Merrill."

Now she knew why most of his employees were afraid of him. He looked so formidable standing there that she wanted to turn tail and run. How could she ever explain what had happened yesterday between her and Colin? It would sound as though she was trying to excuse her own ineptitude.

Trying to tell herself that was ridiculous, she reasoned that agencies lost clients all the time. After all the publicity Geneticon had been receiving, Clendenin should be relieved that they were no longer connected with such a troublesome account. She'd told herself last night that she was, but now with him glaring at her like that, she knew she'd lied. She wasn't relieved at all; she was bitterly disappointed. This was the first account he had given her to manage on her own, and she had failed. Miserable at the thought, she said, "It doesn't matter because Mr. Hughes decided yesterday that he no longer needs our services."

Clendenin's eyes narrowed behind the thick glasses he'd donned again. "Did he decide that, or did you?"

She was taken aback by the question, not sure what to answer. She didn't want to admit at this point that she'd lost her temper and quit, but anything else was admitting that Colin had fired her. Her pride had been battered enough already. "It was . . . a mutual decision, Mr. Clendenin. Mr. Hughes and I couldn't seem to agree on the right approach for the account."

"I see."

She wasn't sure what that meant, but she didn't want to ask. He was still standing there, but at least he didn't look quite as angry. Relieved, she considered apologizing for not consulting him about it before she took action, but then she decided the wiser course was to say nothing.

"Auguste Weidmar called me this morning," he said.

She looked up in alarm.

"He threatened to withdraw from the agency unless we dropped Geneticon."

She didn't want to say it, but the words forced themselves through her lips. "He said the same thing to me a while ago."

"And what did you say?"

"I . . . I told him that I would take his suggestion under advisement," she said uncomfortably.

"Under advisement? Well, I must say *that's* an interesting approach. Didn't you intend to do anything about it?"

She couldn't have heard the chuckle in his voice; his expression was too grim. Even more uncomfortable, she had to admit, "Well, I thought I would handle it when the time came."

He surprised her by going to the door, where he paused. "I think," he said, before he went out, "that the time has come. Give him a call, Reya. Assure the old—assure him that the...problem has been taken care of."

As the door closed quietly behind him, Reya slumped in her seat. She couldn't believe that she was still here, that this was still her office, and that she wasn't packing in tears to find another job. She felt as though she'd just come through a trial by fire where she'd only gotten singed in a few places. When she heard Sally's hesitant knock on the door a few minutes later, she was still almost too breathless to tell her to come in.

"What happened?" Sally asked as soon as she entered. She closed the door and perched anxiously on the edge of the chair Joseph Clendenin had abandoned.

"I'm not sure," Reya said. "I think...I think everything's all right."

"He didn't—"

Reya shook her head.

"Oh, I'm so glad!" Sally breathed. "I thought—"

"So did I," Reya said. She didn't want to think how close she had come to being forced to find another job. She sighed. "At least we don't have to worry about Geneticon or anyone connected with it any longer."

"Uh-oh."

Reya looked at her sharply. "What?"

Sally wrung her hands. "Well, there's just one problem...."

Reya thought if she heard about one more problem today she was going to scream. She'd been in the office less than half an hour and already it felt like three days. She wondered how she was going to endure until six o'clock when she could go home. Cautiously she asked. "Do I want to hear this?"

"It's about Richard Carlyle."

Reya frowned. "What about him?"

"You've got an appointment with him at five," Sally said unwillingly.

"What!"

"I'm sorry, Reya. I didn't know."

Reya was sorry, too. She didn't want to see Richard. She knew what he wanted, and she didn't know what to say. "Call him back and tell him I just can't see him today," she said. "No, tell him I'm out of the office and you don't know where to find me."

Sally stood. "All right," she said reluctantly. "But he's such a nice man I hate to disappoint him."

"I'm afraid you'll have to," Reya said flatly, "considering that Geneticon is no longer one of our accounts."

"Okay, okay," Sally said, turning dejectedly toward the door. "I get the picture."

Reya felt like a heel. Wondering why she was giving in like this, she said impatiently, "Oh, all right. I'll see him."

Sally turned to her with a smile. "Oh, thanks, Reya. I hoped you would."

Reya shook her head as Sally went out. She didn't know why she had agreed to see Richard. She knew it wouldn't do either of them any good. As far as Joseph Clendenin and the agency was concerned, the Geneticon account was history and she, for one, was glad. Someone else could handle that impossible man from now on; someone else could try to make him listen to reason. She was relieved it wasn't her. In fact, she pitied the person who took her place. It had been a mistake to get involved with him in the first place—personally *or* professionally—and she was well rid of him.

That decided, she opened her briefcase and got to work. Or tried to. She called Auguste Weidmar and soothed his irrational fears about Geneticon; she talked to other clients and assured them of the same thing. She told them all that their accounts were uppermost on her agenda, but the whole time she was saying these things, she was seeing Colin in her mind: Colin, as he'd been at the ranch, not as he was at Geneticon.

It was maddening, but every time she tried to concentrate on details that needed her attention that day, she'd remember something else about him. An image would flash into her mind, and she'd picture him with the horses, grinning as he gave his mount extra grain. Or she'd remember him as he'd been around the campfire that night, his lean face burnished by the firelight, laughing at something one of the guests had said. Oh, she could see him in so many guises, none of them remotely connected with the man she knew as the owner of a troubled research center. How could he be so different? He was like two separate men, one hostile and withdrawn, the other like someone she had only fantasized about, a man she had conjured in her dreams. Which was the real Colin?

Then she told herself angrily that it didn't matter. Colin and his problems were no longer any of her concern, and if she didn't get to work, none of her other accounts would be of concern, either, because she would have lost them all. Resolutely she settled down again, and didn't look up until Sally knocked on the closed office door precisely at five. By then she was sitting at her drafting board intently studying an advertising layout for an exercise apparel account. The drawings Sid had given her weren't right, and she was trying to decide on a better approach. If she'd been thinking, she would have wondered why Sally knocked instead of buzzing on the intercom, but she was too preoccupied with the layout.

"Come in," she said, and then promptly forgot about Sally and what she wanted. Suddenly she saw what was wrong with the layout and grabbed a pencil to correct it. With a few quick lines, she created an entirely different picture, and she was so absorbed she didn't realize someone was standing behind her until he spoke.

"I didn't realize you were an artist, too."

She was so startled she nearly fell off the chair. Strong hands reached out to steady her when she started to lose her balance, but she didn't want him to touch her. Wondering why Sally hadn't warned her, she whipped around and gazed into dark eyes far too near to hers. Disconcerted, she reared back and almost lost her balance again. "What are you doing here?" she demanded, surprise making her voice rise. "I thought Richard was supposed to—"

Colin smiled slightly. "He was. But, I er, persuaded him it might be better if I saw you myself."

"Why?"

He didn't seem offended at her ungracious tone. "Because I thought we should talk."

"We have nothing to talk about," she said stiffly. "I thought you made that perfectly clear yesterday."

His eyes darkened. "Yesterday I wasn't...myself."

"Oh, really? Well, you certainly gave a credible imitation, then."

Despite her curt tone, she knew she had to put some distance between them, if only the width of a desk. He was too close. She felt . . . cornered.

Wondering why that thought had occurred to her, she jumped off the high drafting stool and reached the haven of her desk. Standing tautly behind it, she gestured him to the chair in front, and watched as he went around. When he didn't sit immediately, she realized he was waiting for her, and she sank down into her own chair with a thump. What was he *doing* here?

She had to remain calm. Vowing to give Sally a piece of her mind for putting her on the spot like this, she willed her voice under control and said, "What can I do for you, Mr. Hughes?"

When Colin raised an eyebrow at her question, she was even more annoyed. What did he expect, that she'd greet him with open arms?

"You can come back to work for Geneticon," he said.

It was her turn to raise an eyebrow. "And why would I want to do that?" she asked. "You made it very clear yesterday that you didn't need—or want— my help."

His jaw tightened, but he seemed determined to control himself. "That was yesterday. I said I wasn't myself."

She clasped her hands on the desk so that he wouldn't see they were beginning to shake. His unexpected appearance had unnerved her more than she wanted to admit, and even though he was sitting across from her and hadn't touched her but briefly, she felt his impact all the way to her toes. He was dressed in a suit and tie, far removed from the Western garb he'd worn at the ranch, and he was still the most handsome man she had ever seen. Whenever she thought of that hard, strong body underneath the tailored clothing, she almost felt faint.

That thought strengthened her somehow, and she told herself fiercely that she was not going to weaken. If he expected her to come running just because he'd deigned to put in an appearance today, he was going to be surprised. She'd said she was relieved that they were finished, and she meant it.

"Well," she said coolly, her heart beating a tattoo inside her chest, "whether you were or not really doesn't make any difference today, does it? By the way, I meant to ask Richard when he came about the security guard who was injured—Wayne Bellows, wasn't it? I heard this morning that he was released from the hospital."

Annoyance flashed in Colin's eyes, and she knew that he wasn't thinking about the security guard. He was irritated by her manner, but she didn't care. In fact, she wanted him to be annoyed. If she made him angry enough he might leave before she weakened and forgave him anyway.

"Yes, he was released," Colin answered, swallowing his irritation to annoy her by playing along with her game. "He wasn't seriously injured, though he does have a nasty bruise."

"I'm glad he's going to be all right. I suppose it's too soon to have any idea who was responsible."

Colin made an angry gesture. "The police said they'll try, but they're doubtful they'll find anything."

She was surprised at that. "Why? They have the evidence—"

"Some graffiti spray-painted on walls? What kind of evidence is that?"

"What about the guard, then? He must have seen something—"

"He heard a noise, that was all."

Wondering why she was pursuing this, since it was no longer any of her concern, she frowned. "Then what about the video cameras at the gate? Didn't they pick up anything?"

"Whoever it was knew enough to knock out the cameras," Colin said, his voice tight. "That's what made Wayne drive out to the gates to investigate in the first place. He was watching the camera in the office when it suddenly went dead. By the time he got there most of the damage was done, and he was trying to find out what happened when he was struck from behind. Apparently whoever was responsible didn't want to take the chance of being seen."

She shivered. "It's a good thing they were only up to mischief. Otherwise—"

"Mischief?" he repeated caustically. "I'd say that assault and battery is a little more serious than that, wouldn't you?"

"Yes, of course it is," she said, annoyed that he had deliberately misunderstood her. "What I meant was that you were fortunate no one got inside the complex. Just think what a loss it would have been if the laboratories themselves had been vandalized. Or—" she added with a shudder "—something more serious had happened to Wayne."

He was silent a moment. "You're right," he said finally, then surprised her by adding, "and I'm sorry I jumped at you. It's just that this whole business has irritated me no end. No one seems to know what's going on, and even the police can't give me any satisfactory answers."

She was determined not to feel sympathy for him. If she did, she knew she'd forgive him, and after the meeting with Joseph Clendenin this morning, she couldn't do that. Reminding herself again that Colin and his problems were none of her affair, she avoided his eyes and said weakly, "I know how difficult it is—"

"Do you?" he asked. His eyes suddenly looked bleak. "Do you know what the worst part is? It's not knowing why. Why is this happening now? I've owned Geneticon for five years. Stefan Benadi was working on experiments there even before that. So why are we having all this trouble now?"

"I don't know, Colin."

He startled her by shooting to his feet. "I just don't understand it," he said angrily. "It's not as if we're on the verge of a big breakthrough that's going to transform genetic engineering, you know. Any form of gene therapy is years off. So why now? And why Geneticon? It doesn't make sense!"

She could see that he was working himself up to a rage, but she didn't know how to help. She couldn't understand it either, but there had to be a reason, and she muttered, "Where there's smoke, there's fire...."

Colin turned and looked at her. "What?"

She looked up at him blankly, still preoccupied with the thought that had just occurred to her. ''I said—'' she began, and recalled again that it was no longer any of her concern. She shook her head briefly. ''Never mind. I was just thinking out loud.''

He came and sat down. ''About what?'' he said intensely.

She shook her head again. ''It wasn't important.''

''If you've any ideas about this, Reya, I'd appreciate hearing them. I . . . I'm at my wits' end.''

She stared at him, unable to believe he'd said that. Suddenly, to her dismay, she wasn't seeing the stubborn, overbearing owner of Geneticon, but the man she'd met at the Double Ott. The harshness had gone from his eyes, and in its place was a pleading that tugged at her heart. Quickly she glanced away. ''I'm sorry, Colin. I can't help you.''

It seemed she'd been mistaken about the expression in his eyes. ''Can't . . . or won't?'' he challenged.

That demanding note was more like the Colin she knew, and she stiffened. ''I'm not sure I care for your tone, Colin. As I recall, you were the one who was so eager to terminate our arrangement yesterday.''

''You recall it incorrectly, then,'' he said bitterly. ''*You* were the one who said you wanted nothing more to do with me!''

''With you *and* with Geneticon,'' she flung back at him. ''Let's at least get our facts straight!''

They were glaring at each other by this time, and she thought fleetingly that she was going to get her wish. He was getting angry enough to walk out—if she didn't throw him out first. In anticipation of that satisfying thought, she shot to her feet. He stood, too,

and to her outrage, leaned over the desk, forcing her
to back up a step.

"I never said anything about you not working for
Geneticon," he said through his teeth. "You were the
one who quit."

She was furious at that. "Only after you said that
hiring me was a mistake!"

"I never said that!"

"You most certainly did!"

"When?"

"Right after you told me my entire approach to
solving the problems at Geneticon was wrong!"

"When did I say that? Are we talking about the
same conversation?"

She wanted to slap him right across his arrogant
face. "How like you to resort to sarcasm when you're
in the wrong!"

"And how like you to employ a selective memory!" he flung back at her. "I didn't say anything of
the kind and you know it!"

She'd had enough of this. In another few seconds
she'd lose her temper completely and say something
she'd regret. Marching around the desk, she stalked to
the door. He got there before her, blocking the way.
"Oh, no," he said, "not so fast. We're going to get
this straightened out right now."

She looked up, angry all over again because he
towered over her and made her feel insignificant and
small. "There's nothing to straighten out!" she
snapped. "It doesn't matter anymore!"

"It does to me!"

"Why? Because you can't find anybody else to take
over the publicity for Geneticon?"

His eyes flashed at that. "Is that what you think?"

"What else can I think? Why did you come here today, Colin, if it wasn't to—"

Before she realized what he intended, he'd grabbed her by the arms. "I came here for two reasons, Reya," he grated. "One was to ask you to come back to work for me—"

She shook her head wildly. "Oh, but—"

"And the other was to tell you...to tell you... Oh, hell!" he said, and lowered his head to kiss her.

She didn't have time to think, only to react, and her response rocked them both. Involuntarily her arms wound around his neck and she returned his kiss so fiercely that he tightened his embrace and practically lifted her off her feet. She could feel his entire body quivering against hers and she pressed closer, wanting to mold her form to his. She'd never expected to be kissed by him again, and the feeling was so euphoric that she didn't want it to end. It was some time before she realized that the noise she heard wasn't the thundering of her heart but someone knocking on the door.

"Excuse me," Sally said, poking her head tentatively around as Colin and Reya sprang apart. When she realized what she had interrupted, her face turned as red as theirs were. "Oh, dear," she said, and started to back out again.

Reya pulled herself together. She didn't dare look at Colin. She focused all her attention on her assistant—her ex-assistant, she thought blackly, if Sally didn't have a good reason for interrupting just now.

"What is it?" she asked, her voice short.

Sally came reluctantly back in. "I'm sorry, Reya, but Darren just called."

Reya stared at her. Sally had interrupted to tell her *that*?

Sally saw the look Reya gave her and glanced quickly in Colin's direction before she looked at Reya again. "I think you'd better call him," she said, her voice low. "He sounded a little . . . upset."

Reya wasn't thinking clearly. She was still too overwhelmed by what had just happened between her and Colin. She didn't want to talk to Darren right now; in fact, she never wanted to talk to him again. "All right," she said briefly, "I'll take care of it."

"But—"

"I'll take *care* of it," Reya repeated. "Right now, I'm having a conference with a client."

Sally's eyes widened. "A . . . client?"

Reya threw all caution to the wind. She hadn't the faintest idea how she was going to approach Joseph Clendenin with the news, but she'd worry about that tomorrow. "Yes," she said, "a client. Hold my calls, Sally. Mr. Hughes and I have some planning to do about the best way to handle his account."

Colin stirred as Sally glanced nervously at him before closing the door again. "Better yet," he said with a twinkle in his eye, "why don't we go somewhere where we won't be interrupted?"

Reya didn't hesitate. Now that she'd committed herself, she felt reckless and abandoned, so outrageously happy she would have gone anywhere with him. "I take it," she said with a smile, "you have someplace in mind?"

He gallantly took her arm. "I do, indeed."

CHAPTER TWELVE

THE PLACE COLIN HAD IN MIND was the Cherry Hills area, a few miles south of downtown. Reya had been so carried away by that explosive moment in her office when Colin had kissed her that she didn't question what she was doing until they were actually on their way. Then she began to feel nervous.

Was she doing the right thing? She'd promised herself that she wouldn't get involved again with him, but now she was sitting beside him in the Porsche as he expertly threaded his way through traffic, and she knew without asking where they were going. She had never thought about where Colin might live, but she assumed it was a magnificent apartment somewhere, and she kept up an anxious chatter as he drove, not even caring that he seemed amused at her disjointed conversation.

She glanced at him covertly from time to time, thinking that he looked more relaxed than she. Well, why shouldn't he? *He* didn't have to face Joseph Clendenin tomorrow and tell him that she wanted to take on the Geneticon account again, nor did he have to explain to Auguste Weidmar and some of her other clients why, after she had spent a major part of the morning reassuring them that Geneticon was no longer a client, she'd changed her mind and taken back the account. What they would all say to that she could only imagine.

Then she told herself she didn't care what anyone said. Her undeniable attraction to Colin aside, Geneticon was a worthwhile account, more than deserving of the agency's attention. The work they were doing there was certainly more valuable than promoting the newest lip gloss, or coming up with a best way to package trash bags, she thought irritably, and if her other clients refused to understand that...well, it was just too bad.

And was it too bad if Joseph Clendenin refused to understand too?

She winced. She hadn't decided what to do if her boss absolutely refused to sign Geneticon again; she'd handle that when the time came. In the meantime, she realized that Colin had just turned off University Boulevard into the Cherry Hills area, one of the most exclusive sections in Denver. The homes here were like country manors, each with at least a dozen rooms, many with servants' quarters. Every one sat majestically in the middle of a plot of land, separated from its neighbors by several valuable acres. He couldn't live here, she thought, and glanced around wide-eyed as he drove along the winding street. When he finally turned into one driveway and pulled up in front of a huge rambling brick-and-wood ranch-style house, she couldn't prevent an exclamation. "Is this yours?"

Smiling at her expression, he got out of the car and came around to open her door. She was still awed when she stepped out, and as she gazed at the broad expanse of windows and the three chimneys rising from various areas in the shake roof, she couldn't help saying, "It's certainly...big."

He looked sheepish. "It's a long story."

She was still looking at the monolith in front of her. "I can imagine."

"Let's go in, and I'll show you around."

The spacious entrance hall was tiled in Spanish adobe with a beautiful Navaho rug adorning the wall. A hand-carved telephone table displayed a Remington bronze, and Reya stopped to admire it.

"Only a few hundred of those were struck," Colin said when he saw her looking at it. "This one's called *Bronco Buster*, but I have a few others scattered around the house."

"It's beautiful," she said, tracing the lines with a finger. She glanced up with a smile. "It reminds me of the horses at the ranch."

"Ol' Thunder and Lightning, perhaps?"

She cocked her head. "You don't really have a horse by that name, do you?"

He grinned. "No ranch would be complete without one. I'll have to introduce you the next time we go there."

She couldn't help feeling a thrill at that. His casual words implied that there *would* be a next time, and she had to bring herself up short as she followed him into the contemporary living room. *It was just a remark,* she told herself. *Don't start imagining there's more to it than he intended.*

To distract herself, she glanced around the room as he went to the bar in the corner. The furniture was long and low, the upholstery a mixture of soft leather and wools in earth tones, the coffee and end tables made of pine. The room would have looked overwhelmingly masculine if it hadn't been for the Tiffany lamp on one table, and a beautiful stained-glass window set into one of the walls. She smiled appreciatively as she looked around. It wasn't her style, but it looked like him—or at least, it looked like the man she had met at the Double Ott.

"What would you like to drink?"

"White wine, if you have it."

Naturally he did, a Chenin Blanc that she knew Darren would have approved of. Wondering why she'd thought of Darren at a time like this, she remembered that she still hadn't returned his call. Then she dismissed it. Sally had said he was upset, but if he was, it was probably because she hadn't called to say that breaking their engagement had been a mistake. She knew he had expected her to call, but the fact was that since she'd talked to him last, she'd hardly given him a thought. She was almost ashamed to admit it, but it was true. She hadn't realized until their final quarrel that little by little, what feeling she'd had for him had eroded until finally there was nothing left. The only reason she'd kept their relationship alive as long as she had was because she kept hoping that his attitude would change. It had been a futile hope, she knew that now.

"Would you like to see the rest of the house?"

Colin's question interrupted her thoughts, and she looked at him over her wineglass. "Do you think we have enough time? This place is so big we could be wandering around here for days."

He laughed. "Don't worry. I've got a map."

A few minutes later she thought they might need one. From the living room they looked into the kitchen with its gleaming tile and chrome, and a collection of shining copper pans decorating one wall, then he showed her the sun room, a glass-enclosed porch filled with plants and boasting a huge spa sunk into the brick floor. She was still marveling at the whirlpool when they entered the family room with its pool table and long mahogany bar, then Colin led the way down the hall and paused before a closed door.

"This is the real reason I bought this barn of a house," he said, and proudly opened the door.

For a second or two, she thought she was seeing things. But when she looked at him for confirmation, he smiled and gestured her inside. "The music room, madam," he said. "Do you like it?"

"Like it?" she exclaimed, her eyes going to the majestic grand piano standing in the center of the room. "It's wonderful!"

There were other classical instruments in addition to the piano: a gilded harp, several flamenco guitars, a mandolin, a violin. One entire wall was devoted to recording and stereo equipment, and among the array of complicated machinery, she recognized a computerized drum set and a synthesizer. Glancing from one to the other, she finally turned to him and said, "Do you play any of these instruments?"

He laughed at the note of awed disbelief in her voice. "Not all of them," he said, "and some of them very badly."

"Oh, play something!"

Smiling, he reached for the nearest guitar. When he ran his fingers over the strings, the notes floated sweetly throughout the room, and she closed her eyes to appreciate the melody more fully. He played so skillfully that she could almost hear the castanets in the background and the staccato accompaniment of the flamenco dance. The sound seemed to surround her, and when she opened her eyes again he stopped playing and laughed at her bemused expression.

"Now you know the reason I was so taken with the place," he said, replacing the guitar in its stand. "The acoustics in here are perfect."

Her eyes shone. "The *room* is perfect!" she exclaimed. "Oh, please play something else!"

He was flattered by her excitement. "What? You choose."

It was inevitable that she chose the centerpiece of the room, the grand piano. He nodded when he saw her eyes go to the beautiful instrument, and he sat down, his long-fingered hands poised above the keys. "What would you like to hear?"

"Anything!"

He thought for a few seconds and then began to play. The clear notes of a Brahms waltz filled the room, and Reya didn't know whether to be more entranced with the glorious sound or the fact that Colin was creating it. She listened in silence, not moving, hardly daring to breathe, until the last note drifted away. Even then she could barely speak. "That was...beautiful," she whispered. "Where did you learn to play like that?"

"Everyone in my family is a musician," he said, and ran his fingers idly over the keys. A complicated scale rippled out, perfectly cadenced, and she was freshly amazed. "My parents, my younger sister, Lucy. It was inevitable that I learned to play something myself."

"That's more than just playing!" she exclaimed. "You should be performing at the Boettcher Concert Hall, at the very least!"

He laughed. "Let's not get carried away. That's the home of the Denver Symphony Orchestra, you know."

"I know. I told you I loved music. I never miss a performance there." She looked at him accusingly. "Why didn't you say anything when we talked about music before? I had no idea you played—"

"There are a lot of things you don't know about me, Reya," he said, and suddenly the atmosphere changed.

His eyes never leaving her face, he began to stand. But she wasn't ready yet, and she whispered, "Don't get up. Play something else...."

He gazed at her for an instant longer, then he turned and flicked one of the switches on the vast wall of stereo equipment. "I've got a better idea," he said, and bowed slightly as the notes of another waltz, this one by Mozart, began to waft through the room. "Would you like to dance?"

Dazedly, because she hadn't expected this, she moved into his arms. He was a wonderful dancer, light and graceful on his feet, whirling her around the room so effortlessly that she felt as though she were floating. His arms were strong around her, and even though their bodies weren't touching, she felt him so powerfully that she closed her eyes and let the moment flow over her like honey. The music caressed them; the waltz was perfect, a dance she never wanted to end. But then she felt him slowly come to a stop, and when she opened her eyes, he was looking down at her with an expression that took her breath away.

"Reya..." he murmured, and touched his lips to hers just as the last notes of the waltz drifted sweetly away.

Reya knew she would always remember this moment, for it was the first time she accepted the fact that
she loved him. Standing there in his arms, her heart
began to pound with the knowledge, and when he
raised his head and looked deeply into her eyes, she
was sure that he could hear the hammering beat in this
acoustically perfect room. She didn't care. The only
thing that mattered at that instant was him, and when
she looked up into his eyes, his expression changed.
Without a word, he snapped off the light and led her
down the hallway to the master bedroom.

She had only a fleeting impression of the colors of
sunset bathing the room in a warm glow and of a big
bed draped with a heavy velvet spread before he took
her in his arms again. There was nothing gentle about
his kiss this time. One hand at her waist, the other
cradling the nape of her neck, he crushed her body to
his. His mouth descended hungrily on hers, and every
muscle in his body seemed taut with desire. Her response was just as passionate. Moaning with anticipated pleasure, she pressed herself against him, and
they fell backward onto the bed.

Clothes were an encumbrance, and they reached for
each other almost frantically, tossing garments aside
until they were both naked. The velvet bedspread caressed her back while Colin's body warmed her above,
and this time it was she who reached for him, pulling
his head down to hers. Her hands began to move all
over his body, seeking desperately to draw what she
needed from him, and he responded with a fierce passion of his own. There wasn't time for slow, languor-
ous caresses. The moment his body had covered hers,
she'd felt desire rage to life inside her, demanding instant release.

"Oh, Colin..." she moaned, her breath hot against his ear. "I don't want to wait..."

He couldn't have delayed, either; hunger for each other was their master. Every ounce of feeling was being wrung from their writhing, perspiring bodies, and they rolled back and forth on the bed, clutching each other as that tide of feeling swept over them and carried them away. She felt that glorious sensation of pleasure spreading through her, and she clung to him savagely, her body no longer her own, but transported to another plane where they met, joined together as one heart, one mind...one body. She heard his hoarse cry of triumph as she reached the apex, and felt his mouth on her breast. With his strong arms trembling around her, she held his head and laughed in glorious abandon and release.

A long time later, he rolled off her and put his arm around her waist, drawing her close. Sometime during their frenzy the bedclothes had been disturbed, and the velvet bedspread was trailing onto the floor. When he grabbed a corner of it and covered her so she wouldn't be cold, she smiled and rested her head against his chest.

"What are you thinking about?" he murmured finally, one hand idly stroking her shoulder.

She'd been thinking that if someone had told her last night she'd be here with him tonight, she would have laughed in their face. "I was wondering what time it was."

He raised his head to see her face more fully. "Why? Do you have a date?"

She smiled. "No, but I was thinking about dinner...."

He frowned. "Are you hungry?"

She hesitated, then decided to be honest. "Starving," she admitted ruefully.

"Trust a woman to be practical at a time like this!" he said with a laugh. "All right. Let's go see what we can rustle up."

Twenty minutes later, dressed in a voluminous terry-cloth robe he had given her, the sleeves rolled up, the belt wrapped around her about five times, she had managed to rustle up enough to set a fluffy omelet before him. Taking a place opposite him in the breakfast nook, a cheerful area set into a deep bay window overlooking the terrace, she shook her head and said teasingly, "You'll have to make do with this. Judging from the cavernous emptiness in your refrigerator, you haven't been to a grocery store in months."

He looked at her indignantly. "You found some eggs, didn't you?"

"Four is all," she said dryly. "And I have a feeling I was lucky to find those. I won't ask how old they are."

He took a forkful of omelet and then looked at her appreciatively. "Hey, this is good."

"Don't sound so surprised," she said, trying not to smile. "It's not that hard to make eggs."

He took another bite. "Beautiful and creative and a great cook, too. What other talents are you hiding?"

"I might ask you the same thing."

He looked embarrassed as he took a sip of the coffee she had made. "Just because I can play the piano a little?"

She raised an eyebrow. "A little?"

"A little," he repeated with a smile. "My parents would be the first to tell you that they gave up trying to make a musician out of me and wisely decided to concentrate on Lucy instead. I practiced because they insisted, but I was always more interested in other things.''

"Like what?" He rarely talked about himself and she was fascinated.

He looked even more uncomfortable. "Oh, like producing electricity from a waterfall in the backyard when I was eight, or changing the garage door opener to work with voice command when I was ten...things like that."

"Oh, I see. Things that any child occupies himself with when he's bored, right?"

He smiled at her gently mocking tone. "I always did have an inquiring mind," he said, and grinned. "Especially when my mother wanted me to come in and practice the piano."

"When did you become interested in computers?" she asked. When he frowned, she went on gently, "It's no secret that you owned your own computer company at one time, Colin. I believe you were even considered something of a child prodigy."

He looked annoyed at the term. "Hardly. I was twenty-five when I took out my first patent."

She couldn't help it; she laughed. "Practically an old man, then, I agree."

He had to laugh, too. "Well, all right. I wasn't exactly ancient. I did have four years' experience working as an analyst for General Data, and if they hadn't bought that first patent, I never would have been able to start my own company. But I still insist I wasn't really all that young, especially in the computer field. Remember that fourteen-year-old who started his own programming company several years ago? Now he owns one of the largest software companies in the country.''

She had to agree. ''Unfortunately, I wasn't that driven when I was fourteen,'' she said with a laugh. ''I'm afraid the height of my ambition at that time was to become a ballerina and dance with Nureyev.''

''You wanted to be a dancer?'' he asked, intrigued. ''What happened?''

''Torn knee ligaments playing basketball with my brother and his friends, of all things,'' she said with a grimace. ''Oh, I recovered, of course, but that effectively ended any idea of a serious career in ballet. The doctor didn't have to tell me that the knee wouldn't hold up under the strain—I knew.''

''That's too bad.''

She shrugged. ''These things happen, I guess. Anyway, I had to decide on another career—''

''So you chose public relations.''

She laughed. ''No, not right away. I wanted to be an artist first.''

He looked confused. ''What happened to that ambition?''

Her eyes twinkled. 'I really couldn't see myself starving in a garret somewhere waiting to be recognized, so I decided on something a little more practical. *That's* when I chose public relations.''

''Are you ever sorry things didn't work out the way you first intended?''

She heard the wistfulness in his voice and hesitated, wondering if she should be honest. She decided she had to be; it seemed to be a night for telling the truth.

"Sometimes," she said slowly, aware of his eyes on her. "When I hear a beautiful piece of music and think how wonderful it would be to dance to it, or when I see a painting I wish I would have painted." She shook her head slightly, thrusting away the remembered pain her decision had cost her when she put her ballet shoes away for the last time. With an effort, she went on. "But on the whole...no. I'm happy with what I do. It's very satisfying."

"You're fortunate, then."

She looked at him thoughtfully, hearing that wistful note again. "Why, are you sorry you sold Hughes TechCraft?"

"Sorry?" he repeated thoughtfully, and shook his head. "No, it was time for me to get out...to move on to other things."

"To Geneticon, you mean," she said quietly.

He looked down at his coffee cup, and nodded. "To Geneticon."

There was a moment of silence during which she wasn't sure what to say. Before things could become too tense, she reached for his cup and said brightly, "Let me get you some more coffee."

She rose from the table and was just lifting the coffeepot off the stove when she felt him come up behind her. He reached around and took the pot out of her hands, setting it back on the element again. "Forget the coffee," he murmured, and put his hands on her shoulders. Pulling her close to him, he kissed the back of her neck. "I want you...."

He slid the robe from her shoulders so that it fell to her waist, held there by the belt she'd wrapped tightly around herself. She closed her eyes when his lips moved from her nape to the curve of her shoulder, and she was helpless to resist when he gently turned her around to face him. Cupping one breast in his hand, he lowered his head to brush his lips gently over the soft flesh.

"You are so beautiful..." he murmured. Her legs began to tremble at the caress, and she tried to press against him. He held her slightly away, his mouth moving to her other breast. "So beautiful...."

She couldn't bear it. Longing for him was racing through her like a wildfire, and she tried to raise his head. "Colin..."

He looked at her, his eyes burning with the same passion she felt, and when she literally threw herself into his embrace, he crushed her against him. Trembling anew, she raised her mouth to his. Her arms, freed of the confines of the heavy robe, wound themselves around his neck, and she moved against him, feeling the rise of his erection. He had tossed on old jeans and a T-shirt before coming into the kitchen, and she pulled up his shirt to run her hands over his bare back, luxuriating in the play of his muscles as he held her. Lowering her hands, she fumbled at the waistband of his jeans, and he groaned and pulled her back to kiss her again when she slid her hand inside and found him.

He was just reaching for her belt when the phone rang.

And rang.

The noise shattered the mood, and Reya pulled back. Sensing the change in her, Colin cursed and glanced up. He looked so irate when he lifted his head that she couldn't help giggling, and when he looked even more annoyed, she laughed and shrugged back into the robe. "Maybe you'd better answer it," she suggested when it rang for the fourth time.

He tried to reach for her again. "Whoever it is will call back," he said. "Right now, I've got more important things to do...."

Eyes twinkling, she eluded him and handed him the phone. Glaring at her in mock anger, he muttered another curse and snatched the receiver. His voice was somewhere between a bark and a growl when he answered, and she leaned against him, arms circling his waist. Gazing up into his face, she was amused at his irate expression, the more so because with his free hand, he was holding her tightly. Unfortunately she wasn't amused for long.

"It's Richard," he muttered to her, obviously waiting for Richard to come back on the line. "Something's—"

His expression changed just then as he listened to whatever Richard had started to say, and he hardly noticed as she drew away from him, sure now that something was wrong. Cursing the playful mood that had made her insist he answer the phone, she huddled into the thick terry robe, suddenly cold. She watched in dismay as his expression darkened.

"No, I haven't heard anything," Colin said impatiently into the phone.

He listened a moment longer, his face becoming more forbidding by the second, then demanded angrily, "What are you talking about? What lawsuit? When? No, forget that. Who... *Who?*" he shouted, his face turning crimson with anger. "Why, that—"

Remembering that Reya was standing right next to him, he swallowed whatever it was he'd been about to say. "All right," he said with a quick glance in her direction. "What do we do?"

While Reya waited tensely, he listened to what Richard was telling him, then, abruptly, he turned and hung up. His back was to her, but she could see the tremendous effort it was costing him not to explode, and she said tentatively, "Colin? What happened?"

"What happened?" He turned toward her, his expression so enraged that she wanted to shrink back. "I'll tell you what happened," he said, his voice rising with every word. "In addition to everything else, now Geneticon is being sued!"

"Sued!" She couldn't believe it. "Why?"

His face was suffused. "Because some incompetent moron of a man who quit months ago has decided to take advantage of all this publicity about Geneticon and get in on the act, that's why!"

She looked at him bewilderedly. "I don't understand."

"There's nothing to understand!" he shouted. "This...this *idiot* maintains that he was fired because he refused to sign a secrecy agreement!"

"A secrecy agreement! Do you require such a thing?"

"Of course not!" he said scathingly. "What do you think?"

"Then why—"

It was as though she hadn't spoken. "I don't believe this," he said furiously, looking as though he wanted to smash something. "I just don't believe this! How anyone could take the man seriously is beyond me!"

"But why is it so important?" she asked "What difference does it make if you required someone to sign a secrecy agreement or not? You have a right to protect the experiments you're doing at Geneticon. A judge would surely grant that."

He looked at her as though she was a simple-minded fool. "Not if he thought we required a secrecy agreement to hide the fact that we're doing illegal experiments at Geneticon!"

She looked at him, aghast. "What?"

He slammed his hand down on the counter, making her jump. "That's what this moron maintains."

"But that's crazy!"

"Is it?" he asked, his eyes like fierce black coals. "Not according to the papers, who've been bleating about this very same thing for weeks now!"

She wanted to comfort him, to assure him that everything would be all right. She wanted to touch him, but because his expression was so furious, she didn't quite dare. "If this lawsuit is as ridiculous as you say," she said tentatively, "surely Richard will be able to prove it in court."

"I know," he said angrily. "It's just the nuisance of the thing. And why now? Don't we have enough problems at Geneticon?"

She was struck with a sudden thought. "Do you think this is the reason why? Maybe this man is the one who's responsible for stirring up the press."

He looked at her. "You might be right," he said slowly, and then shook his head angrily again. "But so what? What good is that information now? He's hired an attorney who obviously thinks he has a case."

"Who is the attorney?"

"Some man named Enderly," Colin said as Reya's face drained of color and she looked at him appalled.

He didn't see her expression. He was frowning as he muttered, "Enderly. Now why does that name sound so familiar?"

CHAPTER THIRTEEN

"WOULD YOU MIND saying that again?" Joseph Clendenin asked the next morning. "I'm not sure I heard you correctly."

Reya was sitting opposite him in his office, and at the disbelieving expression on his face, it was all she could do not to sink down into her chair. She'd gotten up early this morning to prepare herself for this meeting. She knew how difficult it was going to be to convince him to let her revive the Geneticon account. But even the logical arguments she had so carefully marshaled on the drive in seemed childish now, and she was beginning to feel a little desperate.

Then she straightened. She had to make a case. After what had happened last night, taking on Colin's account again was even more important to her than it had been before. Even if they hadn't been...involved...she had to talk Clendenin into it. Because now, in addition to everything else, she felt so guilty, as though this lawsuit against Colin and Geneticon was somehow partly her fault. She knew that was absurd, but she still couldn't help feeling a twinge every time she thought about it. She cringed even more whenever she thought about how she had deliberately avoided telling Colin why the name Enderly was familiar to him, but last night she just couldn't make

herself confess that her ex-fiancé was the attorney
bringing suit against him. Even though she and Colin
seemed to have reconciled, she didn't want to take the
chance that this would drive them apart again.

Don't you trust him?

The question slithered into her mind, and she
squirmed. It wasn't a matter of trust, she argued; it
was that he'd been under so much pressure lately. She
didn't know what his reaction would be, and even
though he had to be told sooner or later, there was no
harm in making it as late as possible, was there?

When? the mocking little voice asked. *On the day
of the trial?*

She cringed again, remembering how shocked she'd
been last night when Colin told her about the lawsuit.
She thought for a horrified few seconds that she was
going to faint when she heard Darren's name; she
didn't know even now how she had managed to hold
herself together until Colin drove her back to the
agency to get her car. She knew he'd been surprised
when she insisted on leaving, but even though she'd
given him some lame excuse about having work to do,
he hadn't really protested. She suspected that he
wanted to be alone, too, and she was too grateful at
being able to escape to feel shut out. She had to talk
to Darren and demand to know what was going on,
and she couldn't do that with Colin around.

But Darren hadn't been home last night—or he had
chosen not to answer his phone. Grimly, she suspected the latter. He would have known she'd try to
call the instant she heard the news, and he was deliberately keeping her on tenterhooks as revenge. She'd
felt a little vengeful herself last night, and had tried to
call until long past midnight, purposely letting the

phone ring twenty times or more before she hung up. It was childish, but she couldn't help herself. She pictured him listening to that incessant ringing and couldn't help feeling pleased at the thought that it had to be driving him utterly mad.

But when he still wasn't answering this morning when she'd tried to call, she didn't feel like playing childish games. On the way to work, she'd vowed that she was going to talk to him today if she had to have Sally call every five minutes. She was going to find out why he was doing this, or she wouldn't go home.

But in the meantime she had to convince Joseph Clendenin to reconsider *his* decision, and because she felt so intimidated by that disbelieving stare, she squared her shoulders and looked him directly in the eye.

"I've decided I don't want to give up the Geneticon account," she stated.

"How interesting," he said. "Forgive me, but I was under the impression that we already had."

Trying to ignore the sarcasm, she took a deep breath. "Yes, but I talked to Col—to Mr. Hughes again yesterday, and we agreed there had been a... misunderstanding."

He sat back in his chair. "A misunderstanding."

She flushed at his tone. "Yes," she said quickly. "Mr. Hughes was understandably upset about the vandalism at Geneticon, and he—"

"I see. And is he even more upset at the news of this impending lawsuit?"

She didn't ask how he had heard about that so quickly; there was really no point. It hadn't been in the papers this morning, but he had contacts all over town, and she could just imagine how delighted some of them would have been to spread the news. He had probably heard all about it before breakfast. That didn't make her present task any easier, but she was determined to convince him that they couldn't abandon Geneticon now. She wanted to make him see that if she was successful in deflecting all this negative publicity, it would not only be a feather in the agency's cap, it would be a coup. Geneticon could be a lucrative, important account to them if they could just get beyond the current crisis.

"This lawsuit is just a nuisance suit," she said, crossing her fingers in the hope that it really was. "In fact—"

He leaned forward so suddenly that she was startled into silence. "The fact of the matter, Miss Merrill," he said heavily, "is that nuisance suit or not, Geneticon is going to be dragged into court, forced to defend itself against charges ranging from coercion to illegal experimentation."

"Those charges are ridiculous!"

He raised a thick eyebrow. "Are they? It seems we'll have to let the court decide that."

She wasn't going to give up so easily. "But in the meantime, there are things we can do—"

"We?"

She nearly cringed at that tone. "Yes, we…me. I've devoted a lot of thought to this, Mr. Clendenin, and I think—"

This time he held up a hand to silence her. "No," he said flatly. "I've had misgivings about this account from the beginning—"

"You never said that before!"

He shrugged. "I hoped you could handle it. You seemed confident enough, didn't you?"

She wasn't going to fall into that trap. "I still am," she said. "If you would only let me—"

"Didn't you hear me, Reya? I said no."

So exasperated she had to grip the arms of the chair so she wouldn't spring up and pound her fists on top of the desk, she made herself take a deep breath. "I think you at least owe me an explanation why."

She had made him angry. "I don't *owe* you anything," he said, glaring at her. Then he relented slightly. "However, since it was your account, let me just say that I prefer not to jeopardize all our other accounts for this single one. Does that satisfy you?"

She was too upset to guard what she was saying. "No, I'm afraid it doesn't, Mr. Clendenin. I still don't understand why—"

He slapped his hand on the desk. "Do you know how many clients have called me since this business with Geneticon started?" he said. "Do you know how many people I've had to cajole and soothe and pacify? Auguste Weidmar called again just yesterday—"

"After I talked to him?" She was outraged at the thought.

"Yes, after you talked to him. He wanted my assurance—*my* assurance, Reya—that we were no longer connected with Geneticon. He made it quite clear that if we were to reconsider, he would place his business with another agency."

"And so because of Auguste Weidmar you're going to abandon Geneticon!"

He seemed suprised at her choice of words. "Abandon, Reya? That's certainly an interesting way of putting it."

"Well, how else can I put it?" she asked bitterly.

"Into some perspective, I should think," he answered severely. "Geneticon has an excellent attorney in Richard Carlyle, and as far as I'm concerned, he is more than capable of handling this situation."

"Legally, you mean!"

He looked at her in astonishment. "What other way is there? Especially under the current circumstances?"

She couldn't sit still any longer. Jumping up from the chair, she leaned over his desk. He sat back, staring up at her in surprise. "There's our way," she said fiercely. "You know as well as I do that a publicity campaign, properly conducted, could turn public opinion just like that!" She snapped her fingers. "Why won't you let me try?"

He obviously didn't care for the fact that she was leaning over him. Slowly, placing his hands on the top of the desk, he got to his feet so that she had to look up at him. "Are you questioning my judgment, Miss Merrill?"

She heard the warning note in his voice and decided to ignore it. She'd gone too far to back down now. If she gave in, things would never be the same and she knew it. Lifting her chin, she said, "No, I'm not questioning your judgment, Mr. Clendenin. I'm asking you to reconsider your decision. You said this account was mine—"

He interrupted her with an angry wave of his hand. "I don't intend to discuss this any longer, Reya. I've made my decision, and you'll just have to live with it. Now, if you don't mind, I'd like—"

"I'm afraid I can't do that, Mr. Clendenin," she said.

"I beg your pardon?"

She knew she couldn't give herself time to think or she'd never go through with it, so she raised her chin again. "I said that I can't live with that decision, Mr. Clendenin."

He didn't say anything for a moment. Her heart was thundering away in her chest, and she could barely breathe. She had the dreaded thought that she'd just burned all her bridges behind her and she was standing all alone on the edge of a precipice with no way to go but down.

"I see," he said at last. "Well, I'm sorry to hear that, Reya. Are you sure you won't change your mind?"

Some part of her mind was shrieking at her to reconsider. He was giving her the opportunity to retract her hasty words, but even though she wanted desperately to say she'd made a mistake, she couldn't do it. Her feelings for Colin aside, she believed in Geneticon. She wanted others to believe in it, too. But no one could do that in this atmosphere of lies and confusion and unease, and it was up to her to change the situation—not because of Colin, not even because of her love for him, but because it was *right*. Facing Joseph Clendenin now, she had the feeling that everything she'd ever done had led to this moment, and that if she betrayed it, she'd never get another chance to do something this worthwhile again.

"No, Mr. Clendenin," she said clearly. "I won't change my mind."

He seemed taken aback again. Obviously he'd been sure she'd rethink her position and realize how foolish her decision was. Perhpas it was, she thought, but it was too late to go back now.

"I see," he said again. "All right, then, if that's the way you want it...."

From somewhere she dredged up the courage to say, "It's not the way I want it at all, Mr. Clendenin, but since we can't agree on this matter—"

"No, I'm afraid we can't," he said flatly, dashing her last hope.

She wasn't going to beg. "I'll have Sally type up a status list of my current accounts. You'll have it on your desk before I leave today." She paused. "I assume you won't require the usual two weeks' notice...."

It was small satisfaction that he couldn't seem to look her in the eye. "No, that won't be necessary," he muttered.

She nodded. "Fine. I imagine I can have all the details wrapped up by...noon, if not sooner."

She went to the door, but she hesitated there again. Turning to look at him, she said quietly, and meant it, "I'm sorry things had to turn out this way, Mr. Clendenin. I enjoyed working here."

He had the grace to look at her, then. "I'm sorry, too, Reya. And don't worry about a reference, you'll have one before you leave. Until this distasteful Geneticon business, I had no quarrel with you as an employee."

And why was that? she wanted to say. *Because until now, I agreed with everything you said?*

She didn't say it, of course; she merely nodded and went out. By this time her throat was clogged with emotion and tears were brimming, and she started back to her own office, she knew she could never make the rounds and say goodbye to everyone. It was going to be difficult enough telling Sally she was leaving. To her dismay, she met Sid just as he was coming out of the art department. She was so blinded by tears that she literally bumped into him.

"Don't worry about it, I walk on 'em, too," he started to joke, then he saw her face. "Uh-oh. What's wrong, Reya?"

She didn't want to talk about it. She knew if she tried to explain, she *would* dissolve into tears. So she shook her head and started to hurry away. He grabbed her firmly by the arm and yanked her into his little cubbyhole of an office. Closing the door, he stood like a guard against it and said, "All right, let's have it."

Sniffing, she looked around the cluttered space for a box of tissue and couldn't find one. "Here," he said, handing her his handkerchief. "I knew if I carried one long enough, I'd get to use it some day."

"Thanks," she said, her voice muffled behind the coarse cotton. Groping for a chair, she sank into it and tried to get herself under control.

"It's this business with Geneticon, isn't it?" he asked after a minute.

There was no point in lying, so she nodded. "How did you guess?"

He pulled up the high stool he used when he was sitting at his drafting table. "I read the papers, too, you know," he said, and hesitated. "What happened? Did he tell you how to handle the account?"

The sympathy in his voice was almost her undoing. She felt fresh tears gathering and willed them away. "He told me he didn't want me to handle the account at all."

Sid raised an eyebrow. "He pulled you off to take over himself?"

She crumpled the handkerchief into a tight little ball. "Not exactly. He's decided that we're not going to handle Geneticon, period."

"You're kidding!"

She shook her head.

"What are you going to do?"

"I don't know," she said. "I was so angry I quit."

Sid leaned back in astonishment and almost fell off the stool. She made a grab for him as he tried to catch his balance, and by the time he had righted himself, she was able to offer him a shaky smile. "I didn't mean to bowl you over," she said, making a feeble attempt at a joke. "Are you all right now?"

"Are *you*? What do you mean, you quit? Just because the old man decided to drop an account? But he's done that before, Reya, and you—"

"It wasn't that," she said slowly, trying to find the words to explain. "It was the way he did it, the *reasons* he had for doing it. None of them made sense to me. I mean, it's not as if Geneticon is hyping a new kind of toothpaste or—"

"Boy, he really impressed you, didn't he?"

"Who?"

"That guy—Hughes. I've seen you fired up before, Reya, but never like this."

She knew her face was turning red. "It's Geneticon that impressed me," she insisted. "Colin Hughes has nothing to do with it."

"Right."

"Well, he doesn't!"

Sid threw up his hands. "Okay, okay. But now what are you going to do?"

She hadn't thought that far until now, but an idea suddenly occurred to her and before she lost courage, she said, "What can I do? I'm going to handle Geneticon's account myself."

He gaped at her. "Are you out of your mind?"

She was so excited at the thought that she began to pace back and forth in the tiny office, forcing Sid to shrink back against the wall. "Why not?" she said, talking more to herself than to him. "I can do it. I've got the contacts...."

He stepped in front of her to get her attention. "Aren't you forgetting something?"

She looked blankly at him. "What?"

He jerked his chin again, this time in the direction of the big office down the hall. "Him."

"What about him?" she asked with a toss of her head. "He told me just a few minutes ago that he didn't want anything to do with Geneticon."

"Yes, but that didn't mean he expected you to go out and scalp his accounts."

She looked at him scornfully. "According to him, Geneticon is no longer one of his clients. That makes it fair game in my book."

"Yeah, but what about his?"

"Are you trying to tell me you don't think I should do this? Because if you are—"

"No, no. It's not that. It's just that I don't want to see you get hurt."

She was about to snap back a reply when she noticed his woebegone expression. He really did care, she realized, and touched his arm. "You worry too much," she said with a smile. "I'm not going to try to take away his entire client list, you know."

He still looked glum. "No, just the one who could destroy your entire career."

"What's left of it, you mean," she said, trying to make him smile and failing utterly. He looked like he was the one who had just lost his job, and she shook his arm a little. "Come on, it's not that bad."

"But what are you going to do?"

Her eyes gleamed. *In for a penny, in for a pound,* she thought, and said, "I'll tell you later."

"But—"

She went to the door, hesitated, then turned around again and gave him a quick kiss on the cheek. "Thanks for everything, Sid. You've been a good friend."

He had blushed crimson at her gesture, so embarrassed that it was hard for him to look her in the eye. "I hope everything turns out all right for you, Reya," he said. "You'll let me know, won't you?"

She grinned at him from the doorway. "If things turn out the way I intend, I won't have to let you know—you'll see it for yourself."

She wouldn't tell him any more than that. She waved a quick goodbye and went back to her own office. By this time she had herself under better control, and she briefly explained what had happened to Sally.

"I don't believe it!" Sally exclaimed, sinking down onto the edge of the desk, staring at her numbly as Reya flipped quickly through her files. "He actually *fired* you because of the Geneticon account?"

"He didn't fire me, I quit," Reya corrected, and slammed the filing cabinet door shut again. She brought an arm load of folders back to the desk with her and dumped them on top. "There's a difference, you know."

"What difference?" Sally wailed. "The result is the same, isn't it? You're not going to work here anymore! Oh, it isn't fair! What am I going to do?"

Reya didn't want to talk about it. Thumbing briskly through the folders to distract herself, she said, "It's not as if I'm going to the North Pole, Sally. We'll still get together for lunch—"

"No, we won't! Once you leave, that'll be it, and we both know it. Everybody always promises to get together for lunch, and they never do!"

"We will," she said firmly, and gave Sally the clients' files she had chosen with instructions on what she wanted done. Then she began to gather her own things: the pictures she had scattered around, the knickknacks she'd found amusing. There wasn't much to take. She had never believed in an office cluttered with personal effects at the expense of important things, so she was ready to leave in minutes. Sally stood watching mournfully the entire time, so Reya said brusquely, "I hate goodbyes, so let's just pretend that this is the end of another workday, all right?"

"All right," Sally said, and promptly burst into tears.

Reya was emotional herself by the time she mopped up the last of Sally's tears, and she was just starting out the door when her phone rang. Sally had gone to the ladies' room to freshen up, so she answered automatically, forgetting for an instant that she was no longer working here. When she recognized Darren's voice, she immediately became angry.

"Where have you been?" she demanded. "I've been trying to call you since last night!"

"I thought you might want to talk to me."

She heard the satisfaction in his voice and her own became more sharp. "I certainly do! I'd like you to tell me what's going on. Is it true that you're involved in this ridiculous lawsuit against Geneticon?"

He was his usual overly controlled self. "In the first place," he said patiently, "the lawsuit against Geneticon is not ridiculous. We wouldn't be going to trial if it were."

Swallowing her irritation at his pedantic manner, she said coldly, "And in the second place?" She knew from past experience with him that there had to be one.

"And in the second place," he said, ignoring her sarcasm, "the man has an excellent case, one which I fully intend to win."

"What man is that?" she asked acidly. "The one who quit Geneticon because he was passed over for promotion?"

Darren's tone was just as caustic. "Where did you get that piece of erroneous information?"

"Where do you think?"

"From the defendant, no doubt. Well, I'm sorry to say, but the man is lying, Reya—"

"Your man is," she interrupted furiously. "And before you go to court, maybe you'd better investigate your facts a little more closely!"

"I have all the facts I need to prove my case in court!" he replied sharply. "And I would appreciate it if you didn't try to tell me how to do my job!"

"Perhaps someone should," she snapped. "The last I heard you were a corporate attorney. Isn't this change of careers somewhat sudden?"

"About as sudden as your breaking our engagement," he snapped back.

"Our engagement! What does that have to do with this!"

"What do you think?" he said nastily. "It's all his fault, isn't it?"

"His fault? Who? What are you talking about?"

"Oh, don't play the innocent with me, Reya. I know that Colin Hughes is responsible for your sudden change of heart. He's the reason you broke our engagement, and we both know it!"

"That's not true!" she cried. But even as she denied it, she wondered if it was, and they both heard the guilty tone of her voice that she couldn't quite disguise. Hastily she tried to repair the damage. "Darren, listen to me. . . ."

"Why? Have you changed your mind again?"

"No, I—"

"Then I really don't want to talk about this anymore. Oh, there's just one more thing," he added, unable to hide his enjoyment. "I know you won't mind, but I've subpoenaed you as a witness in the trial."

"What!"

"Think of it this way. You're the only outsider who's been through those labs at Geneticon. I'm sure you'll be able to shed some light on what's going on out there."

She was gripping the phone so tightly she thought it might snap in two. "Nothing's going on out there, and if you think I'll make something up for you, you're out of your mind!"

"Oh, I didn't expect you to be on our side. I knew you'd be a hostile witness."

"You're right about that!"

"But a witness all the same," he went on, his voice turning hard. "I know you, Reya, and no matter what you think of me, you'd never perjure yourself. So goodbye. I'll see you in court."

He hung up before she could swallow her anger long enough to make a reply. Smashing her own receiver down into the cradle, she drummed her fingers agitatedly against the top of the desk in an effort to calm down. This wasn't happening, she thought. It couldn't be. It was like something out of a bad soap opera, where the rejected suitor plots his revenge against the hero for some imagined slight. She knew that nothing she could ever say would convince Darren that he was mistaken about her reasons for breaking their engagement. Even though they'd had their final quarrel right after she'd taken on Geneticon's account, that didn't mean that Colin was responsible.

It was no one's fault, really. People fell out of love all the time, and she knew with certainty that she'd been falling out of love with Darren for a long while before she met Colin Hughes. Their marriage would never have lasted, and that was why she had broken the engagement. Colin had nothing to do with it—not then, anyway.

That thought brought her back to the reason Darren had called, and she shook herself. It was even more imperative now that she follow through on her own plans for Geneticon, and after looking up the phone number she wanted, she made the call. A feminine voice answered, and she said pleasantly, "Serena? This is Reya Merrill. How would you like the real story on Geneticon?"

CHAPTER FOURTEEN

REYA WAS DETERMINED to turn the tide of public opinion in favor of Geneticon, so her phone call to Serena Jackson was not the only one she made that day—she called in favors all over town. In fact, she called in some on the way home, the first when she stopped by the offices of the *Rocky Mountain News* to talk to Rudy Sabin.

"Reya!" Rudy exclaimed warmly when he saw her. He stood up, nearly spilling a cup of cold coffee all over his desk. Grabbing it with one hand, he embraced her with the other, bussing her loudly on the cheek. "It's been a long time since you graced these offices with your lovely presence," he said with a grin. "What do you want?"

Waiting until he'd swept the files and papers stacked on the desk side chair grandly onto the floor, she sat down with a laugh at his theatrics. She'd always liked Rudy. If she'd had to write a description of a harried newspaper reporter, she would have written about him. But even though his shirt pocket was invariably stained with ink, and his hair stood up in peaks from running his fingers through it, Rudy Sabin was no caricature. He was sharp, perceptive, and one of the best feature writers the *News* had. Even though she needed him as a reporter now, she was still glad she'd cultivated his friendship. They had worked together before, and she knew he'd be fair.

"What makes you think I want something?" she teased as he perched on the edge of his cluttered desk. "Can't I just stop by to visit?"

He took out a cigarette. "You can," he said with a twinkle in his eye. "But you usually don't unless you have something on your mind. What is it now? No, don't tell me. Geneticon, right?"

She wasn't surprised that he had guessed; she would have been more surprised if he hadn't. Her expression sobering, she nodded. "Yes," she said. "I need your help, Rudy—"

He held up both hands. "Oh, no, you don't. You're not going to drag me into the middle of *that* controversy!"

"But you're a reporter—"

"A feature writer. It's not necessarily the same thing."

"But you covered the press conference, didn't you?"

He raised an eyebrow. "Oh, is that what you called it? I thought it was more of a reaming up one side and down the other."

She wasn't going to let him get away with that. "Yes, I thought you people were pretty rough on Mr. Hughes that day."

He gave her a quelling look. "I thought it was the other way around."

She returned his look with one of her own. "Maybe we should call it a draw and forget it, all right?"

"All right," he said with a grin. "So what now? Don't tell me you're going to try again!"

Trying not to shudder at the thought, she smiled. "No, this time I thought we'd start out slow, and *then* work our way up to the grand finale."

He looked at her suspiciously. "What does that mean?"

"What do you think about an article or two on the benefits of genetic engineering?" she asked persuasively.

"Are there any?"

She ignored the mock sarcasm. "I have all the information you need," she said. "More than enough for a feature in Sunday's edition."

"Are you out of your mind?"

She laughed. "Maybe. Will you do it?"

He looked at her for a moment, then he shook his head resignedly. "All right," he said, and tried not to smile at the sparkle in her eyes. "But I'm not going to promise a feature. Contrary to the impression I've deliberately given you, I don't write whatever I please. I'll have to talk it over with the managing editor first."

"Thanks, Rudy," she said gratefully, and then to his surprise, kissed him lightly on the cheek. "I know you'll do what you can."

He was still staring bemusedly after her when she paused at the door to look back. Smiling again, she waved goodbye and practically floated out of the building on a wave of euphoria. If all her interviews went like this, she thought, Colin wouldn't have anything to worry about.

Her next stop was to talk to Corrine Castault of Denver's educational radio station, KLST. She'd made an appointment, and when she walked in, Corrine jumped up from behind her desk and gave her a hug. She was a small woman, dark haired and dark eyed, and Reya had worked with her many times before. She knew what an inquiring mind Corrine had, so she plunged in with her idea of devoting some air time to a program on biotechnology.

Corrine's dark eyes glowed. "I've been waiting for you to ask," she said with a smile. "What took you so long?"

"You wouldn't believe it if I told you."

"Long story, huh?"

Reya smiled. "Someday I'll tell you. Right now, I'm just trying to get things straightened out with Geneticon. I have to say, though, that I'm not working with the agency anymore. Will that make a difference?"

Corrine was the manager of the station; her husband owned it. "Not to me," she said with a laugh. "And if it does to Brad, which I doubt, well, I do all the programming, so..." She spread her hands and shrugged.

Reya laughed and impulsively hugged the tiny woman. "Thanks," she whispered. "I owe you one."

"Who keeps score?" Corrine said, and then pushed her out the door. "Go on, now. I'll call you when I have a time slot open. It should be soon."

Reya was practically skipping when she went back to her car, but after she'd climbed in and started driving to the last appointment she'd made, her expression sobered. Parking outside the coffee shop where Serena Jackson had agreed to meet her, she drew a deep breath to steady herself. Rudy and Corrine were going to be a big help, but it would be Serena's participation that would make the vital difference. Survey after survey indicated that television was the most powerful medium of the three, and she had to convince Serena that running a series of special reports after the nightly news would benefit everyone. Serena had been cautious on the phone, but once Reya had reminded her that the current publicity had made genetic engineering a "hot" subject, she began to see the possibilities.

"Well, it's controversial, that's for sure," Serena said a while later, over their third cup of coffee. "We should be able to pick up a stray fraction of a percentage point here and there by running the series. I'm just not sure it will hold audience interest that long."

"Of course it will," Reya said, and leaned forward to give her the list she'd written up. Before she'd left the office for the last time, she'd dashed off a page of suggested topics to cover, and she had even provided the names of experts from various fields who might guest on the programs.

Whistling softly when she glanced over the sheet Reya had given her, Serena muttered admiringly, "You've obviously done your homework. I guess it's time to do mine."

"Does that mean you'll do it?" Reya tried, but she couldn't keep the excitement out of her voice, and Serena smiled.

"I'll try. But you know I have to talk to the station manager first."

Reya sat back. "I'll be glad to come and talk to him with you," she said casually. "Brian and I are old friends."

Serena looked up quickly. "Then why didn't you go to him first? You might have been able to ram this through over my head."

"I might have," Reya agreed. "But I figured after hearing several of your editorials about this subject that you would be my toughest audience. If I could convince you, the rest of the population would be a piece of cake.''

Serena laughed, and after a moment, Reya joined her. Ordering fresh cups of coffee, they began working out the rest of the details about the series, and several hours later left the coffee shop. To their mutual surprise, they left it as friends.

"You know," Serena said as they walked through the parking lot toward their cars, "none of this would have happened if Colin Hughes would have been open with us in the first place. All we wanted was the truth.''

"I know," Reya said with a sigh. She still wasn't sure how Colin was going to accept this latest scheme of hers, but since their relationship seemed to have entered a new phase, she hoped she could convince him this was right. After all, if he didn't have to appear on any of the programs himself, he shouldn't have any objection, should he? Shaking her head wryly, she felt like crossing her fingers, just in case.

They reached Reya's car first and she was about to say good-night to the reporter when Serena dismayed her by saying thoughtfully, "If we could film part of the series at Geneticon, it would have a much greater impact. Do you think you could talk Colin Hughes into letting me bring a crew into the labs? We could sign something saying we'd only film what he wanted us to.''

Reya drew in a deep breath. She knew it was a good idea; in fact, she had thought of it herself right away. But she knew she was going to have a difficult enough time convincing Colin that Serena would be fair in her reports without asking him to let a film crew into the research center, so she said cautiously, "I'll try.''

Serena smiled wryly. "I know from experience how difficult he can be, but give it your best shot, okay? It really would make a difference if we could show some actual experiments going on. There's nothing like a visual image to convince an audience."

"Yes," Reya said dryly, "unless they expect to see Frankenstein monsters roaming around out there."

"Are there any?"

Reya looked at her indignantly and Serena laughed. "Just kidding. But try to talk to him, all right?"

Reya agreed that she would, but it was a few days before she could summon the courage to think of an approach. She tried to convince herself that there were too many other things to worry about, too many other details to take care of first, but the truth was that she was enjoying Colin too much to take a chance on spoiling their new relationship. Even worse, she still hadn't told him that Darren Enderly had been her fiancé. She knew she couldn't keep it a secret forever, but with every day that went by, it became harder and harder to broach the subject. She knew he'd want to know why she hadn't told him before, and because she really didn't have a reason, she just wanted to avoid the topic. Whatever price she had to pay later, she couldn't take the chance now of destroying this glorious time with him.

Typical of the way things had changed between them was the morning he arrived at her apartment bearing fresh croissants and a single red rose. It was several days after she'd quit the agency and she hadn't told him yet that she wasn't working for Clendenin anymore. She knew she had to say something when he kissed her and said he wanted to have breakfast with her before she went to work.

"I'm . . . not going in to work this morning," she stammered.

He put his arms around her waist. Nuzzling her neck, he murmured, "That suits me just fine. I'll play hooky, too, if you like."

It was tempting to keep up the fantasy, to pretend that she had decided to take a stolen day off, but then she knew she had to tell him. Slipping out of his embrace, she took a deep breath. "I'm not playing hooky, Colin," she said quietly. "I . . . I don't work at the agency anymore. I quit the other day."

He looked at her in astonishment. "Quit? But I thought you liked it there."

She glanced away. "I do—I did," she said. She knew that she couldn't tell him the entire truth, so she shrugged and added, "But I've been thinking for quite a while now about striking out on my own, and this seemed the right time to do it."

He must have heard the hesitation in her voice, for he frowned slightly. "You don't sound very excited."

"Oh, I am," she said quickly. "I guess it's just going to take some time getting used to the idea."

To her relief, he decided not to question her further. "Well, if that's what you really want. . . ."

"It's what I want," she said, and made herself look at him again. "Now that I'm on my own, I'll understand if you want to stay with the agency, Colin, or even if you want to go with someone else—"

He reached for her and pulled her close, tipping her head up with one finger under her chin. "I don't want anyone else," he said. "As far as I'm concerned, you're doing just fine."

She looked up at him, into those penetrating dark eyes. Her own were uncertain. "Are you sure?" she asked, and laughed shakily. "I mean, I don't even have a real office yet. As of now, I'm working out of my apartment."

"That's fine with me."

"But—"

He stopped her protest with a kiss, and a long time later they finally remembered the croissants he'd brought for breakfast. Since it was almost noon by then, they decided to go to lunch instead, and Reya couldn't remember ever being so happy as they walked hand in hand to a small restaurant nearby. Sitting under one of the green and white striped umbrellas that shaded tables alfresco, she looked across at Colin and knew she'd always remember this moment. He looked so handsome that even the waitress was making eyes at him as she took their orders, and Reya smiled privately to herself. She knew how the girl felt.

When their coffee was served, Colin leaned back with a sigh of contentment and pushed his plate away. "I can't remember when I've had a day like this."

"Not going into the office, you mean?" Reya asked. "It is different, isn't it?"

"Feeling guilty?"

She looked at him quickly, the guilt she did feel making her wonder if he'd found out about Darren and was giving her an opening. Then she realized it had just been an idle comment, and she made herself laugh. "Not so much that as...displaced," she admitted. "I guess I haven't gotten used to the idea of working for myself yet."

Absently stirring his coffee, he said, "It sounds as though your decision to quit was a sudden one."

She looked up at him sharply again, wondering this time if he knew—or guessed—the real reason she

wasn't with Clendenin anymore. Even more reluctant
than before to tell him the truth about quitting her job,
she didn't want to ruin the lovely morning they'd had,
so she forced a smile. "Not so sudden," she lied.
"Didn't you feel this way when you first went out on
your own?"

He looked thoughtful at that. "You mean when I
first started Hughes TechCraft? Yes, I guess I did. It's
a big step starting your own business, but—" he
grinned "—you'll do fine. I've no doubt of that."

"Thanks for the vote of confidence. At least one of
us thinks so."

"Look at it this way...you already have one client."

This was the opening she'd been seeking, and she
knew she had to take it. She wanted to laze away the
rest of the day, pretending that they had no concerns
but each other, but they didn't have that luxury.
Though they hadn't mentioned the pending lawsuit
against the research center, she knew it wasn't far from
either of their minds—nor were the disastrous consequences if by some miracle Darren won.

She refused to consider that possibility, so she said
carefully, "Speaking of clients, there's something I
wanted to talk to you about."

"All right."

Since she'd already arranged for what she was pro-
posing to him, she crossed her fingers and took a deep
breath. She didn't know what she'd do if he flatly refused to go along with her strategy for Geneticon, so
she plunged in confidently, as if his agreement was
assured.

"I've been thinking about the situation," she said,
"and I believe that what we need to do is start educating the public."

He frowned. "Didn't we discuss this before?"

"We did," she agreed calmly. "And my opinion hasn't changed." She paused. "Has yours?"

He looked wary. "That depends on what you have in mind...."

She wasn't going to start off by telling him she had enlisted Serena's support and that they wanted to film some of the special reports at Geneticon; it was too soon for that. She knew from experience that the groundwork had to be carefully prepared, so she said, "I've already started some of the wheels rolling. A friend of mine at the *News* has promised to do an article or two on the benefits of genetic engineering—"

"How did you manage that?"

She smiled, deciding to tease him a little. "You're not the only one who has friends in high places, you know."

"If I had friends in high places, Geneticon wouldn't be in the trouble it's in now."

"Well, it's not going to be in trouble for long," she said blithely. "By the time we're finished, the only people who won't be able to form an educated opinion about the subject will be those who don't watch television or read newspapers or listen to the radio."

He sat back, his expression guarded. "And you're going to do all this by having your journalist friend write a couple of articles for the paper?"

"Of course not," she said indignantly. She almost told him about Serena then, but she sensed the time still wasn't right. "KLST is going to devote some radio time to the topic, and I have some other ideas, too." She smiled brightly. "So you see—"

"You mentioned television," he interrupted, his eyes intent on her face.

She forced a laugh. "Did I?"

He didn't laugh with her. "You did."

It was an effort to hold that penetrating gaze. She had the uncomfortable feeling that he knew she was hiding something, but things were going so well that she didn't want to make him angry by mentioning Serena. She knew he disliked the reporter, and before she and the other woman had had a chance to talk the other night, she hadn't blamed him. But she felt that Serena was trying her best to be objective now, and that she'd do everything she could to present an unbiased viewpoint on her special reports.

The only problem would be convincing Colin of that, she thought with an inward sigh, and reached across the table to touch his hand. "I know how hard it is for you to deal with the press, Colin," she said quietly. "That's why I'd like you to leave it up to me. You trust me, don't you?"

His eyes were very dark as he took her hand in his. "You know I do," he said simply.

"Then let me handle it. I'll let you know when I've arranged all the details."

He hesitated a moment while she held her breath, but finally he nodded. "All right," he said, and looked wry. "As you've reminded me so many times, this is your job."

Pleased that this hurdle, at least, had been overcome, she laughed. "Then I'd better get going and do it, otherwise my only client is going to think I'm just wasting his time."

She'd started to rise, but he held her hand fast. "Let's waste a little more time...."

They went back to her apartment, sauntering down the street, purposely prolonging the anticipation of being together again. Reya could hardly believe this was happening. Walking alongside Colin, she glanced at him again and again, and every time he met her eyes, and he smiled. It was as though they were sharing some delicious secret, and by the time they entered the courtyard of her apartment building, every nerve in her body was taut with expectation.

She knew that he felt that way, too; she could feel it in the slight trembling of his hand as his fingers held hers. And she wasn't surprised when he suddenly stopped under one of the Spanish arches lining the courtyard and pulled her to him; she could tell he wanted her as much as she wanted him. She melted against him, thrilling to the way he whispered her name. The kiss they exchanged was fierce and passionate, and when he laid a hand briefly against one of her breasts, she twined her fingers in his hair and kissed him again.

"Let's go upstairs." she murmured into his ear, and drew away from his embrace. She knew if she stayed within his arms one second more, she'd be lost. Already her entire body felt flushed with desire, and her legs trembled as she climbed the stairs. The scent of the flowers in the courtyard surrounded her, mixing with the masculine scent of him, and she knew that she would always associate that fragrance with him. Her hand shaking, she unlocked her apartment door.

It was late afternoon by this time. The rays of the sun, filtered by the gauzy curtains, slanted into her bedroom when they entered, turning everything golden. The bed was still rumpled from their lovemaking that morning, and she was reaching automatically to straighten the covers when he grasped her wrist and pulled her to him. His mouth descended hungrily on

hers, and she no longer cared about the bed. She clung
to him passionately, pulling and tugging at his clothing as he was pulling at hers, until they were both naked and trembling in each other's arms.

She wanted to lie back on the bed, to feel his weight
over her, to hold him in her arms, but he shook his
head when she tried to coax him down. He made her
stand while he caressed her with hands and lips and
tongue until she was so weak with desire her legs
wouldn't hold her any longer. She half fell against
him, clutching his hair as he knelt before her. She
pleaded incoherently, "Colin, I can't . . ."

He looked up at her then, his eyes like black dia-
monds, fierce and sparkling in that strange golden
light. He looked like a bronze statue at that moment,
and when he slowly stood, she shook her head. This
was like a dream, the culmination of all the fantasies
she'd ever had.

Except that Colin was no fantasy. She felt it in the
hard, broad muscles of his chest when she placed her
hands there; she felt it in the crisp texture of his hair
when she twisted her fingers in it so she could pull his
head down to hers; and she felt it in the glorious
weight of his body when he fell on top of her at last.
The flame he had ignited burst into a conflagration
then, and she could no more have held herself back
than she could have doused a fire with a teaspoon of
water. She didn't even realize that her nails had made
marks down his strong back, or that he had cried out
with her, grabbing her and rolling back and forth on
the bed in an ecstasy of pleasure that never seemed to
end . . . until it was over. Even then he wouldn't let her
go. By the time the last ripple had faded away, she lay
exhausted in his arms. Damp tendrils of hair clinging

to her face, she listened to the thundering of his heart beneath her ear.

Gradually that pounding beat quieted, and they both slept. The rays of the sun lengthened and dimmed and finally vanished altogether. Reya was in the throes of a dream when she heard a ringing sound. It seemed to go on and on, and she frowned and shifted in her sleep.

"What's that...?" Colin muttered, his face buried in the pillow.

His voice brought her abruptly awake. Groping for the phone, she murmured, "Never mind. Go back to sleep."

Pushing her tangled hair from her eyes, she sat up and muttered a hello. What had he done to her? she wondered, trying to wake up. She couldn't remember ever falling into such a deep sleep after making love. She felt as though she'd been drugged.

"Reya? This is Serena," the brisk voice said, and hesitated. "I didn't wake you up, did I?"

Reya glanced at the bedside clock and saw to her horror that it was nearly seven. Clutching the sheet to her, she glanced quickly at Colin. "No, of course you didn't."

Serena hesitated again. "You sound so sleepy. Look, if this is a bad time..."

Wondering what the reporter would say if she knew that Colin Hughes was sleeping right beside her at this moment, Reya tried to slide out of bed so she wouldn't disturb him. He shifted position and put his arm over her, muttering, "Don't go...."

"What?" Serena said. "Did you say something? Why are you whispering, Reya? Is somebody there?"

Reya felt as though she'd been pinned between the two of them. "Don't worry about it," she said hastily. "What did you want, Serena?"

She knew immediately that she'd made a mistake mentioning that name, for Colin glanced up just then and, seeing the guilty look on her face, started to get out of bed. Reya was just about to tell Serena she'd call her back when the reporter went blithely on. Sounding like the cat who'd found the cream, she said, "I'm calling to tell you that Brian thinks the special reports are a great idea. He's already assigned air time for me."

Reya was aware that Colin had thrown back the covers and stood, but she was so thrilled at Serena's news that she couldn't help exclaiming, "That's wonderful! When?"

"Every night next week after the evening news."

"Next week!" Reya bolted upright in bed. Colin had begun gathering his scattered clothes, and though she made a frantic gesture for him to stop, he ignored her.

"That doesn't give us much time, I know," Serena said. "But you pointed out yourself that this is a hot topic, so Brian feels that we should air it as soon as possible."

Reya made another gesture to Colin, but he jerked his head in the direction of the bathroom and she gave up. Wrenching her eyes away as he disappeared down the hall, presumably to dress, she tried to force her attention back to what Serena had said. "I agree."

"So when do you think we could get together? We've got a lot of details to work out before we air on Monday, and I think we should have a strategy meeting right away. Besides, with that lawsuit pending—"

"Lawsuit!" The word burst from her before she could stop it, and she glanced quickly in the direction of the bathroom door. Lowering her voice again, she said, "How did you find out about that?"

She could almost see Serena's upraised eyebrow. "I'm a reporter," she said loftily. "I'm supposed to find out these things." Then she relented. "Besides, that lawyer, Enderly, called me. Can you believe he actually said that since we'd devoted so much time already to Geneticon, he wanted equal air time for his client?"

Reya couldn't believe it. That didn't sound like the Darren she knew at all, and she was furious with him all over again. If this was all to make her change her mind about breaking their engagement, he was certainly going about it the wrong way. "What did you say to that?" she asked quickly.

Serena scoffed. "What do you think? Can you imagine what would happen if we did that? We'd have every screwball and crackpot in the city suing someone just for the chance of getting on television."

Reya let out the breath she'd been holding. It could have been worse, she thought, and muttered, "Yes, I see what you mean."

"You know, his name is so familiar. Weren't you going to marry him a while ago?"

"Oh, don't tell me he made an issue of that, too!"

Serena laughed at her irritation. "No, but he did mention it."

"I can't imagine why," Reya said, suddenly too angry to notice that Colin had appeared again at the bedroom door. She didn't see his eyes narrow when she snapped, "The fact that Darren and I were engaged has nothing to do with the case against Geneti-con!''

"Maybe he thinks it does."

"What do you mean?"

Serena's response was dry. "Well, I got the definite impression that he felt your involvement with Colin Hughes was the reason you broke your engagement."

"That's the most ridiculous thing I've ever heard!" Reya exploded. She closed her eyes, wondering if Darren had been telling that lie around town. If he had, she thought blackly, he might find himself in the middle of a lawsuit for slander, or defamation of character, or libel, or whatever the hell it was. Colin had enough to worry about without adding that to the list, so in an effort to staunch whatever rumors were rising, she said firmly, "My relationship with Colin Hughes is strictly business, Serena. He's a client, nothing more."

"Hey, don't get mad at me. I'm just passing along the news."

Still angry at the thought of Darren spreading gossip in order to get even with her, she tried to rein in her temper. It wasn't Serena's fault that Darren was reacting like a child, and she was sorry she'd snapped at her. "I'm sorry," she said. "It's just that he said the same thing to me, and it made me furious. The idea is completely absurd!"

"Is it?"

"What do you mean by that?"

"Oh...I hear a certain something in your voice when you talk about our infamous Mr. Hughes," Serena said slyly. "Could it be that the lady protests too much?"

Wondering if she had inadvertently said too much, Reya shot back, "It could be that the lady is too inquisitive for her own good!"

Serena laughed. "I thought so," she said. Before Reya could reply, she asked, "Do you think we can get together tomorrow morning? I'd really like to get started on this right away."

"Yes, that will be fine. How about nine o'clock at your office?"

"Sounds good to me. Oh, by the way, did you get a chance yet to ask our Mr. Hughes if we can film at Geneticon?"

"No, I—" Reya began, and just then became aware of Colin standing in the doorway. When she saw his thunderous expression she forgot what she'd been about to say.

"Reya . . . ?"

Reya couldn't take her eyes off him. "I . . . I'll see you tomorrow," she said to Serena.

"Is something wrong?"

"No, I just have to hang up now. I'll see you tomorrow."

Colin came into the bedroom as she dropped the receiver in its cradle. She saw that he had dressed, and because she felt so exposed sitting there with only the sheets covering her nakedness, she reached for the robe at the foot of the bed. "What is it, Colin?" she asked, wrapping it quickly around her and getting out of bed. She didn't feel so vulnerable now that she was facing him, but the expression on his face still made her quail. "What's wrong?"

He didn't answer for a moment; he was obviously trying to control his temper. She must have said something to offend him, and she was casting franti-

cally back over their conversation when he finally
spoke.

"Now I know where I heard the name Enderly," he
said, his voice low and beginning to shake with anger.
He looked at her, and his eyes practically shot sparks.
"You were engaged to him, weren't you, Reya? Why
didn't you say something?"

Appalled at this turn of events, she took a step in his
direction, but he tensed so visibly that she stepped
back again. "I'm sorry, Colin, I—"

"Sorry!" he exploded. "You were engaged to the
man who is taking me to court, and all you can say is
that you're *sorry*?"

She wanted to look away from that furious expression in his eyes, but she couldn't. Desperately she said,
"What else can I say? The fact that we were engaged
doesn't have anything to do with—"

He looked so enraged that she was afraid for a horrified moment that he might actually destroy something. But he had better control of himself than that,
and when he looked at her again, it was with such
contempt that she nearly cringed. "Doesn't it?" he
asked caustically. "I wonder how I could have been so
stupid!"

"I . . . what do you mean?"

"I get it now," he grated. "It was all part of a plan,
wasn't it? What were you supposed to be—his spy?
Did he think that by getting close to me you could get
the *real* story about Geneticon?"

She was appalled. "No! How could you even think
such a terrible thing?"

"How could I?" he repeated scornfully. "Well, it
seems obvious, doesn't it, Reya? You and that woman
reporter and Darren Enderly are all in this together."

"No!" she cried again, desperate to reach him. "Serena is trying to help!"

"Help!" His lip curled with derision. "She's certainly proved that, hasn't she?"

"Colin, please listen to me! The reason Serena called me tonight is because we've gotten permission for station KRDA to go ahead with a series of special reports about genetic engineering."

His eyes flashed again at that. "What? More Frankenstein stories? Is that what you have in mind?"

Despite her desperate desire to make him believe her, she was beginning to get angry at his deliberate refusal to understand—or even listen to her. She could feel her temper slipping and tried vainly to control it. She knew nothing would be accomplished if they both became angry, so she took a deep breath and debated quickly. She hadn't intended on telling him this soon what she and Serena had planned, and she certainly hadn't intended on telling him in these circumstances. But things could hardly get worse, so she said boldy, "No, it isn't. What we have in mind is filming a series of special reports at Geneticon."

He looked at her so incredulously that at another time his expression would have been comical, but she didn't feel like laughing now. She was too close to losing her temper as completely as he'd just lost his.

"You . . . *what*? Film at Geneticon? Are you out of your mind?"

Her last shred of self-control vanished. "Why are you being so stubborn about this?" she cried. "Don't you see that I'm trying to help?"

"By trying to talk me into letting reporters swarm all over Geneticon?"

Her eyes sent out sapphire sparks of fury. She was so angry at his obstinacy that she didn't care any longer what she said. "Look, Colin, I know what you went through with your wife and daughter. I know what the press dragged you through—"

He stiffened, his face suddenly looking as though it was carved from granite. "Leave my wife and daughter out of this," he warned.

She was too furious to heed the warning. "Why?" she shouted. "They're at the root of this, aren't they? They're the reason you're stuck in the past. They're the reason you've developed this unreasonable aversion to the press!"

"Unreasonable?" His eyes were like black pits. "What do you know about it? What have *you* suffered because of the press? Do you know what it's like to be hounded by some reporter anxious to make his name by cashing in on suffering?"

She knew what he was going to say, and instantly her anger disappeared. Her own face white, she saw the anguish in his and tried to stop him. "Colin, please..."

It was as though he hadn't heard her. His voice taut with remembered pain and suffering, the words tumbled out like a ghastly litany they were both powerless to stop. He went on, and she listened, transfixed. It was as though her own heart was being torn in two.

"Do you know what it's like to watch your daughter dying before your eyes, and to turn around and be blinded by some flashbulb going off in your face, or how it feels to have your wife collapse in your arms because she can't bear the strain of public scrutiny any longer?" His voice rose again, until Reya wanted to clap her hands over her ears to shut out the terrible sound.

"Do you know what it's like to have everything that ever mattered to you taken away, destroyed, and to have some reporter breathing over your shoulder, recording it all? Do you, Reya? *Do you?*"

He stopped abruptly, drawing in a shuddering breath. Before she could say anything, before she could begin to recover from that terrible emotional assault, he said, his voice low, "Don't tell me about the press, Reya. I've been there before. Just as I've been betrayed before—by the best. So you take your little sideshow somewhere else, all right? I just can't be the center of one again. I won't! Because this time I have a choice, do you hear me? *This* time I have a choice!"

He turned on his heel and went out before she could stop him. She wanted to go after him, to tell him that she did understand, to beg him to forgive her, to say they'd work out something else. But she couldn't move. She felt paralyzed, frozen in place. She had never heard such suffering in anyone's voice before, and she knew that nothing she could say or do would make any difference to him now.

Slowly she sank down onto the bed. The pillow he had used was by her hand; she grabbed it and hugged it to her. The scent of him rose to tantalize her nostrils, and she bowed her head. Her shoulders shaking, she buried her face in the pillow and wept for them both.

CHAPTER FIFTEEN

"WHAT DO YOU MEAN, you can't reach her at the Clendenin Agency?" Richard demanded. "Why not?"

Colin angrily threw down his pen. He'd known there was going to be trouble the instant Richard roared into his office, demanding to know where Reya was. Of all the cursed luck, he hadn't been here when the call from Corrine whatever-her-name-was came through; Richard had taken it instead, and when he'd heard that Corrine couldn't get in touch with Reya for the radio show they had planned about Geneticon, Richard had flown off the deep end. He'd practically knocked the door off its hinges when he rushed in; sure that something terrible had happened. According to this Corrine woman, no one had seen or talked to Reya in days.

"Well?" Richard said.

Colin stiffened at that tone. His voice curt, he said, "She quit the agency."

"What?" Running his hand agitatedly through his hair, Richard dropped into a chair. "When?"

"Last week."

"Why?"

Colin looked at him angrily. "How should I know?"

Richard's expression darkened even more. "Don't give me that—" he began furiously, and then stopped. "Never mind. Just tell me if you've seen her since then."

"I told you—"

"I know what you *told* me!" Richard shouted, angry all over again. "But there has to be something else. Something," he added pointedly, "that you're not telling me."

Trying to hide his guilty flush, Colin pretended an interest in the papers on his desk. But the lines swam before his eyes, and suddenly all he could see was an image of Reya's white, shocked face staring up at him. He flinched. Ever since that horrible scene at her apartment last week—had it only been a week?—he'd done nothing but think of her. He'd replayed that fight endlessly in his mind, going over every word, every gesture, every nuance, until he was driving himself crazy. He'd picked up the phone a hundred times to call her, but hadn't had the nerve. He'd made a terrible fool of himself, and now Richard was giving him a bad time, reminding him of it all.

As if he needed to be reminded, he thought blackly, and glared at Richard again. "I've told you all you need to know," he growled.

Richard wasn't about to let him off as lightly as that. "You haven't told me anything beyond the fact that she quit the agency," he declared. "I know you, Colin. You're hiding something. Now, what happened? What went wrong?"

To his fury, Colin couldn't hold his friend's eyes. "What makes you think something went wrong?"

"Because it's not like Reya to disappear like this!"

"How do you know what she's like?" Colin demanded angrily. "You hardly know her at all!"

"I know her well enough to know she'd never drop out of sight without having a damned good reason!" Richard stated, and glared at Colin again. "Especially now that things are finally starting to turn around for Geneticon. Even if she doesn't work for the agency anymore, I know she's responsible for that article that appeared in Sunday's paper. You *did* notice that, didn't you?"

He had, and that made him feel like an even bigger fool. Reya had promised him that things were going to change for Geneticon, and it seemed they were. As much as he wanted to deny it to make himself feel better, he could see Reya's hand in that article. Rudy Sabin, feature writer for the *Rocky Mountain News*, had done a great job covering genetically engineered products, and he knew he had Reya to thank. It wasn't a coincidence, either, that that woman from KLST had called. Reya had mentioned something about a radio program, and he knew he had her to thank for that, too. That made him feel even more enraged and helpless.

"I saw it," he growled.

"Then you can't think that the media here suddenly had a change of heart and decided you were a good guy after all," Richard said angrily. "No, Colin, Reya had something to do with that, and I can't—"

Colin suddenly slammed his hand down on the desk. Papers flew, but neither man noticed. "Do you have to keep on about her?" he shouted. "Maybe she just decided to take a vacation! Maybe she went to visit her family! Maybe she just needed some time off. How do I know?"

Richard's gaze was direct. "You know."

"Damn it all!" Colin turned away from him, swiveling in his chair so violently that it creaked in protest. He could feel Richard staring relentlessly at him, and finally he muttered, "All right. We had a fight."

"A fight!"

Colin swiveled back. "Yes, a fight!" he exclaimed angrily. "But that doesn't have anything to do with her leaving the agency. She quit before that!"

Richard was obviously trying to hold on to his temper. "How convenient for you."

"What does that mean?" Colin demanded, and then thought better of it. He didn't want to listen to any more of this. He already knew that Richard would cheerfully have boiled him in oil right now, and the way he felt, he probably would have handed him the match. "Never mind," he said brusquely. "You can keep your opinions to yourself. Don't we have an appointment with that lawyer this afternoon?"

"Yes, we do," Richard said coldly. "There's something in the air about a settlement."

"A settlement! That'll be the day!"

Richard looked even more grim as he stood. "I agree. But in the meantime, I would appreciate it if you would try to find out where Reya went."

Colin looked up at him sharply. "Why?"

Richard glared down at him. "Because for one thing, you no doubt owe her an apology. And for another, I'm not about to spend another week with you like this past one has been. I knew something was wrong—"

"Of course something's wrong!" Colin shouted. "It's not enough that Geneticon's been hounded by the press—"

"A situation for which we have you to thank!"

Colin's face reddened. "I don't think that's fair."

"Fair?" Richard was a little red himself. "Fair? After the way you've behaved, I'm surprised the media hasn't banded together to run you out of town on a rail! I don't think you've been exactly *fair* to them, either!"

His face suffused, Colin slowly got to his feet. Richard held his ground, refusing to be intimidated into an apology. His voice shaking with anger, Colin said, "How dare you say something like that to me! Have you forgotten what happened before? Of all the—"

Richard held up his hand. "I haven't forgotten, Colin," he said evenly. "But when are you going to forgive—"

"Forgive!" Colin was livid at that. "After what the press did to me?"

Richard lost his temper. "Damn it, Colin!" he shouted. "You're not the only one who's ever been raked over the coals, and I think it's time you faced up to that. All right, it happened. It wasn't right. It wasn't even fair! But it happened. And now it's in the past. Are you going to let it ruin your whole life? Are you going to let it destroy what you have with Reya?"

Colin had blanched at this attack; now his face reddened again. "You don't know what you're talking about!"

"Don't I?" he demanded. "You forget, I've known you for a long time, Colin. I've seen the way you look at her, and if ever there was a man in love, you're the one."

"That's absurd!"

Richard didn't even listen to the protest. Leaning over the desk for emphasis, he went on, "After the shabby way you've treated her, I'm tempted to find her myself and tell her never to speak to you again! But I can't do that, Colin, and do you know why? Because she's the first woman who has ever been able to stand up to you. Claire never did, you know. Oh, Claire was a lovely woman, I agree. I loved her myself. But she couldn't set you straight, and that's what you need, my friend—someone to set you straight. So if you lose Reya because of your stubborn pride, you'll have only yourself to blame!"

"That's the most ridiculous thing I've ever heard!"

"Is it? Well, maybe you should think about it while I go and prepare for the meeting this afternoon. You do intend to be there, don't you? I can't imagine you'd rather spend precious time trying to find Reya."

Despite himself, Colin flinched at the sarcasm. "You worry about the legal issue," he said tightly, "and let me worry about Reya."

"Does that mean you're coming to the meeting, or what?"

"I wouldn't miss it for the world."

The thought of meeting with Darren Enderly filled him with rage again, and as Richard angrily left the office, Colin had the irrational thought that if it hadn't been for Enderly, none of this would have happened. He'd lost his temper with Reya when he realized that the attorney bringing the lawsuit against Geneticon had once been her fiancé; he couldn't understand why she hadn't mentioned it before. Then, after he'd become so angry and made all those ridiculous accusations, he realized why she hadn't said anything. She had obviously anticipated such a childish reaction on his part, and he certainly hadn't disappointed her. Wincing at the memory, he wondered what had been wrong with him that night. Then Richard's words came back to haunt him, and he had to admit that he knew what had been wrong. He'd been terrified. That was the plain truth of it.

He'd never thought to fall in love again after Claire died; in fact, he'd done everything he could to guard against it. But Reya had somehow managed to slip past his defenses, and when he was with her, the shadows of the past seemed to recede.

That was what had scared him the most. He never wanted to forget Becky and Claire; it seemed so disloyal, such a betrayal after all they'd been through. He never wanted to forget their pain. He never wanted to forget that he had lived, and they had . . . died.

Slowly his eyes went to the only painting in his office, the rendering of the DNA molecule, with the entwined threads that contained the meaning of life. He had devoted the past five years of his life to unraveling its secrets, as though by such fanatic devotion he could make what had happened less painful . . . less senseless. But the death of a child was always senseless, and so, to him, was the taking of a life. Claire hadn't been able to bear her pain; she had ended it. But had he really done anything so different?

His lips twisted as he stared at the painting. How ironic it was, he thought, that he had been surrounded by life here in all its most basic forms, but for the past five years, he hadn't allowed himself to live. It was as though he had willed himself to die with Becky and Claire, and he had buried himself here.

Until the day Reya had breezed into the office. He could see her in his mind's eye now: that glorious mane of sable hair, those beautiful, expressive eyes. But it wasn't only her physical beauty that had attracted him, it was something within her—a vitality that couldn't be denied, a sense of *life*. She had made him feel alive for the first time in five years, and he had despised her for it. He didn't want to feel alive, because to him life meant pain.

And love?

The question flashed into his mind without warning, and he bowed his head. He had loved Claire with all his heart; he had loved Becky even more. But they were gone, and nothing he could do would bring them back. Weren't five years of mourning enough?

Slowly he bent forward and rested his head on his folded arms on the desk. He felt overwhelmed by the loss he had never acknowledged emotionally before, and as his shoulders began to shake, one agonized sob escaped him, a heart-wrenching sound all the more excruciating because it came from a man who rarely cried. He stayed unmoving in that position for a long time, but when he finally raised his head, there was a new acceptance in his eyes. Richard was right. He couldn't change what had happened any more than he could bring his wife and daughter back. But there was something he could do, one way to make amends. Reaching for the phone, he dialed Reya's apartment.

There was no answer. He waited until the fifteenth ring before he finally hung up, and then he got up to pace. Where was she? Trying not to think that Richard's concern hadn't been misplaced, he wondered what to do. If something had happened to her, he'd never forgive himself, and on that thought, he jerked open his office door.

"I'm going out," he said tersely to his secretary.

"But you have a meeting in an hour with—" she started to say.

"Tell Richard to start without me if I'm not back. This is more important."

"But where will you be? How can I reach you?"

He didn't hear her; he was already on his way out. Thirty minutes later, he was knocking at Reya's apartment, praying she'd answer the door.

"If you're looking for Reya, she's not here."

Colin whirled around at the sound of the voice. When he saw Serena Jackson standing there, he was so surprised he couldn't think what to say. The reporter had been the last person he expected to see, and as he stood there staring at her, Serena brushed by him. Fitting the key into Reya's front door lock, she opened the door and stepped inside.

"Didn't you hear me, Mr. Hughes? I said Reya isn't here."

She was closing the door behind her when he pulled himself together. "Wait—"

She gave him a cool look. "Yes?"

He could see the hostility in her eyes. Feeling his old aversion to any member of the press rising in response, he told himself not to get angry. If she had Reya's key, she obviously knew something, and he couldn't afford to alienate her. Finding out where Reya had gone was more important than his pride.

"Do you have a minute?" he made himself ask. "I'd like to talk to you."

Her eyes narrowed. "About what?"

He was determined not to get angry. "About Reya, of course. I assume since you have her key you know where she is."

"So?"

He took another grip on his temper. "So," he said carefully, "I'd like to get in touch with her."

"Why?"

He clenched his jaw. "I'm not sure that's any of your business, Miss Jackson," he said. "In fact, I could ask you what you're doing here."

"It's no secret," she said, and smiled nastily. "I'm watering the plants. Reya didn't want them to die while she was gone."

He fought to hide his dismay. "How . . . how long is that?"

Serena shrugged. "She didn't say."

He felt so exasperated he wanted to shake her. "What exactly *did* she say, then?"

The blue eyes narrowed again. "Nothing that concerns you, I'm sure."

He couldn't help himself. His voice harsh, he said, "Let's not play games, all right, Miss Jackson?"

"Games?" Serena repeated, her voice going from cool to frigid. "You're the one who does that, Mr. Hughes."

He looked at her sharply. "What does that mean?"

"You've been playing games this whole time with Geneticon, haven't you? It would have been so simple to tell the truth, but no, you had to make an issue out of privacy."

He told himself he wasn't going to be diverted, but he couldn't let that pass. "Privacy *was* an issue."

She gave him that cool look again. "Whose?" she asked. "Yours, or Geneticon's?"

"Geneticon's, of course!" he snapped. "I—"

He stopped, questioning it for the first time. Had he confused the two? Uncomfortably, he had to admit it was possible. He had vowed that he would never again go through what he had endured with the press in California, but as Richard had pointed out so succinctly this morning—and Reya that night—he had allowed that experience to color his reactions here. Whose privacy had he been protecting?

Aware of the knowing expression in Serena's eyes, he stiffened. "I didn't come here to talk about Geneticon, Miss Jackson," he said tautly. "I came to find out where Reya is. If you know, I'd appreciate your telling me. If you don't, I'm sorry I wasted your time."

He waited, but when she didn't reply, he knew she wasn't going to tell him. Tightening his lips, he turned to go. He'd taken three steps before she exclaimed impatiently. "Oh, all right!"

He glanced back at her. She stared at him suspiciously for a few seconds, then made up her mind. Opening the door so that he could enter, she said ungraciously, "You might as well come in while I take care of things."

He started to thank her, but she raised a hand. "I don't know if I'm going to tell you where she is," she warned. "I'm not sure you deserve to know."

He had no reply to that, and stood awkwardly as she wandered around, watering can in hand. She deliberately ignored him, letting him—as the saying went—stew in his own juices. A part of him couldn't believe he was standing here allowing her to do this to him, but he knew that if he tried to press her, she wouldn't tell him anything. He'd seen that evil gleam in her eye, and under other circumstances, he would have been furious. Today he knew he deserved it. So he waited, watching her as she sorted through the mail and the newspapers, stacking the one just so in a pile on the rolltop desk in the corner, placing the other on a chair, making sure the edges were perfectly straight. He knew she was taunting him, and though his jaw tightened, he didn't say a word until she finally turned to him.

"Now that everything is arranged to your satisfaction," he said, and couldn't prevent a trace of sarcasm from creeping into his voice, "do you think you could answer my question?"

She looked at him innocently. "What question was that?"

His jaw tightened again. "The question about where I can find Reya, that's what question."

She looked at him a moment longer. "Do you know she lost her job because of you?"

He stared at her. "What are you talking about? She didn't lose her job—she quit the agency!"

"That's what she told you."

"That's what happened!"

"Are you sure?"

"Of course I'm sure!" he declared, though suddenly he no longer was. He looked at her belligerently. "Why would she lie?"

"To protect you," Serena said disgustedly. "Although I can't imagine why."

"I . . . What do you mean, to protect me?"

Serena sat on the arm of the couch. She was enjoying this, he could tell, but right now he didn't give a damn. He was too anxious to get to the bottom of this. Something was wrong here, and he didn't know what it was.

"I asked you a question," he said through his teeth.

"I know," she said calmly. "I'm trying to think how to answer."

"Why don't you just try the truth?"

She looked at him. "That's a good one, coming from you."

"What does *that* mean?"

Serena shot to her feet again, her idle pose forgotten. "What do you think it means, Mr. Hughes?" she demanded. "You know, if you gave a thought to anyone but yourself, you'd see that none of us—with the exception of that sleaze Jim Naughton—ever wanted anything but the truth! All you had to do was answer our questions and none of this would have happened. Reya wouldn't have been fired from her job—"

"She wasn't fired. I told you, she quit!"

Serena's eyes blazed, her fist actually clenched. "She quit because she was about to be fired! And do you know why, Mr. Almighty Hughes? Because of you—because of Geneticon! That's why she's no longer with the agency. It's because of you!"

Colin's face had gone white. "That's a lie!"

"Is it? Well, you're the expert on lies, so you should know! My God, can't you see—" She couldn't finish; she was choking with anger. She went to the door and jerked it open. "You'd better go. I'm not sure Reya would want you here."

"Wait a minute...."

"No, you wait! I've had just about enough of you, Colin Hughes! Because you still don't get it, do you? Reya really put herself out for you, you know? She's the one who talked Rudy into doing those articles in the *News*; she's the one who persuaded KLST to do an educational spot on genetics." She gave a short laugh. "Hell, she even talked me into doing a series of special reports on Geneticon. Me, the one who's been sitting behind that desk for weeks now, spouting off about all the mysterious goings-on out there!"

Colin ran a hand through his hair. "She told me about the special reports," he muttered. "But I—"

Serena had regained her breath. "Yeah, yeah, I know. But you wouldn't allow any reporters to set foot on Geneticon's precious soil, right?" She looked at him disgustedly again. "And this was after she got fired from her job for defending you!"

He looked up quickly, but Serena raised her hand. "Oh, sure. She told me she quit, too, but that doesn't change the fact that Clendenin gave her the choice— give up Geneticon as an account, or give up the agency." Serena's lip curled. "Some choice, huh? Well, we both know which one she picked, and right now for the life of me, I can't imagine why."

Right now, Colin couldn't imagine why, either. He despised himself for being so blind, so preoccupied with the past that he hadn't glimpsed what was happening in the present. Now it was too late. He couldn't doubt what Serena had told him; her words rang with truth. Reya had given up everything for him, and he'd been so engrossed in his own concerns that he hadn't even noticed. Cursing, he wondered how he could have been such a fool.

"Serena," he said, "I have to know where she is."

The reporter looked at him warily. "I'm not sure I want to tell you," she said. "She didn't want anyone to know."

Colin suddenly thought of a way out of this dilemma. It might not work, but he had to give it a try. To Serena's astonishment, he smiled and took her arm. "I think we should talk about this," he said, leading her to the couch. "And then when you've heard what I have to say, maybe you'll change your mind."

"I doubt that," she said suspiciously, but a few minutes later, after he had outlined his plan, she was smiling, too.

"Then it's agreed?" Colin said.

Serena didn't hesitate. "Agreed."

"Now you can tell me what I want to know," he said, and looked at her in complete surprise when she told him.

"Are you sure?" he asked.

Serena nodded. "Of course I'm sure. I had to ask her twice before I believed it myself." She gave him a hard look. "Remember, I only told you because—"

"I know," he said hastily, and happened to glance at the clock. He was already late for his meeting, but he didn't care. What he'd learned today was far more important than any lawsuit could ever be, and he stood. "Thank you, Miss Jackson," he said, and meant it.

Serena stood, too. "I think," she said, "that under the circumstances, we could be a little less formal, don't you?"

Colin smiled and held out his hand. "I'll be in touch . . . Serena."

The reporter took his hand. "I'll hold you to that, Colin," she said, and winked.

RICHARD WAS WAITING when Colin got back to Geneticon, agitatedly pacing back and forth in his office. He halted the instant Colin opened the door and demanded, "Where in the hell have you been? I thought you were going to attend that meeting with me!"

"I was," Colin said calmly. "But I had something more important to do."

"What?" Richard asked suspiciously, and then waved his hand. "Never mind. I'm not sure I want to know."

Colin smiled, knowing that Richard was bursting with curiosity and determined not to show it. "How did the meeting go?"

Richard looked balefully at him. "Do you care?"

"I've got every confidence in you. I'm sure you handled things superbly."

Richard threw himself into a chair. "It would serve you right if the whole thing was an unmitigated disaster."

"Was it?"

Richard glared at him again and Colin laughed. "You convinced them to drop the suit, didn't you?"

"I did," Richard said shortly, and gave him another dire look. "But it wasn't easy."

"You're too modest."

Richard couldn't stand it any longer. After Colin congratulated him and went to the bar to pour them both a drink, he asked cautiously, "And what have *you* been doing while your legal counsel has been working hard to save your company from being dragged into court?"

Colin came back with a highball glass in each hand. He handed Richard one and raised the other in salute. "Taking your advice," he said, and grinned.

CHAPTER SIXTEEN

THE CALL CAME just as Reya was helping Matilda with the last of the dinner dishes. Charlie answered the phone, and he held the receiver out to her.

"It's fer you."

Warily, Reya put the wet dish towel aside. No one but Serena knew she was at the ranch, and she couldn't imagine why Serena would call, unless it was to relate more bad news about Geneticon. They had promised to keep in touch, and Serena had said she'd keep her posted about events the last time they had seen each other, the day after that terrible scene with Colin at Reya's apartment. The last thing she'd wanted to do that next morning was keep her appointment with Serena, but she felt she owed it to her to explain why the genetic engineering specials had to be indefinitely postponed. She hadn't told her the real reason, of course. She had used the excuse that because she was no longer working for Clendenin, she hadn't the authority to go through with the project. But Serena, with her reporter's instinct, had seen through that ruse right away.

"Did you quit over this, or were you fired?" Serena had asked flatly.

Reya had hesitated, then reluctantly admitted, "I quit." She tried for a smile that failed dismally. "Right before he fired me."

"I thought so," Serena said, and shook her head angrily. "Damn it. It's not fair."

Reya's smile was wry this time. "No one ever promised us fair, did they?"

Serena frowned. "No, but it's a hell of a thing when you can't hope that someone will do what's right."

Reya shrugged. "We just had a difference of opinion, that's all. And it is his agency, remember that."

Serena wasn't impressed. "Well, if you ask me, he made a big mistake letting you go. What are you going to do now?"

That was when she told Serena she was going to the Double Ott. She hadn't realized until that moment that she'd made the decision, but once she said it aloud, she knew that's what she wanted to do. Serena, the devout city girl, had been horrified. She had immediately invited Reya to stay with her, but even though Reya had been grateful for the offer, she had gently refused. She needed to be alone for a while, to sort things out.

And now she'd been here almost a week, and she still hadn't decided what she wanted to do about anything. It seemed a lifetime since she'd arrived at the Double Ott, so confused and dejected she wasn't even sure why she had come, except that the ranch held so many happy memories for her. Charlie and Matilda had been wonderful to her. They had welcomed her without questions, and upon her request, reluctantly included her in the chores. She had even helped with the horses, but though she kept busy every minute of the day, she couldn't get over this horrible depression. She had hoped all the activity would exhaust her to the point where she fell into bed each night, too tired to do anything but sleep, but it didn't. Charlie had found her sitting out on the porch one night long after she thought he'd gone to bed, and she'd been embarrassed by her tears. It seemed that all she did during the long, empty nights was cry.

Charlie hadn't said much as she surreptitiously wiped her eyes; he pretended to be involved with the ceremony of lighting his pipe. Waiting with that uncanny instinct of his until she had collected herself somewhat, he asked, "Mind if I sit a spell?"

She tried to laugh; it was his porch, after all. "Of course not," she said. "I'll be glad of the company."

He gestured with his pipe. "Looks like you already have some."

Smiling tearfully, she looked down at the dog by her feet. Fergus seemed to have adopted her since she came. He followed her around during the day, and the instant she came out to sit on the porch at night, he climbed the steps and threw himself down, his muzzle atop her shoe. Fondling his long, silky ears now, she knew that in his own way the dog was trying to comfort her, and she was grateful.

Fergus sighed at Reya's touch and settled himself even closer to her. Charlie shook his head. "Ne'er thought I'd see the day," he commented.

Reya looked at him curiously. "What do you mean?"

Charlie shrugged. "Fergus is a good dog, but he's always been Colin's dog. Sort of keeps to himself unless Colin's around, if ya know what I mean."

"I thought he was your dog, Charlie."

"Nope. Colin's the one who found him. Abandoned by the side of the road, he was. Just a pup then, sorriest thing you ever saw. Skin and bones, near starved t'death. I told Colin he wasn't goin' to make it, but he wouldn't listen. Stayed up with that pup night and day, feedin' it with an eyedropper 'cause it was too weak to lift its head. And darn if the little thing didn't live." Charlie hesitated, and then chuckled. "Course, that's not the first time Colin's proved me wrong."

Reya lowered her head to fondle the dog's ears again, wondering why she wasn't really surprised at the story. But then, why should she be? Remembering that night in the music room when Colin played the guitar, and then the piano for her, how could she doubt that the man who could create such beautiful music wasn't kind and compassionate, too? That was the man she loved—not the arrogant, suspicious businessman who owned Geneticon and was so mistrustful of the press and everyone connected with it. When he assumed that persona, she didn't know him at all.

Charlie cleared his throat. "I know it's none of my business, Reya," he said quietly, "but Tilda and I can't pretend we haven't noticed how unhappy you are. Is there anything we can do?"

Grateful for the offer, Reya reached out and squeezed his arm. To her dismay, tears began to sting her eyes again, and she had to glance quickly away. "You're already doing it," she said, her voice choked, "by letting me stay here."

"Aw, that's not so much," he said, touched by her gesture. "Besides, you're paying your way. You know

you don't have to, but you help in the house, and
you're gettin' pretty good at working with the horses.''

She smiled weakly. ''As long as they don't decide to
go one way and me the other, I'm fine. I'm afraid I'll
always be a tenderfoot, Charlie.''

''Not if Ol' Thunder and Lightning has a say.''

She did laugh at that. Colin hadn't been kidding
when he'd insisted that the ranch had a horse by that
name, but the first time she had seen him, she'd burst
out laughing. Ol' Thunder and Lightning was an ancient gelding, so gentle that even she could handle
him. He'd amble agreeably along, calmly stepping
over and around and across any obstacle as long as he
could snatch a blade of grass here and there. It was the
perfect partnership: she allowed him to graze whenever he wanted, and in turn he gave her confidence as
a rider. Charlie had assigned him to her—or the other
way around, she thought wryly—when she came, and
after a week, she was even looking forward to her daily
ride with Charlie when he went out to round up stray
cattle.

No, it wasn't the days that were difficult for her; she
kept herself too busy to think much about Colin. It
was the nights that were the hardest; the long hours
when she'd toss and turn, his face always in her mind.
She knew now it had been a mistake to come here—the
memories overwhelmed her, and she could see Colin
everywhere. She'd reached the point where she had
even considered leaving Denver and taking another
job somewhere else. The thought of starting over
again was depressing, but there was nothing now to
hold her here. Depressed even more at that thought,
she took the phone from Charlie when he told her the
call was for her.

"Hello?"

"Hi! This is your friendly neighborhood reporter calling to see how you're doing," Serena said cheerfully.

Reya glanced quickly at Matilda. She didn't want to hurt the kindhearted woman by allowing her to overhear a thoughtless remark, so she said carefully, "Okay, I guess."

"Well, that certainly sounds enthusiastic. Dare I hope that you're disenchanted with the bucolic life already and long for the city?"

Reya leaned despondently against the counter, staring at the floor. Out of the corner of her eye, she saw Matilda gesture to Charlie, and the two went out and left her alone. Silently blessing them for their thoughtfulness, she said, "I don't know. I've been doing some thinking about that."

"And?"

She sighed. "I'm just not sure."

"Well, before you make your decision, maybe you'd better watch the six o'clock news," Serena said. "You *do* have a television there, don't you? I mean, you're not confined to wireless reports from the outside world, are you?"

Reya refused to be diverted. She had heard the undercurrent of excitement in Serena's voice, and she tensed. "Don't be sarcastic," she said. "Why do you want me to watch the news? Has something happened? Is it—"

"You'll see," Serena said, and to Reya's complete astonishment, actually giggled. "I'll talk to you later."

"Wait!"

But Serena had already hung up. Wondering what had happened now, Reya put the receiver down and darted a glance at the big kitchen clock. It was almost six now, and she rushed into the living room to turn on the ancient TV. She'd been amused by the old set when she first came, but as she waited for it to warm up, she prayed that it would work tonight. It sometimes didn't, she'd discovered, but that hadn't mattered. No one at the ranch stayed up late to watch television when they were all up in the morning with the rooster's crow.

"Come on...come on..." she muttered, willing the picture to emerge. At last it did. "Thank God," she said, and perched tensely on the arm of the couch.

She was still sitting there a half hour later, getting a little angry with Serena for playing a joke on her. The newscast had been filled with the usual recital of world and national events, but for once there had been nothing disastrous or earthshaking. Even the local news had seemed tame, and she was just getting up irritably to snap off the set when the night news anchor at KRDA, Mel Clayburn, looked solemnly into the camera and intoned, "And now a special report from Serena Jackson...."

She'd been reaching for the knob when Serena's face filled the screen, and her hand froze in midair. Disbelievingly, she heard Serena say, "In a sudden reversal of its former 'hands-off' policy, the owner of Geneticon, the genetic research center that's been so much in the local news lately, called an open press conference today. Mr. Colin Hughes, president and director of the beleaguered company, invited reporters to tour the facility and was on hand to answer questions. This reporter was honored with an exclusive, which we will air at a later date, but for now, we take you to Geneticon, and the press conference filmed earlier today. . . ."

"I don't believe it," Reya said, and couldn't look away from the screen long enough to find her seat again. Groping backward, she touched the arm of the couch and sat down, her eyes riveted on the television as the camera opened with a shot of Colin, the Geneticon logo in stark relief behind him. She recognized the employee cafeteria, where that other disastrous press conference had taken place, and she tensed again, wondering what had happened today.

But this was a different Colin than even Reya had seen before. Standing behind the podium, he was relaxed and confident as he opened the conference with a short statement, and there was nothing abrasive in his manner as he began to answer the questions fired at him.

"What made you decide to call another press conference, Mr. Hughes?" someone asked. "Does it have anything to do with the lawsuit that's being brought against you?"

Colin didn't hesitate. "The suit was withdrawn today," he said, "when we were able to prove that the litigant left the company of his own accord. We have his letter of resignation on record, along with his reasons for resigning—none of which had anything to do with his refusal to sign a nonexistent secrecy pact." Anticipating the next question, he added calmly, "The document in question was a simple security agreement, and when these facts, along with the evidence in the man's own writing, were presented, his attorney advised him to drop the suit."

Reya lifted an eyebrow at that. She knew Darren, and the evidence against his client must have been overwhelming for him to advise withdrawal. He must be grinding his teeth in rage right now, she thought, and couldn't feel any sympathy for him. If he hadn't been so anxious to have his revenge on Colin, he would have prepared more carefully and investigated the facts before he humiliated himself this way.

"Then security agreements are required as a condition of employment, Mr. Hughes?"

"Yes, of course," Colin answered naturally. "But I'd like to point out that that's as much to protect our employees as it is to shelter the results of their research. Genetic engineering is a highly competitive field, as you know, and it would be foolish not to recognize that fact and take appropriate steps to guard the work being done here."

"In case a mutant strain of some super-bug gets out, you mean?"

Listening, Reya closed her eyes. There was only so much Colin could be expected to take, and so far the reporters weren't giving him an inch. Worse, they were practically attacking him. She knew it wouldn't be long before he exploded and the press conference turned into another disaster, but Colin surprised her.

With no trace of temper, he said, "I assume you're referring to research in germ warfare, which has been banned in this country. But even if it hadn't been, there are enough deadly bugs occurring in nature to worry about. We certainly don't need to create them in the laboratory."

To Reya's intense relief, Serena spoke up then. "I'd like to get back to the reason you called this press conference, Mr. Hughes. Geneticon hasn't been exactly friendly to reporters.... What made you change your mind?"

Colin hesitated. Reya, who knew him so well, saw the pain flash across his eyes, and she tensed in response. But his voice was calm when he answered, and he looked at Serena directly. "I have had occasion in the past to resent the press, Miss Jackson," he said quietly, "and I don't deny it. But Geneticon and the work we're doing here is more important than...than my *unreasonable*—"

He emphasized the word so slightly that for a moment Reya wasn't sure she had heard correctly. Remembering the painful words they had exchanged about that very subject, she bit her lip. Was he trying to tell her something? She wished it were so, but knew that was impossible. He was just answering the question Serena had put to him.

"—attitude toward the media and their right to know," he finished, and smiled slightly. "This unreasonableness on my part has been pointed out to me rather forcefully lately," he went on ruefully, "and so I decided to...to make amends."

Jim Naughton of the *Tribune*, the newspaper that had deliberately fueled the present controversy, spoke up. "Does this mean that you're starting to feel some of that ethical and moral responsibility you denied before?" he asked nastily.

Colin looked at him coolly. "Ethical responsibility?" he repeated. "I find that a strange question coming from you, Mr. Naughton. Weren't you the reporter who eagerly rushed into print the lies and distortions that Geneticon's ex-employee gave you?"

Naughton flushed and lowered his head quickly to scribble something in his notebook. The camera held on him mercilessly for a few seconds, then swung back to Colin as he said quietly, "I would like to amplify my answer to that question, if I may. No one realizes more than I the dangers inherent in this kind of research. There are always the unscrupulous, the unethical, the immoral, who take advantage of any new technology or achievement or invention that has any potential for misuse at all. We all know that includes just about any discovery ever made—''

"So how can you justify—"

Colin held up his hand. "I don't pretend to be a philosopher, or a theologian, or a bioethicist," he said somberly. "Better minds than mine will debate those issues for generations to come. I prefer to concentrate on the enormous benefits genetic engineering and biotechnology can provide—"

"And what are those?" someone asked.

Colin didn't hesitate. "Here at Geneticon, we have already developed bacterially produced insulin and vaccines that are saving thousands—perhaps millions—of lives. We're working on agricultural technology that will increase crop yields and productivity, which will eventually eliminate hunger in the world. Scientists all over the country are working around the clock to identify genes that cause cancer and heart disease, to name but two. New discoveries are being made every day—"

"And isn't that the problem?" someone asked. "Don't you think we should have more control, slow down a little? Aren't things moving too fast?"

Colin looked thoughtfully at the speaker. It was a few seconds before he answered, and when he did, no one moved. "Too fast?" he said softly. "Tell that to the child who is dying from an inheritable disease for which there is no cure. Tell that to the parents who unknowingly gave her that disease. Ask them if they would like to wait and debate." He paused, his glance touching everyone in the room. "Would you, if you were those parents, and the child was yours?"

A profound silence fell, and the picture dissolved to Serena's serious expression. "During the following week," she said, "we will be examining those issues and more in a series of special reports. Mr. Colin Hughes of Geneticon, whom you have just heard speak so eloquently on the subject, has graciously consented to be one of our guests. He will be accompanied by other experts who will debate both sides of the biotechnology issue, a subject that affects us all. So until tomorrow night at this time, this is Serena Jackson wishing you and yours . . . a thoughtful good night."

The station's logo came up, and Reya got slowly to her feet. She felt dazed by what she had seen, so proud of Colin she could have burst. Reaching to turn off the set, she heard booted footsteps in the big entry beyond the arched doorway of the living room, and she turned, her eyes shining. "Charlie, did you—"

It wasn't Charlie.

Colin was there, dressed in old jeans and a plaid Western shirt. For a few seconds she just stared at him, unable to believe he was really here. She'd promised herself she'd be cool and detached when—if—she saw him again, but her heart began to hammer so hard she could barely speak. "What . . . what are you doing here?" she stammered.

He came down the single step into the living room. "I'd like to ask you the same question."

She stiffened. "This is a guest ranch," she said defensively. "I have the right to be here if I want."

He didn't answer for a moment. "So you do," he said. "I have to admit, it's the last place I would have looked. If Serena hadn't told me—"

"Serena told you I was here?" She was immediately furious with her friend.

Colin smiled. "Don't be too hard on her. I held out a carrot she couldn't resist."

Reya suddenly understood. "Ah.... The exclusive interview," she said bitterly. "I might have known."

"I had to do something."

"Why?"

He looked at her. "You're not going to give me an inch, are you?" he said softly.

Her heart leaped at that, but she ruthlessly quelled the thrill. She wasn't going to jump to conclusions, not again. She had suffered too much for her foolishness already.

"I don't know what you mean," she said, and tensed when he took a step toward her. Trying desperately to maintain her composure, she tried to think of something safe to say and happened to glance at the television. "I saw the press conference on the news tonight," she said quickly. "I thought you did a wonderful job."

"Better than last time, I hope," he said, and took another step closer.

She wanted to smile, but her lips felt too stiff. "Much better," she agreed, and wondered what else she could say. He took another step, and she turned hastily toward the fireplace. Grabbing a poker, she jabbed at the dying fire.

"I was glad to hear the news about the lawsuit being dropped—" she started to say, and then cried out in dismay when he came up behind her and took the poker out of her hand. Before she could escape, he had grabbed her by the shoulders and turned her around so that she had to look up at him.

"Why didn't you tell me that you quit the agency because of Geneticon?" he asked.

"I . . . I didn't."

He held her eyes. "That's not what Serena told me, or Joseph Clendenin when I spoke to him today."

"You talked to him, too?"

He smiled slightly at her indignation. "I had quite a few fences to mend, Reya," he said softly. "Not the least of which was to explain things to him. He was eager to make amends himself when I made it clear that I had been too . . . stubborn to follow your excellent advice. He called me back, in fact, after the press conference today. It seems that he's anxious to sign Geneticon again."

"I find that hard to believe," she said bitterly. Still, she couldn't prevent herself from asking, "What did you say?"

"I told him I couldn't possibly consider it unless you handled the account, which, I added, you had done superbly on your own."

She looked at him disbelievingly. "You told him that?"

"Call him and ask. He wants to talk to you anyway, since if you decide to go back to the agency you'll be working in a new capacity. Account executive, I believe it's called."

She ignored the thrill that raced through her at the idea. She didn't need his help, and she wanted him to know that. "I can take care of myself, thank you," she said haughtily. "I certainly don't need you to blackmail Joseph Clendenin into—"

He smiled again, wryly this time. "Independent to the last, right?"

Her chin came up. "There's nothing wrong with that!"

"On the contrary," he said calmly. "I wouldn't have it any other way."

She swallowed when his hands tightened on her shoulders. Their bodies were only inches apart, and she had the overpowering impulse to close the distance between them by throwing herself into his arms. Her heart was beating so hard that she was sure he could hear it; her pulse seemed to thunder in her ears. She hardly dared to look up into his eyes; she knew if she did, she wouldn't have the courage to pull away.

"Why are you here?" she asked, and tried to free herself.

He held her fast. "Because I wanted you to know that I agreed with two friends who told me that I'd be a fool to let you go."

Once again she felt that thrill, but she couldn't allow herself to believe him...not yet. She'd trusted him once, and he'd thrown her feelings back into her face. She was not going to make that mistake again. "Is that really why you came, Colin?"

He shook his head, and her spirits plummeted. She wanted to break away from him, to run from the room before she betrayed herself by bursting into bitter tears, but he held her tightly.

"No," he said. "I came to say that I love you."

She had dreamed so often of hearing him say those words that for a precious moment or two, she was sure she had only imagined his saying it now. "What?"

"I do love you, Reya," he said again, as though the knowledge surprised him. "I never thought I'd say that to anyone again, but I do. I tried to prove it to you today by calling that press conference. I knew that if anything would convince you that I was no longer living in the past, that would."

She could hardly speak. "I . . . I know how difficult that was for you, Colin, but . . ."

He looked down at her, his expression so filled with love that her heart soared. "Not half as difficult as the thought of losing you," he said quietly. "I think I knew I loved you the day you walked into my office, so full of life, so alive." He laughed tenderly. "I knew I was tempting fate to hire you that day, but I couldn't help myself."

"But you're in the business of tempting fate," she whispered. "You and your scientists do it every day."

"Not without you," he said, and pulled her close. "Never again, without you. If I don't have you on my side—"

He stopped, too choked with emotion to go on. She looked up into that handsome face and couldn't doubt the love she saw in his eyes. The knowledge of their future together was in that one glance, and at last she believed. Reaching up, she brought his head down to hers. Smiling through sudden tears, she raised her lips to his and murmured, "But darling, I always was...."

Harlequin Superromance

COMING NEXT MONTH

#242 LOVE CHILD • Janice Kaiser
Jessica Brandon desperately needs money to care for her
crippled son. Chase Hamilton desperately wants a child
of his own. Surrogate motherhood seems the perfect
solution for them both—until love creates a whole new
set of problems.

#243 WEAVER OF DREAMS • Sally Garrett
Growing up dirt-poor on a Kentucky farm has instilled
in professional weaver Abbie Hardesty the need for
financial independence. She dreams of overseeing every
aspect of her own crafts business, but she needs to learn
about wool production first. So she becomes Montana
sheep rancher Dane Grasten's intern student, and they
both end up learning more than they'd bargained
for...in each other's arms!

#244 TIME WILL TELL • Karen Field
Attorney Corinne Daye no longer knows whom to
trust: Derek Moar, the devastatingly attractive stranger
who bears an amazing resemblance to her dead
husband, or Margaret Krens, her loyal assistant, who
insists that Derek is on the wrong side of the law. She
only hopes that when the dust finally settles, Derek will
be there to fill the emptiness that stretches endlessly
before her....

#245 THE FOREVER BOND • Eleni Carr
With her daughter grown up and her career finally
established, Eve Raptis is ripe for a change. Carefree
Carl Masters supplies it, but the responsibilities of
Eve's past unexpectedly reappear to dim her precious
freedom....

AUTHOR'S CHRISTMAS MESSAGE

To all our Harlequin Readers:

I wish you and yours the best at this time of year—the joy of giving, the pleasure of receiving, the warmth that only families together can bring.

But most of all, I wish you a moment in all the rush and bustle of the holiday season when you look across the room at that special person and share a secret smile or two. . . .

Because seasons come and go, but romance should always be with us.

Season's Greetings and many happy hours of reading, wherever you are.

Brian Koch

WILLO DAVIS ROBERTS

To Share a Dream

A story of the passions, fears and hatreds of three sisters and the men they love

Well-known author Willo Davis Roberts captures the hearts of her readers in this passionate story of Christina, Roxanne and Megan. They fled England in 1691 in search of independence, only to find a harsh new life in Salem, Massachusetts.

Available NOW at your favorite retail outlet, or send your name, address and zip or postal code along with a check or money order for $5.25 (75¢ included for postage and handling) payable to Worldwide Library to:

In the U.S	In Canada
Worldwide Library	Worldwide Library
901 Fuhrmann Blvd.	P.O. Box 609
Box 1325	Fort Erie, Ontario
Buffalo, NY 14269-1325	L2A 5X3

Please specify book title with your order.

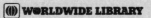 **WORLDWIDE LIBRARY**   SAD-H-1RR

Take 4 books
& a surprise gift
FREE

SPECIAL LIMITED-TIME OFFER

Mail to   **Harlequin Reader Service** ®

In the U.S.   In Canada
901 Fuhrmann Blvd.   P.O. Box 609
P.O. Box 1394   Fort Erie, Ontario
Buffalo, N.Y. 14240-1394   L2A 9Z9

YES! Please send me 4 free Harlequin American Romance®
novels and my free surprise gift. Then send me 4 brand-new novels
as they come off the presses. Bill me at the low price of $2.25 each
—a 11% saving off the retail price. There are no shipping, handling
or other hidden costs. There is no minimum number of books I
must purchase. I can always return a shipment and cancel at any
time. Even if I never buy another book from Harlequin, the 4 free
novels and the surprise gift are mine to keep forever.

Name   (PLEASE PRINT)

Address   Apt. No.

City   State/Prov.   Zip/Postal Code

This offer is limited to one order per household and not valid to present
subscribers. Price is subject to change.   DOAR-SUB-1RR